"Ma... *the Open...* an enthralling, nonstop read. Looking for depth, emotion, and history? You'll clamor for more."

—*RT Book Reviews*

"The action-packed story line uses real persona and a period of dangerous unrest as a backdrop to this excellent love story.... one of the subgenre's top novels of the year."

—*Midwest Book Review*

"What a completely engrossing tale!... Ms. MacTavish once again [writes] a dynamic and vital story that captured my imagination from the first page to the last."

—*CK2S Kwips and Kritiques*

THE PRIVATEER

"Dawn MacTavish transports readers back in time with this enchanting tale. *The Privateer* is full of characters you'll either love or love to hate but I can guarantee you won't be bored as you immerse yourself in this Regency story line. Beautifully written Ms. MacTavish! This is Regency storytelling at its best!"

—Romance Junkies

"I readily recommend *The Privateer*. It's an exciting book with a fresh plot and likable, lifelike characters."

—Romance Reviews Today

"Adventure on the high seas, family drama, rescue from a fate worse than death, passionate love; what more can a romance reader ask for? Dawn MacTavish draws us right in and paints her absorbing story with authentic historical detail in *The Privateer*."

—Single Titles

MORE PRAISE FOR DAWN MacTAVISH

THE MARSH HAWK

"*The Marsh Hawk* is historical fiction at its very best. A breathtaking, sweeping adventure. No one does period romance with such style and panache. *The Marsh Hawk* stole my heart!"

—Deborah MacGillivray, Author of *Riding the Thunder* and *The Invasion of Falgannon Isle*

"If you're looking for something fresh and lively . . . Dawn MacTavish's tale of a London beauty of the ton who isn't afraid to impersonate a masked highwayman, including robbery and possible murder, and the real, sapphire-eyed highwayman who pursues her, will keep you up reading all night. The love scenes are luscious. *The Marsh Hawk* is a winner."

—Katherine Deauxville, National Bestselling Author of *Out of the Blue*

"*The Marsh Hawk* will enchant the reader from page one. This sweeping Regency will capture the reader's imagination and make you fall in love with the genre all over again."

—Kristi Ahlers, The Best Reviews

"A master of vividly accomplished tales, the author ups the ante yet again with *The Marsh Hawk*. From the first suspenseful page, I was captivated!"

—Kenda Montgomery, official reviewer for The Mystic Castle

"Brilliant! . . . A breathtaking historical romance. *The Marsh Hawk* will run the gamut of your emotions—from laughter to tears. . . . You won't want the story to end."

—Leanne Burroughs, Award-Winning Author of *Highland Wishes* & *Her Highland Rogue*

A QUESTION OF COURAGE

"You're a coward, Trace Ord. Oh, you'll face down Jared, guns blazing, but you're afraid of what you feel, afraid to reach out for the future we could have together."

He was so close. His body heat scorched her, and his raw male scent was dizzying. His hot breath puffed in her face. For a moment she thought he was going to kiss her. The mere thought of it and she was aroused. So was he. The proof of it pressed heavily against her belly, and his eyes were dark and hooded with passion. If he would only kiss her . . .

He didn't. Instead, he scooped her up in his arms and plopped her down on Duchess. Mounting Diablo, he pointed her down off the mesa toward the valley below and rode off.

Her shout chased him. "You're a coward, Trace. But I'm strong enough for both of us."

Other *Leisure* books by Dawn MacTavish:

COUNTERFEIT LADY
PRISONER OF THE FLAMES
THE PRIVATEER
THE MARSH HAWK

Writing as Dawn Thompson:

THE BRIDE OF TIME
THE RAVENING
THE BROTHERHOOD
BLOOD MOON
THE FALCON'S BRIDE
THE WATERLORD
THE RAVENCLIFF BRIDE

DAWN MACTAVISH

Renegade Riders

LEISURE BOOKS NEW YORK CITY

A LEISURE BOOK®

March 2010

Published by

Dorchester Publishing Co., Inc.
200 Madison Avenue
New York, NY 10016

ISBN 10: 0-8439-6322-0
ISBN 13: 978-0-8439-6322-9
E-ISBN: 978-1-4285-0819-4

Visit us online at www.dorchesterpub.com.

Renegade Riders

Foreword

Renegade Riders is the earliest of my sister's works, before Dawn decided Regency and paranormal romances were where her heart belonged. Her love for the Old West came from our father, who loved the novels of Zane Grey. She took his passion for those stories of the West and made it her own, and *Renegade Riders* was written as a tribute to him—and to our mother, too, as the heroine is named after her.

Since Dawn died before she had a chance to edit this book, I wish to thank her close friends Deborah Mac-Gillivray, Diane Davis White, and Monika Wolmarans for helping me with that process. Their efforts were a true labor of love for my sister.

I especially wish to thank Chris Keeslar and Dorchester Publishing for giving Dawn her dream and for putting out this book, preserving Dawn's story for her many fans. I hope everyone enjoys my sister's very first novel, for it is special in so many ways.

This book is also dedicated to Miss Fuzz, who cared for and defended Dawn for many years.

Diane "Candy" Thompson
New York

Chapter One

Canyon country,
Arizona Territory, 1875

Trace Ord holstered his smoking gun. The horse thief he'd just shot wasn't mortally wounded. Judging from his build, the would-be rustler couldn't be more than a boy, so he hadn't aimed to kill.

He whistled for Diablo, the mustang with which the thief had nearly ridden off—without a saddle, no less. Impressive. Trace had to give the boy that. If he hadn't come back to camp from hunting when he did, and then drilled the hombre with one shot, the low-down varmint would've been halfway to Utah by now. Diablo could run like the wind; Trace could testify to that. Hadn't it taken him five long years and more than one broken bone to capture and break the stallion?

Red rock gravel crunched under the soles of his spurred boots as Trace climbed down from the rocks he'd scaled to take the shot. The last blaze of a fiery copper sunset was disappearing behind the rim above. Like a descending window shade, it robbed light from the canyon floor every night with a crushing disregard for whatever was left undone. His captive would have to wait. Diablo was spooked, milling aimlessly, ready to bolt. Trace approached with caution and practiced skill. He wasn't about to risk losing the horse now, not with night coming on so quickly and him with nothing but a stubborn pack mule to give chase.

"Come here, you black imp of Satan!" he bellowed at the beast. His voice rang back in echo, ricocheting off the darkening canyon walls.

The high-stepping horse pranced toward him, snorting, breath visible in puffs from flared nostrils in the cool spring air. His hooves clattered on the table of flat rock as he advanced, bridle dragging, head bobbing, black tail tossing and sweeping—the longest tail Trace had ever seen on a mustang, wild or otherwise. What a sight! Even now the beast thrilled him.

However, he'd been a wild horse wrangler long enough not to be fooled by the glamour. He'd learned the hard way that, while it was possible to bend a mustang to your will, there would always be a bit that remained wild. There was always the elusive part that pricked up its ears to answer the call of another wild horse riding the wind, the ingrained drive to recapture freedom. Trace had a healthy respect for that, so, while he handled his mustangs with playful banter and gentle whispers, he never let a beast he'd broken think it had gotten the better of him.

Fondly but firmly, he stroked the dusky horse's rippling neck and withers. "What? You forget who's boss around here?" he asked. Snatching the bridle, he wound it around a clump of brush jutting from a crevice in the rocky wall, narrowly missing the prickly needles of a reddish-tinted *bisnaga* cactus in the same fissure, jerking his hand back just in time. "Now see what you nearly made me do?" he complained. "You stay put, you ungrateful cayuse."

That accomplished, Trace strode to the body sprawled facedown on the canyon floor a few yards away. He squatted next to it. All that remained of the day was a flare of azure, rose, and gold on the horizon, and the wide brim of his Stetson cast purple shadows over the inert figure. He pushed the hat back for a closer look. No blood on the man's back. The bullet must still be in him.

He rolled the horse thief over, dislodging a dust-covered tan sombrero and revealing the culprit's face and hair—long, wavy hair the color of the sunset. Staring down at the unmoving form, Trace grimaced. "By damn, a woman. If that don't beat all. I've shot a woman!" And she was armed. Out of self-preservation, he relieved her of the gun in her holster and then felt for a pulse in her neck. "Thank the good Lord, fool woman's still alive."

Blood was seeping from a hole in her shirt at the shoulder, and a sizable lump was forming on her forehead where she'd struck a rock when she fell off Diablo. Both needed attention. Trace lifted her into his arms, snatched the horse's bridle, and strode off toward the lee of the canyon wall and his camp.

Trace had shot men before. A renegade rider couldn't live past thirty in the Territories without coming up against some bandit, some cardsharp or rustler or claim-jumping varmint itching to throw lead. Not in post–Civil War Arizona. But a woman? Never in his thirty-nine years had he ever succumbed to that, by accident or otherwise. A man of principle in general, he had an ingrained respect for the gender that was a by-product of his Southern planter upbringing. No matter what stamp he put on it, what he'd just done—albeit lawful—was a stain on Trace's reputation that couldn't be blotted out. That sorry realization played havoc with his equilibrium.

He cradled the woman to his chest, plowing through the sage and scrub in his path, evicting unsuspecting critters along the way, his heart keeping a ragged rhythm with his long-legged stride while he pondered her situation. What was she doing way out here alone on foot at sunset, and without an outer garment to protect her from the cool canyon night? Only a fool ventured forth after sundown in canyon country dressed as she was. And why in the garb of a man? What event had pushed her to become a horse thief? That was a hanging offense. Was she running to something, or away?

There was a more pressing matter, too. What had to be done had to be done quickly, now, while she was still unconscious. This woman was in need of medical attention, and Trace was the only living soul in a day's hard ride in any direction. He'd dug out his share of bullets over time—some from his own body—but he was no doctor. Nevertheless, there was no one else to save her. The one thing for which he was thankful was that he hadn't aimed to kill. Shooting a woman was bad enough; killing one was something his conscience would never forgive, horse thief or no.

Trace hadn't put up a tent. He never did in spring or summer, when the weather was good. Camp consisted of a fire to cook over and ward off predators, and a blanket roll, with his saddle as a pillow. Fortunately, he'd put that in place when he built the fire earlier, so he could now lay the woman down upon the bedding. He had nothing to ease the coming pain but whiskey, and precious little of that; it had been a while since he'd ridden to civilization for supplies. He hoped she didn't wake up.

Though a lantern was part of his gear, he couldn't remember when he'd last lit the thing. He did so now, and carried it closer. The canyon had quickly grown black as coal-tar pitch, and there was no moon, so he'd need all the light he could get. His fingers trembled as he adjusted the wick to a proper level and then placed the light down by her shoulder.

He tossed his Stetson atop his saddle and reached for his pack to take out a narrow-bladed knife kept for just such a situation. As he stared at it, he grimaced at the prospect of it cutting into her flesh. A cold oily roiling began in the pit of his stomach. With a long sigh, he next unstrapped the bowie knife from his thigh and hardened himself to what he must do. He leaned down and thrust both blades in the coals.

She had lost a lot of blood. Her blue plaid shirt was soaked with it. He unbuttoned the garment and gingerly stripped it away. The camisole beneath was also saturated. Trace hesitated, working his fingers nervously, then reached out and pulled it off, proprieties be damned. He sucked in a breath.

"Sweet Jesus. . . ." The words of awe came unbidden. The woman's breasts were full and round. Her skin was translucent and delicate, like pearl glistening in moonlight. For modesty's sake, Trace snatched another blanket and covered her. As he did, her tawny nipple grazed his wrist, its tumescent roughness in the cold night air causing a wash of scalding heat through his loins. The sensation rocked him back on his heels. Considering the urgency of the situation, his reaction took him by surprise. He tried to shake it off the way a dog sheds water—unsuccessfully. Lust surged through him. How could he ever have mistaken her for a man?

He focused again on his task. The bullet in her arm was likely lodged against the bone, which was why it hadn't passed through. There was no choice; it had to come out. Then the wound needed to be cauterized, to stop the bleeding and prevent infection.

"Damn it!" He looked up at the night sky in frustration, almost in supplication. "This needs a doctor." But there was no way around it; she might die if not properly treated.

He snatched his smaller knife from the fire, poured water over the blade, and waited for the hissing, spitting steam to evaporate. Without further hesitation, he pushed the thin, razor-sharp blade into the wound. Probing for the bullet, he glanced up at her ashen face, fearing she might somehow awaken.

Beads of sweat formed on his brow, trickled down his face. He wiped them away, trying to keep his vision clear. The woman didn't stir. He took note of the lump on her brow, larger now than when he'd first laid her down, the bruise already darkening from red to blackish purple. That, too, needed attention, but it would have to wait.

He swallowed hard as his knife struck metal. Carefully, he dug around the bullet, meanwhile pressing down with the fingers of his left hand alongside the entry hole. The hardest part was working the bullet free without causing more damage. Fortunately for her, the bullet wasn't too deep and hadn't ricocheted off bone and plunged deeper into her body.

"Thank the good Lord for small miracles."

Trace breathed a ragged sigh of relief, again thanking God when the bullet came free without too much effort. She'd lost so much blood that he wanted to minimize the amount of time he poked around. Reaching for his bottle of rotgut whiskey, he pulled out the stopper and poured some over the wound. Hesitating a second, he next put the bottle to his lips.

"I think I earned that," he said after downing a slug. Then, taking a clean bandana from his pack, he folded the cloth and pressed it to the wound. His eyes strayed to the fire, and he laughed, shaken. He'd been so relieved to have the bullet out, for a moment he'd forgotten the ordeal wasn't over. "Damn. Wish I'd taken a bigger drink."

His stomach muscles flexed as he pulled his bowie knife from the fire. Gritting his teeth, he pressed the glowing blade against the woman's oozing wound and gave a slow count of three. The smell of singed flesh hit his nostrils, and he had to swallow back bile. The woman finally stirred, writhing against the press of red-hot metal, but she moaned and lapsed back into unconsciousness without ever opening her eyes. The sound of her agony ran through Trace like the Yankee saber that had pierced his side when he rode with the Nathan Bedford Forest's cavalry during the War Between the States. Only, this was worse.

A strange mix of euphoria and desperation moved

Trace. Almost dizzy with it, he marked it as concern for the woman. Removing her boots and bathing her face with cool water from his canteen, he hacked off the head of a nearby cactus, stripped off his kerchief, and soaked it in the cactus juice, making a compress that he applied to the lump on her brow. Even so, his edginess was far from spent. The night was cool—too cool for the way she was dressed. Ignoring his body's reaction to touching her bare flesh, he eased her into his spare shirt and then tucked both blankets around her. When that was done, he set about gathering enough dead wood to erect a crude lean-to out of his rain slicker, a shelter for her from the wind. Only then did he permit himself to sink down cross-legged beside the fire.

Reaching for the bottle, he took another drink: a small one, just a swallow to still the memories clamoring inside his head. He would not sleep, not until he was certain the woman was out of danger.

Her face was ash white in the firelight; the full, bowed lips bore no trace of color. In stark contrast were the ribbons of strawberry blonde hair spread out like a fan about her. He recalled its fragrance, like blooming wild clover. It wouldn't leave his nostrils. Not even the pungent sagebrush fed to the campfire could chase it.

Somewhere he'd heard that people who suffered a blow to the head should not be allowed to sleep; they often didn't wake up. Where had he heard that? At his mother's knee? Among the Navajos? He couldn't remember. And, truth or not, he wouldn't chance waking her; he didn't have enough whiskey to quell her pain.

He almost laughed. If she were a man, none of this would be happening. Horse thieves weren't coddled in the Territories. What would he have done in that case? Probably not what another man might have. Torturing and killing were both distasteful to Trace Ord. Such tactics were abhorrent to him, though he'd watched many men swing from the end of a rope, seen them pinioned over red ant hills in the desert or staked out in the blazing sun for vultures, seen all manner of debasements for stealing another man's horse. Surely she must have known the consequences of taking such an action. What could have possibly driven her to it?

After a while he began to nod off, each time jerking back awake. When the fire started to dwindle, he fed it more scrub until it flared to life again. He crept close to the woman often, and felt her face for fever. Her skin remained cool to the touch, thankfully, and the gentle rise and fall of her breasts was steady—good signs. She was young, and evidently of sturdy stock. Despite her frail appearance, she was unmistakably a lady of quality.

Admittedly, Trace was hardly a good judge anymore. In the near decade since the war, he'd had scant contact with women. Once . . . Well, he remembered gentler things, like lacy doilies and the sweet scent of violet water, but those had been a lifetime ago. These days, the sorts of women he found were in parlor houses, saloons, and cantinas. They asked for little from a man, and they left him with different sights and smells, ones he would just as soon dismiss from memory once he was out the door.

He based his conclusions about this woman on those distant memories, the ones he pondered on rare occasion when sitting fireside and listening to the mournful cry of a distant coyote. He'd noticed her fingernails were clean and trimmed, her hands soft and unspoiled. They hadn't the telltale markings of hard labor, and she wore a wedding ring. Why did his heart twist at that discovery? He doubted her fine skin had ever been slathered with a whore's paint, or that she'd ever smelled of anything stronger than wildflowers or rosewater—which made her current situation even more bizarre.

Just before dawn she stirred, and Trace surged to his feet. This was what he'd been waiting for, and was also what he dreaded: the answers to all the questions banging around in his brain, not the least of which was what he would do with her. When she groaned and tried to rise, he reached her in two giant strides and prevented her with a firm but gentle hand.

"Easy, ma'am," he said. "You need to rest."

She groaned again. "What's happened to me?" she murmured.

In the gray light, Trace couldn't tell the color of her eyes, only that they were large and doelike. He held the lantern close, but she shrank from the light. He'd seen that many times before in people who'd taken blows to the skull.

"You were making off with my horse," he said. "I called out a warning, but you didn't heed it, and . . . I shot you."

Clearly terror-stricken, she tried to rise in earnest.

"Whoa there!" he said, restraining her again. "I dug the bullet out, and you're going to be fine—unless you undo all my work. You've lost a lot of blood, so you need to stay still and rest if you're going to mend."

"You can't mean you . . . you . . ." She examined the shirt he'd given her. "You . . . ?"

"With you bleeding to death, there was no time to stand on ceremony," he said. "Your clothes were blood-soaked, and I never yet met a man who could dig lead out through frilly undergarments." Her breath caught on a strangled gasp as he displayed her bloody shirt and camisole before consigning them to the fire.

"Wh-what do you mean to . . . do with me?" she panted, sinking back down again with a groan.

"That depends," he said. She had a lot of explaining to do before he could make a decision.

"W-water . . ." she moaned. "Is there water?"

Trace snatched up his canteen and moistened her lips. "Go easy!" he cautioned. "Little sips. We've got enough to deal with as it is." The command sounded sterner than he'd intended; he didn't want to frighten her. By the same token, he needed to keep the upper hand.

She obeyed, and after a moment he set the canteen aside. "You've got some explaining to do, lady," he said, hands on his hips. "But first off . . . I didn't know you were a woman when I fired—"

"And if you had known?" Her eyes flashed.

"I didn't, and that's that," Trace growled. "For your information, if I'd aimed to kill, you'd be dead. I can shoot the wings off a bee at fifty paces." A slight exaggeration, of course, but her wide-eyed expression told him he'd made his point.

"Just for the record," he went on, "I don't hold with hard handling of women—any women, even a horse thief. I'd say you best start with telling me why you were trying to make off with my horse." That fact stuck in his craw. How would it look for a renegade rider—a wrangler who rode from ranch to ranch, returning stray and rustled horses to their owners—to have his own mount stolen right out from under him? His jaw muscle began to tick at the thought.

The woman didn't reply.

"And what were you doing way out here all alone with no coat and night coming on?" he demanded. "Is somebody after you?"

"I don't have to answer you!" she snapped, sounding stronger than she possibly could feel.

"No, you don't," he fired back. "You can answer to the sheriff at Flat Springs if you'd rather. Well? What'll it be? Think careful now. That pretty neck of yours wouldn't look good stretched by a rope."

"You've got your horse back," she pointed out.

Ignoring the remark, he asked, "Where did you learn to ride bareback like that?" She was a plucky little thing, gentlewoman or no.

"Back ho—" Her eyes flew wide, reminding him of a trapped animal. "None of your business!"

"Hmm. What's your name? You can tell me that, at least," he tried.

"Mae C—Mae *Ahern*," she amended.

Mae was true, at least. He was sure of that. But she was frightened and clearly hiding something. Only, this didn't help his problem. What was he going to do with her? How was he going to see her wherever she needed to go once she was fit for travel? He owed her that at least. But if she wouldn't tell him where she was headed in such an all-fired hurry—

"I'm tired," she moaned. "I hurt . . . and I'm tired."

"I have nothing for the pain but whiskey. You're welcome to what's left," he offered.

"I don't drink strong spirits," she huffed. It made him think of those lace dollies again.

"Not even for medicinal purposes?"

"Not for *any* purpose," she flung at him.

Trace shrugged. "Suit yourself. You're a stubborn filly, ain'tcha? Do you sass your husband like this, too?"

"What do you know of my husband?" she flashed.

"Nothing. Never had the pleasure . . . that I know of. How could I? I don't even know who you are. Neither do you, evidently, judging from the way you stumbled over your name just now."

She blanched. "I don't owe you any explanations. You shot me!"

"Making off with my horse. Let's not forget that, lady," he growled.

"I'm tired and I hurt," she sobbed. "And I'm still thirsty."

He sighed. "I told you, you've got to go easy on the water; it's a ways to the next watering hole. I offered you whiskey for the . . ."

She shook her head in refusal, shut her eyes, and shrank beneath the blanket.

Well, wasn't that a fine how-do-you-do? Trace didn't know any more now than he did before, the sun was already sending pink-gold streamers over the canyon wall, and he hadn't shut his eyes all night. He heaved a ragged sigh and stomped to where he'd tethered his burro the night before. Muttering under his breath, he fished the coffeepot from his pack. He groped for his sack of Arbuckle's coffee, his basin, and the fixings for pan biscuits he'd bake over the fire.

Squatting down, he built up the dwindling campfire, prodding it with a stick. This was clearly not the start of the day he'd planned. He'd been trailing wild horses with an eye toward getting an invitation to hire on at the next ranch on his list: the Lazy C. But he wouldn't just be rounding up strays there. On good authority, he had it that the owner was responsible for half the rustled horses in canyon country. All he had to do was prove it. First, however, he needed the bait, and he couldn't concentrate on getting that while he had Mae Whoever-she-was on his hands.

He glanced over to see if she was ready to talk yet, but her eyes were shut and she'd fallen back asleep. A half smile twisted his lips. "Little Renegade," he whispered. His chest heaved with a small laugh.

She rested most of the day, but Trace enjoyed no such luxury. He didn't dare, though he was passing exhaustion. He'd gone without sleep many times before, during the war and after, but he wished he hadn't driven himself so relentlessly these past two days, not stopping to make camp, pausing only briefly to rest his animals in his hurry to reach the canyon; all this was taking its toll on him now. He could hardly keep his eyes open.

To beat back the exhaustion, he scavenged the area, stockpiling brush and firewood. He took advantage of Mae's deep slumber to check her wound and apply a healing poultice made with the medicine bag given to him by the Navajos. They had taught him how to gather and dry roots and herbs, to grind them into powders and potions. These had cured many injuries over the years, from toothaches to bullet wounds. Fortunately, Mae's wound wasn't deep, and she showed signs of healing nicely. So far, there was no taint of infection. Only, out here one couldn't be too careful. He fashioned a sling from his last clean bandana and gently tied it in place.

Every so often he felt her face, but there was no sign of fever; her skin remained cool to the touch. The bruise on her head was a nasty sight, but it would mend. All in all, he was satisfied with his doctoring. He hadn't been forced to do so much since the war, so it pleased him that he hadn't lost his touch. He'd saved his own life more times than he could count.

As the day wore on, Trace repositioned the lean-to in order to keep the sun off Mae. He couldn't help but worry that someone would come looking for her, maybe someone she didn't want to see. It wouldn't do to be taken unawares. Leaving a canteen and a couple of biscuits beside her, he climbed the ridge to scope the lay of the land.

That vista offered an eagle-eyed view for miles in all directions. The canyon wall sheered upward from sandy bottomland, which had a snakelike ribbon of water threading through it. To the north other canyons loomed, each more spectacular than the last, sweeping across the cloudless horizon in varying hues from red to purple to brown to gray. To the south the land fell away into plains and finally wasteland, shimmering like a silvery mirage in the sun. A striking mesa lay to the east, and in the west was more canyon country.

Distant mountain peaks rose like the Amat Avii

Kahuwaaly, Hualapai Mountain, veiled in lavender, a late afternoon haze. Somewhere in that purple distance was the Lazy C. Trace squatted on his haunches at the edge of the ridge for some time, his Winchester across his knees, looking for motion, a cloud of dust kicked up by horses in pursuit. Mae had been heading northeast when his shot brought her down. He looked long and hard to the southwest, but nothing met his eyes save broad-winged condors, silhouetted black against the clear blue sky. Meanwhile, he remained on alert for the wild mustangs he knew inhabited the canyon. They were led by an elusive broomtail sorrel stallion the Indians called Standing Thunder. All Trace had to do was locate them. Nothing met his eye.

Just before sunset he abandoned his vigil and climbed down. Mae was still sleeping—or pretending, since he noticed she'd eaten the biscuits he'd left. He couldn't help the smile crossing his lips as he passed her. Trying to ignore the reaction, he set the kettle of frijoles he'd prepared earlier on a tripod over the fire.

Mae struggled to sit upright, giving a yawn, her brown eyes following his every move. She clearly knew she was in deep trouble for stealing his horse, but there was another story in her gaze: she recognized Trace's guilt at shooting a woman.

"You hungry?" he asked.

She didn't answer, just gave a faint nod.

Trace dragged one of his packs between the bedroll and the fire, and he created a makeshift table for the coming meal. While he worked, he debated on pushing her for answers. Then he recalled taming Diablo. It had been a step-by-step process, allowing the horse to approach him in trust. He figured gentling a woman wasn't too different.

They'd scarcely finished the grub when she set aside her plate and turned away. Blasted woman hadn't even spoken a word, though she'd watched his every move while he ate, her smoldering eyes raking him with unabashed disapproval.

He ran a hand over the stubble on his face. Well, he *could* use a shave, and his hair was a mite shaggy. He usually got it cut when it started to fall in his eyes, but he hadn't been near a town in a month of Sundays. Maybe that was the reason she regarded him with her pretty little nose in the air. He sniffed his shirtsleeve as inconspicuously as possible, then grimaced. There was no doubt about it; he smelled more like a horse than a man.

"Not so fast," he said as she tried to disappear beneath the blanket. Enough of this silence; he needed answers. Too much time had passed already. If she was on the run from someone, which he readily assumed, then trouble was riding up on their heels, fast. He had to be prepared for whatever it was. "We've got to talk."

"I have nothing to say to you," she pronounced. "Do what you will with me and have it over with."

"That's just it," he snapped. "I don't rightly know what *to* do with you, unless you give me some idea who or what you're running from. I figure me shooting you sort of squares us in regard to you stealing my horse. I'll see you safe to wherever it is you want to go, wherever it was you were headed when I—"

"You can't."

Her answer came fast, and with a finality that rocked

him back on his heels. "For a horse thief you're mighty
quick with telling me what I can and cannot do. Maybe
that knock on the head jangled your brain. You can't be
out here all on your own, half dressed with no horse
and no provisions. You need help. Not telling me your
troubles don't change the situation. I'm sorry for my part
in your miseries, and I'm trying to make amends, but—"

"You *can't* . . ." she sobbed.

"There you go again with those can'ts. Lady, you've
got two choices: I can see you safe to where you were
headed when you stole my horse, or I can wash my
hands of you, leave you with the sheriff at Flat Springs
and let him sort you out. There are no other choices,
and if you're half as smart as I think, you know it. Now,
what'll it be?"

"Thanks to you, I'm hardly in fit condition for either
of your choices at the moment," she said. "I need
time . . . to think. It's only fair."

He shook his head. "You know, it amazes me that
you keep forgetting that you're to blame for all of this.
You make me out the villain, when it was you who were
looking to make off with my horse. You just don't go
around stealing a man's horse! It'd be kinder just to put
a gun to his head and kill him on the spot, for that's
what it amounts to, and you damn well know it!"

Her eyes were big and brown, a frightened doe's eyes
staring down the barrel of a hunter's rifle. They had the
power to melt Trace. Something twisted inside—a part
of him he'd thought long dead, belonging to a time
when chivalry still lived—which made him want to put
his fist through the nearby cactus. Maybe pain would
bring him back to his senses.

He growled, "You don't have much time, lady. Unless I miss my guess, and I rarely do, somebody's hot on your trail. It's been a full day since I shot you. A full day's riding for them to catch up. I have an itch crawling up my neck, like when a bunch of Comanches are out for a scalp, telling me we're about to have company. I'd say your time for reflection has just about run out."

Trace jerked up his Winchester. He paused, waiting for a reply. When not one word came, he turned his back on her and stomped off to have a look around. Blasted female was going to be nothing but trouble.

Chapter Two

$\mathcal{M}ae$ wasn't all that steady on her feet, though she'd practiced that afternoon while her captor was up on the ridge. She didn't want the man to know her exact condition. Clearly, she couldn't have left—not then, in broad daylight—even had she found the strength, so she'd bided her time and waited for the right moment.

He was asleep now, his snores a comfort. They'd cover any sounds of her withdrawal from camp. As she tiptoed past, she couldn't help but notice the long, lean length of him, rolled up in that blanket too short for his frame. He'd given her all his other covers, keeping only this for himself, and his horse's worn saddle blanket, which he'd used over his saddle for a pillow. Poor man, he'd likely awaken with a stiff neck.

Divested of his Stetson, his chestnut hair lay in waves and fell carelessly over his brow and around his earlobes. The front locks were streaked by the sun, glinting coppery in the firelight, which also showed faint traces of silver at his temples. His was a strong profile, with rugged, angular features and a handsome cleft chin that three days' growth of beard couldn't hide. Shadows obscured his deep-set eyes. She had noticed them in earlier furtive glances, those steely blue eyes, piercing beneath a ledge of sun-bleached brows. She had avoided looking directly into them as much as possible. No one could hide from such eagle eyes. They had the power to hypnotize. They also made her uncomfortable in ways she didn't want to think about.

More than once on her way to where he'd hobbled Diablo, she glanced over her shoulder to be certain he hadn't heard her. Thankfully, he slept like the dead. Mae breathed a ragged sigh. He seemed a nice man, genuinely sorry he'd shot her. But then, her poor judgment had played her false too many times. Oh, how she longed to trust him—to trust *someone*. She was so desperately alone. He'd shot her, yes, but the man was within his rights. Even so, he'd doctored her. She shuddered to think of her fate if she'd encountered one of the more unsavory sorts that infested the West like fleas.

Her skin still tingled from the gentle touch of Trace's hands feeling her brow for fever and fastening the sling about her neck when he thought her asleep. That's what she'd wanted him to think. She could still feel his body heat and smell his scent: provocative raw maleness, laced with leather and tobacco. Different than any other man. Though the shirt he'd given her was clean enough, it smelled the same. How that scent swam over her! She fingered the soft blue flannel absently, several wishes going unspoken.

All at once blood coursed through her veins, surged hot to her temples, and prickled along her scalp. Have mercy! She nearly lost her footing as she recalled the truth: the man had seen her naked to the waist. Oddly, he hadn't taken advantage of her. Many men would not have been so respectful, so kind. He was evidently cut from the cloth of a gentleman—something to which she was unaccustomed. The fool had even offered to take her wherever she wanted to go. If he only knew where that was! And it was impossible, especially after what she was about to do.

At her approach, Diablo greeted her with a soft nickering. Mae's blood jumped, but she quickly soothed the stallion to silence with gentle strokes and soft words. Bending over, she unbuckled his hobbles, whispering to him all the while and responding with reassuring hands as he nudged her with that velvety black nose. Taking the bridle, she eased the bit into his mouth and then fastened it around his ears and forehead.

Casting one last look back, she stared, fixed upon her captor sleeping soundly beside the fire. Sadly, she didn't even know his name. But perhaps it was best that way. For a moment, she'd hesitated, sorry for what she was about to do, but there really wasn't any other choice. One thing he'd said rang true: someone would be coming after her. Indeed, she could already almost feel his hot breath on her neck. No, the stranger was right. She'd run out of time and forfeited her choices.

Her head was reeling. She was by no means up to the task at hand, but there was nothing left but to suck in a deep breath and carry through. She couldn't mount Diablo bareback in her weakened state, and wouldn't even if she could. Not here. The risk of being caught out was too great. Dang wranglers never slept soundly; she'd learned that the hard way long ago. His sitting up and caring for her for a full day gave her a small edge. Poor man was exhausted.

Swallowing dry, she gripped the horse's reins in her right hand and slowly walked him out into the canyon. There was a break in the wall some yards off, where rocks had sheared away from the ridge above, allowing her to climb to a height where she could more easily mount the stallion. Pain seared her shoulder with every movement, and to keep from crying out she bit into her lip until she tasted blood. When at last the dizziness subsided, she took a deep breath of sweet spring air and turned her eyes one last time toward the campfire where her captor slept. Tasting regret, she gently nudged the horse with her knees and disappeared into the starlit night.

Trace awoke, chilled in the darkness before dawn. The fire had gone out, and his first conscious thought was of rekindling it for Mae's comfort. He yawned, stretched, and rolled over . . . only to stop dead, his eyes fixed on Mae's bedroll. Her empty bedroll. As his heart stuttered, he tried to tell himself that maybe she'd slipped off to heed the call of nature.

A quick glance to the far side of the encampment confirmed other fears. Diablo's hobbles lay abandoned on the ground. Trace scrambled to his feet and rushed toward them, wincing at the sharp stones beneath his stockinged feet. Snatching them up in an iron fist, he scanned the black distance in all directions for some sign of Mae. Nothing.

"Hellfire, horse feathers, and damnation!" he roared

as he hurled Diablo's hobbles to the ground. Not content with that, he let loose a string of expletives, which in turn evoked a *hee-haw* from the burro staked nearby. Marching over, he vented his spleen on the fool varmint. "Shut up, you lop-eared jackass! Why couldn't you make that god-awful racket when she was making off with Diablo?"

It was beyond bearing. He was a renegade rider, and he'd had his prize stallion rustled from right under his nose not once but twice—and by a woman, no less. When this got out, and it surely would, he'd never live it down. He'd be the laughingstock of the whole territory.

Trace raked a hand roughly through his hair, trying to think. The blasted hobbles caught his eye again, and he drew back his foot and kicked them into the air with all his strength, remembering too late that he hadn't taken the time to pull on his boots. His yowl, and the one-legged dance that followed, elicited another chorus of braying from the burro. Trace loosed another string of curses, more colorful than the last, and then stalked back to build up the campfire.

He was used to night tracking, but the circumstances were too serious to risk losing the trail in the dark. Dawn was nigh, so after tending the fire he set out a pot of Arbuckle's to brew, awaiting first light.

After drinking half his second cup of coffee, he doused the fire by slinging the remainder into the flames. He'd decided not to break camp. In her condition, he doubted she would stay in the saddle for long. "Stupid woman wants to get herself killed," he muttered, gathering what he'd need. "If she hadn't lit out with Diablo, I might leave her to do just that."

Despite his grumbling, Trace knew that wasn't so. There was something vulnerable and panicked in her brown eyes that touched his heart in a way he couldn't explain. It made a man want to step forward to defend her, no matter what she was running from.

Giving the donkey a glare, he told it, "Don't you go getting yourself stolen, too, you hear?" Then, armed with his pistol, his Winchester, and a full canteen, he put on his Stetson and strode past the burro.

Mae and Diablo's trail was easy to follow, and he tracked them on foot across the canyon to the sheer-faced wall to a shelf where she had obviously mounted. Such resourcefulness encouraged him somewhat, but the fact that she couldn't just jump up on the stallion told him that Mae wasn't up to making any escape. His white-lipped anger dissolved into a troubled frown. He would find her any minute, unconscious on the canyon floor; he was sure of it. He just hoped she was still alive.

Diablo's tracks were clear and fresh; the stallion was running at a full gallop. He wasn't branded, but Trace had notched the horse's hooves and shoes as a means of identification to prove ownership in just such a situation as this. The trail stopped at the narrow stream snaking through the canyon, one of many tributaries that fed the Colorado River farther down. The stream was shallow here, and not too wide to cross on foot. The water barely reached midcalf at its deepest. Frustratingly, the prints didn't pick back up on the other bank.

Looking up at the hot sun rising high in the sky, Trace sighed. "Blamed woman is smarter than I gave her credit for." Mae had evidently ridden Diablo straight through the center of the stream to avoid leaving a trail.

Picking up his pace, Trace waded into the water and zigzagged back and forth from bank to bank for some distance. At a bend in the canyon wall, the rising water reached his hips. Then his waist. The depth and swirling eddies were a growing problem, and Trace had to struggle to keep his balance and to hold his weapons up to keep them dry. This was good news, however. Diablo was water-shy.

Assuming the horse would be too hard for her to handle, Trace crossed over, and just as he expected, he found the beast's tracks again on the south bank. He followed them east-southeast for some time until the canyon wall gave way to flat tables and shelves leading to higher, rockier ground that would cloak Diablo's hoofprints. Mae had ridden straight for it.

"Son of a bitch."

And Trace cursed again when he spotted the other tracks. "One . . . two . . . three, no, *four* riders, riding hard."

A short distance ahead, it was clear where they had overtaken and surrounded Mae. She had almost escaped them. Almost. The violent marks left behind on the sandy canyon bottom told the story. Diablo's tracks, for the most part, were hind-hoof prints, showing he'd reared and spun in a vain attempt to break free of the circle of horses closing in around him. Trace imagined the confrontation only too clearly.

He followed. Mae had not gone willingly. She had fought her attackers, both on and off Diablo. She'd been dragged off the stallion by the look of it, broken free, and run. One man had jumped from his horse and gone after her. She hadn't gotten far. There had been a skirmish then. The imprint of two struggling bodies was clearly visible in the red sand, along with ruts from Mae's boots as she was dragged off.

"Poor, stupid fool. She never had a chance." Trace removed his hat to mop sweat from his brow, blinking back tears. Why hadn't she stayed with him? He could have protected her.

He put together what had happened next. The riders had headed southwest, Diablo with them, bucking and rearing to the last. But Trace lost their trail in the rocks, and blind fury set his blood boiling. How could she have courted this fate rather than confide in him? Double damn, it was his fault. He'd spooked her.

Farther up ahead, a swatch of blue caught his eye: his kerchief. The same one he'd fashioned into a sling for Mae. He picked up the pace and, squatting on his haunches, dragged it from a tumbleweed. The knot was still tied. There was blood on it.

A flaming sun died on the horizon, painting the sky over the western hills with bands of crimson, gold, and turquoise blue, that majestic beauty almost taunting Trace as he limped back toward his camp. He was thirsty, hungry, and sore to the bone.

"On top of that, I must be hallucinating," he grumbled—and pulled up short. The tantalizing aroma of fresh coffee, biscuits, and what smelled like hot son-of-a-bitch stew threaded through his nostrils, riding on the fragrant smoke of burning sagebrush.

Cocking his Winchester, he crept along in the shadows of the rocky shelf. He could have sworn he had doused the campfire. Taking aim, he leveled the rifle on a wizened, rags-clad figure in a floppy slouch hat. He was seated on the ground, stirring part of the afore-mentioned hallucination with a long-handled spoon.

"Don't move a muscle," Trace warned the intruder.

"I heard you coming, young fella," the man replied without turning. "Heard you before you rounded that ridge back yonder. Not too smart. You want to watch that. Could get you killed."

"You're the one courting death, old-timer, messing with another man's camp," Trace growled. "Who in hell are you?"

It was as though Trace hadn't asked the question. "Them Navajos didn't teach you much, did they?"

Trace stood slack-jawed.

The old man did turn then, and presented him with a sly wink and a gap-toothed smile. "No magic. I found your medicine bag," he explained.

Trace shook his head to clear it and tossed the man's words back into his face. "Do you always make free with a man's belongings without so much as a howdy-do? Not too smart. You want to watch that. Could get you killed."

"Now, ain't that gratitude for you?" The intruder laughed. "Here I fix you vittles, feed your jackass, and keep watch over your outfit for you, and what do I get for my pains? Piss and vinegar, that's what. Didn't your mama teach you no manners?"

"Leave my mother out of this. Answer my question," Trace demanded. "Who gave you leave to go rummaging through my kit?"

"Why, nobody," the old man said. "You see anyone around here to say yea or nay, except that fool burro?

I stumbled onto your camp—coffee still warm in the pot, that jackass over there with his tongue hanging out for want of water, hobbles on the ground, with no horse in them . . . and tracks I take to be yours, leading off into the canyon. Seemed you lit out in a hurry. I got tired of waiting for you to come back, so I had me a look-see through your packs to find out if you was worthy of some of my stew. Ain't as good as I usually make, sorry to say—not enough critter parts. Mostly beans, some wild onions. But an empty belly makes everything tastes better, eh?"

"So I passed muster?" Trace asked.

"Well enough," the old man replied with a crisp nod. "I don't break bread with outlaws or rustlers. I got you figured for a man come to hard luck or hard times. Maybe both."

"You still haven't told me who you are," Trace persisted. "I'm pretty careful who I break bread with myself."

"Some folks call me Pappy, but that ain't my real name. Some folks call me Slops, since I done my time as camp cook over the years. Tain't my real name, neither. Take your pick, or call me whatever you like. Truth told, folks have given me so many handles over the years, I don't rightly remember what my real name is." He dosed Trace with a sober stare. "Around these parts, young fella, sometimes it's better that way."

Trace stared at the strange figure patiently stirring his pot. He looked like one of those raggedy leprechauns his mama had told him about at bedtime when he was small. Still, his belly was getting the better of his caution, as the aroma of that stew was sheer torture.

He hadn't had a bite to eat all day, just the few swigs of coffee, since he'd been so anxious to set out after Mae. His stomach rumbled and his mouth began to water. He swallowed back the hunger. Dealing with an old "sourdough" was the last thing he needed. But oh, the smell of that stew . . .

"Well?" The old man brayed a laugh, which set off Trace's burro again. "Are you going to stand there slack-jawed, or put that damn Winchester down and grab a plate?"

With a sigh, Trace leaned the rifle against his saddle.

Chapter Three

Trace didn't know what to make of the new intruder. He'd been a loner too long for trust to come easily. Putting faith in the wrong people often put a cowboy in his grave, and this man showing up so soon after Mae made Trace think twice about trusting him. Still, there was something about the old geezer that seemed harmless, and Trace's guard slowly relaxed.

"You got a name, son?" the drifter asked, taking a final bite of biscuit.

Trace set his plate aside and settled back with his tin cup full of perfectly brewed coffee, watching the old man through the flames of the campfire. Finally he said, "Ord—Trace Ord."

"Not your real handle, though, I'll wager."

"Like you said, old man, sometimes it's better that way."

"Yep, that's what I figured."

"Where'd you come from anyway?" Trace pressed. He wanted answers—or at least some reason to trust the old man's sudden appearance.

"Originally? Back East—"

Trace gave him a level stare. "No, today. Did you happen on a pack of riders—five, maybe six—heading southwest?"

Pappy shook his head. "I'm down from Flat Springs," he said.

"Too far north," Trace grunted. "You wouldn't have seen them. Where are you headed anyway?"

"Just drifting," Pappy replied. "Figured I'd head on out toward California. Heard there's still gold in the desert out there, if a man knows where to look for it."

Trace shook his head at the notion. "Death Valley? You must be addled? That's no place for an old-timer. Not with summer coming on. That desert is hell on earth, a man-killer. How do you think it got its name?"

The old man shrugged. "Prospecting is just about the only occupation I haven't tried my hand at. A man can't brag about what he ain't done, and I aim to brag about it *all* afore I die. Bragging is what I do best, son. Where were you aiming to head before you lit out on foot like you got bee-stung? And where's your horse? You ain't been riding that burro, that's for dang sure."

"I was headed for the Lazy C. A couple rancher friends of mine are looking for some horses that somebody made off with. Rumor has it that more than one herd's made its way to the Lazy C. I aim to see if theirs is among 'em," Trace admitted.

Pappy looked skeptical. "Old Colonel Comstock's place, eh? That's a bad outfit, son. You don't want to be messing around the Lazy C. Word is, it was a pretty square spread when the old man was running it." He paused to sip his coffee, shooting Trace a dark look. "The son's got it now. Ain't no meaner hombre in the Territories than Jared Comstock. Heard tell he ain't above rustling or worse. He'd sooner shoot a man as look at him, is what people say."

"I'm going there just the same. You know where it is?"

Pappy pointed. "See them mountains? That's the Hualapai Range. The Lazy C sits just east of that gap there in the middle. But what—you aiming on walking in there single-handed, expecting him to just hand over all the horses he's stole? And you called *me* addled." He snorted.

"I had planned to cut out a few wild mustangs, maybe even the one the Indians call Standing Thunder if I got lucky, and use them as bait to get myself hired on as a wrangler. Only, now I've got to catch up with those riders I asked about. I tracked them southwest to the rocks, and then lost the trail in the dark. I left a marker. I'll head back to the spot come first light and scour the area until I pick it up again."

"You sure must want them hombres pretty bad," Pappy muttered.

"One of them stole my horse."

"Well, that explains you being on foot. I had you pegged for either a wrangler or a lawman. I can smell the law a mile downwind of a cyclone."

"Is that right? You got problems with the law, Pappy?"

"Nope. I just spot 'em."

"Well, I've done my share of days as deputy," Trace admitted, "but I'm no lawman. Never been on the wrong side of the law, though, if that's what's about to come out of your mouth. But that's likely to change once I catch up with those riders."

"I don't want nothing to do with bounty hunters," Pappy remarked. "Can't trust 'em."

Trace flashed a grin. "You might say I'm a bounty hunter—of sorts. But I hunt horses, not men."

"That why you tote a gun with no trigger guard? You sure you ain't a gunslinger?"

"I'm no gunslinger, Pappy, but I like staying alive. A man has to have an edge to survive out here."

"A renegade rider?" Pappy realized. Trace steeled himself against what was coming. "And you got your horse stole?" The old man shook his head and clicked his tongue, chuckling. "That don't say much for your talents, do it? You ain't been at it long, have you?"

"Long enough," Trace growled, hurling the dregs of his coffee into the fire. A plume of hissing, spitting steam shot up.

"Don't go gettin' your britches in a twist. I'll help if I can," Pappy offered.

"You wouldn't happen to have a horse stashed someplace, would you?" Trace asked. "That's about the only way you could help me now."

"Just that old jackass staked alongside yours over there. Where's your partner? Did he get his horse stole, too?"

Trace blinked. "What partner?"

The old man crooked his thumb toward the two bedrolls.

Trace drew the bloodstained kerchief from the back pocket of his jeans and fingered it absently. "I shot a thief stealing my horse, night before. Turned out to be a woman running from something."

"A woman out here? Alone?"

Trace nodded. "The wound wasn't bad. I wasn't shooting to kill. Whatever she's running from must have scared her pretty bad."

Pappy filled in the blanks: "So she stole your horse again. And you set out after her."

"Yep. And I mean to get that damned horse back," Trace concluded.

The old-timer frowned, scratching his grizzled beard. "A man gets his horse stole, he gets mad. You ain't mad so much as you're worried. I'm guessing that worry is for that little horse thief."

"She's on the run—and I did shoot her, after all," Trace confessed. "And now that pack of riders has her and my horse."

"And you plan on going up against five or six men alone?" Pappy took sand and rubbed the tin plates to clean them. After a moment he added, "She must be something. A man can always wrangle another horse, so I'm thinking you're more concerned about that gal."

Irritation pulsed through Trace. "I spent five years of my life stalking that stallion, tracking him from canyon to canyon and finally cutting him out of a herd single-handed. Snapped a bone in my wrist breaking him."

"You might be proud of the stallion, but it's concern over that gal eating away at your insides. And most likely your conceit is scorpion-bit by her stealing your pride and joy, *twice*. Bad mix of emotions riding you, renegade. You best be careful. When a woman gets under a man's skin, he loses that edge you were talking about."

Trace's jaw flexed. "She ain't 'under my skin.' I just want my horse back."

Pappy laughed. "Then them mules ain't the only thing stubborn around here." He paused before suggesting, "Since we're both heading in the same general direction, maybe I'll throw in with you for a spell."

Trace shook his head. "I travel alone, old-timer. Then I only have to worry about myself."

"Seems to me you could use a hand, seein' as your head's been turned by a female."

Trace settled back against his saddle, stared into the fire. "I don't want you underfoot. Not that I don't appreciate the offer, but I can't afford distractions. And that's what you'd be. I don't want to bury you, either."

"Might be one way to look at it," Pappy mused. "But from where I'm sitting, maybe it was your lucky day when I stumbled upon your camp, maybe it happened for a reason. Maybe having me watch your back would be good——might save your life. You might be glad you brung me. See, no pretty female has me all hepped up like a stallion scenting a mare. A thing like that is mighty distracting. When you throw down against a pack of varmints, another gun protecting your back might make all the difference. Ever think of that?"

Trace ran his hand through his hair and breathed an exasperated nasal sigh. This was not how things were supposed to be. He'd had everything planned before a horse thief smelling of wild clover, with hair like sunset gold and eyes like a doe, crashed into his life. His loins responded to the memories of Mae's soft skin, her full white breasts. Pulling a blanket over his legs, he shifted uneasily.

The old man sniggered, not fooled. "Thinking, are you?"

"I'm going after my horse," Trace responded.

"I figured. The woman has nothing to do it." Pappy began fixing his bedroll. "And that's another thing— I'm a damn fine tracker, nearly as good as an Injun. Might come in handy tomorrow trying to pick up their trail."

"Is there anything you aren't good at, old man?" Trace asked.

"Jack-of-all-trades, master of few," came the reply. "Unless you say otherwise, I'm assuming I'll be heading out with you at first light."

"Even if I said no, I have a feeling you'd just trail along anyways." Trace slid down against his saddle, fighting a yawn. It had been a hard day. He needed to get some sleep.

"Maybe you ain't half as stupid as that damn burro of yours. Been kind of lonely out here. Our paths crossing seems fated, so I reckon I'll be tagging along."

"Just one thing," said Trace, stretching out. "If you're going to tag along, stay out of my way, and when I tell you something, I expect you to listen. I don't want to be repeating myself. A man's life depends on quick thought and even quicker action."

Not waiting for an answer, he rolled over to get some much-needed rest. His feet were sore from the stones and his imprudent assault on Diablo's hobbles, not to mention the miles of tracking Diablo and the woman. Only, sleep didn't come. His blankets smelled of wild clover—of Mae.

He awoke with a start just as the sky began to lighten, to the smell of fresh coffee and a hand like wrinkled leather shaking his shoulder. His gun left his holster before his eyes focused.

"Whooooooa, Ord! It's *me*," the old man chuckled. "Ain't worth wasting the bullet."

"Don't ever do that," Trace growled.

"You'd best hop to," the old man urged. "You made it sound as if you wanted to be off by first light. Maybe we better shake a leg? I don't like the looks of that sky. The air's so thick you could cut it with a knife."

Trace accepted a tin of hot coffee, then took note Pappy had already packed up the rest of the camp. Maybe allowing him to tag along wouldn't be so bad after all.

Pappy pushed a plate at him. "Not much—just some leftover stew and a hard biscuit. Soak it in your coffee and it'll soften it up. You need grub in your belly if'n you plan to catch up to your horse and your woman."

"The woman ain't mine." Trace picked up a fork. "And I've ate coffee-soaked biscuits more times than I care to remember. Daily diet for a Johnny Reb."

"Figured you for one, what with that accent." Pappy studied him with a sharp eye. "Tough to place. Ain't hard like Tennessee, nor heavy on the drawl like Mississippi. Planters stock, I'm a-guessing. Georgia or Alabamie."

Trace gave a faint nod, not really wanting to think about the past or why he'd come out West—to get away from all that had been taken or destroyed in his life. It was easier to forget when you weren't reminded of the way things used to be.

"Louisiana. Not far from Baton Rouge," Trace admitted grudgingly, hoping that Pappy would allow it to drop.

"A renegade rider . . . Hmm, bet you rode for old Nathan Bedford Forrest during the war." The old man's brows lifted in challenge, daring him to deny it. "His boys could *ride*."

Trace shook his head. "You know, Pappy, my mama used to tell me stories back from England and Ireland, where my family hailed from. She said hundreds of years ago they used to burn or hang people for being witches. You better be glad you were born now. You would have been dancin' on the wind."

Pappy tossed sand onto the campfire to put it out. "'Tain't nothin' magic about it. I just watch. A lot of people are too busy flapping their jaws."

Trace chuckled. "Seems to me you do a fair amount of jaw-flapping yourself."

The old man shrugged and studied the pink and purple horizon toward the east. "Well, might just be me flapping my jaw now, but I fear a sandstorm might be kicking up. See how misty it looks back in the canyon? That ain't good. We'd better make tracks, and pray that haze burns off when the sun comes up."

Trace hated to admit it, but the old man was right. Again.

The haze did not burn off. The saffron sun rose, cloaked in a jaundiced gray veil draped like a pall over the entire canyon, and the air was thick despite the occasional gust that whistled through. It was like inhaling near a campfire.

"Where'd you leave that marker?" the old man asked as they led their mules up the rocky draw.

"Not much farther," said Trace. "There's a spring with a stand of cottonwood trees."

"Well, we might reach it too late. See that yellow fog rising from the canyon floor?"

Trace nodded, taking his kerchief from his pocket to wipe his face.

"That ain't haze like before, that's sand, and it's coming our way. We're going to need shelter here, pronto. Afraid your woman's trail is going to get blown away."

Trace pulled his bandana up over his mouth and nose, hating that the old man was right. The storm seemed to hit them from everywhere, a hissing, howling whoosh of wind that sucked up the sand from beneath them and blasted the entire canyon. A great wall of it eclipsed the sun, making day into an eerie gray-green twilight. Despite the protection of the bandana, the sand stung his ears, clogged his mouth and nose, and left grit in his clenched teeth.

Trace tugged the brim of his Stetson down over his eyes, struggling to find shelter. Blind against the wind, he and Pappy trusted their burros' instincts to find water. Suddenly the ghostly trunks of the cottonwoods loomed before them.

He helped Pappy drag a blanket from his pack while the burros huddled together, their faces behind the trunks of the trees. He couldn't help it; he had to laugh. Crouching low, the two men sank down beside the tree and huddled together as the merciless waves of sand swept over them.

Pappy glared. "Damn fool! What's so funny? You have a chaw of locoweed?"

"Sorry. The asses have their asses turned into the wind." Trace tried to regain seriousness, given the gravity of their situation, but then Pappy laughed, which returned Trace's humor. Sometimes life was so damn ridiculous that laughing was the only thing you could do. Here he was, huddled under a blanket with a bossy old coot and about to be buried alive. He was no closer to getting onto the Lazy C than he'd been a few days before, and his horse had been stolen twice—and a certain beautiful horse thief was most likely in the grasp of a gang of outlaws.

The last thought was sobering. Images of the war returned: homes burned, lives destroyed. Women hadn't fared too well, as Mr. Lincoln's war had seemed to set loose an ugliness in men that made respect and gentle manners a way of the past. Trace wondered if Mae was healthy. Had infection set in? His stomach muscles tightened with fear as he pictured her abused by five or six men. He'd encountered women—one woman in particular—in the wake of such brutality. Or, rather, the shells of these women. One had been his sister, Annelee.

Trace might have shed a tear—for his sister, for Mae—but it was hard to tell in the dust storm. All he could do was shake from the painful memories and fear, and pray.

Sand piled up against the blanket Pappy and he desperately clutched, heavy, anchoring them to the spot. The grit worked its way under the edges, sharp as needles against any exposed skin. But while the time was painful and immeasurable, eventually the storm spent itself. The wind slowly died down, picked up again briefly, then gradually carried the driving sand westward. Trace was unsure how long the storm had lasted. It seemed like years. They shoved their way out from under the blanket.

The brim of Trace's Stetson was heavy with sand. It clogged his ears and blurred his vision. It overflowed his boot tops and had collected underneath his shirt collar. The damn stuff had even worked its way under his shirt.

Trace struggled to his feet, took off his hat, and knocked it against his thigh. He tried to spit but lacked enough moisture to do so. "I thought storms like that only happened in the desert," he choked out, again trying in vain to clear his mouth of the gritty particles.

"Damn dust devil. Look at what you're standing on." The old man coughed. "Wherever there's sand, you're going to have sandstorms."

"We never had sandstorms in Louisiana," Trace complained.

Pappy chuckled. "No, but I heard you have big blows called hurricanes."

Trace stared past the trees to the valley beyond, his heart heavy. There was little hope any trace of Mae or Diablo remained. The wind had covered everything in sand; the stuff was knee deep in some places. The horse tracks had vanished as though they never existed.

Chapter Four

It seemed fate had it in for Trace Ord. In the course of the month since he'd left the ranchers up north to locate their stolen horses, his whole life had changed. His horse had been stolen by a baffling female, which had forced him to cancel his plans to capture the elusive wild stallion, Standing Thunder, and now he'd taken on excess baggage in the person of a crusty old wanderer.

He'd dubbed his companion Preacher after a particularly long sermon the old man gave. Damn old-timer rambled incessantly. He'd implied he had a dark past, which sometimes made him contemplative, though he'd shrugged off giving any details. Trace respected that, not being willing to give any details of his own. He liked the old man. Still—and though a lot of what he said had merit—Preacher's constant yammering made it hard for Trace to concentrate. A loner, Trace was used to silence. Preacher talked so much he feared his ears might bleed. Now, when he needed his wits about him as never before, his nerves were frayed to a raveling.

He was at the end of his tether by the time they reached the last semblance of civilization east of the Hualapai Mountains and the Lazy C. It was a strange town, so small that Trace could hardly believe the mail coach even stopped. No dwellings, only establishments. If someone had ever christened it, no one seemed to know the name anymore. "The Outpost" was all anyone knew. It consisted of—and these first things were all under one roof—a general store, a saloon, a hotel, and a bathhouse complete with weathered, steelbanded wooden tubs. Next door was a combination livery and blacksmith. The closest thing to a law officer of the so-called town was a circuit judge who, Trace was told, put in an appearance every three months or so. But even that wasn't set in stone, since a dispute over the territory's western border was still a bone of contention.

Trace spread the word that he and the old man were drifters—a wrangler and a camp cook—looking to hire on with any outfit that would have them. They were quickly directed to the Lazy C, which was precisely what Trace had hoped. There weren't any other spreads in the area, and it had become quickly apparent that Jared Comstock owned the Outpost, lock, stock, and barrel. The place existed almost solely to serve the needs of the Lazy C.

At the general store Trace replaced his spare shirt that Mae had taken when she ran away, and much of his sandblasted wardrobe, then headed for a good long soak, a shave, and a haircut at the bathhouse. Dust and sand coated his body like a second skin beneath his clothes, and he'd nearly scratched himself raw in spots.

Getting his companion to follow suit was another matter entirely, but persistent threats finally won out.

After a filling if not particularly palatable meal, they paid a visit to the livery. There Trace bought himself a respectable-looking sorrel mare that answered to the name of Duchess. She was no Diablo, but she was healthy and fast enough to pass for a wrangler's mount. Preacher balked at the idea of a horse for himself, opting to stick to driving the burros. Though that would slow them down, Trace had to agree that it better suited the old man's image.

It was a half-day's distance to the ranch, and by the time their personal business was done the sun had slipped behind the mountains, capping those hazy purple spires with rivulets of crimson and gold. Trace viewed the flaming sunset with a wistful uneasiness, seeing the exact color of Mae's hair. He hoped to God she was all right. Why that should be, when anger seemed a more appropriate response to the bedeviling little horse thief, he couldn't imagine. But some things just were.

Anxious to reach the Lazy C, Trace decided it was best they not spend the night in town. Instead, they headed out and traveled until night fell. They made camp in the inky blackness and slept under the stars.

When they approached the Lazy C the next day, noon was near. The spread was far grander than Trace expected. A sprawling compound, it boasted a half-timbered ranch house, with bunkhouse, stables, and corrals tucked behind, well out of view. Though he could hear horses, none were visible.

The spread backed up to the mountains. Owing to

the lay in the land, there was only one possible approach to the ranch: the trail they now traveled. All in all, from first impression, the Lazy C had all the earmarks of a rustler's paradise.

Trace's demeanor changed with every step as they guided the animals closer. His eyes—sharp as an eagle's—and keen nose missed nothing, neither the hawks swooping overhead nor the muffled sounds and tantalizing smells of roast meat coming from the ranch house. He sat his horse with spine straight. Every sinew was taut. He was all renegade rider, aloof yet ready for anything.

"Let me do the talking," he said to Preacher as they approached the hitching rail in front of the house. "Just follow my lead and don't volunteer anything. They're probably expecting us after all the noise I made back at the Outpost about looking for work. I did that on purpose. Our coming out here needs to look natural. If Jared Comstock and his riders are what I think, they'll pick up on an ambush quick as you can spit and holler howdy."

"Suppose they take you on and not me?" the old man asked.

Trace growled. "Let's just take things as they come, eh? Don't go borrowing trouble. We've been lent enough as is."

He was about to swing out of his saddle when a wiry, hatless man strode out onto the ranch house porch, spurs jangling, and sized them up with a hooded gaze that turned Trace's blood cold. "You have a purpose for being here, you better state it quick," the man snarled.

"We're looking for work," Trace responded. "Folks

back at the Outpost said you might be looking to hire a wrangler and camp cook. Said to see Jared Comstock. Would that be you?"

"It would not," the stranger replied, raking them with skeptical eyes. "He'll be along, but we don't need no help."

"Well, since we've come this far, we'll stick around and ask him anyway—if it's all the same to you," said Trace.

The stranger shrugged. "Suit yourself. I don't much care how you waste your time, but I'm foreman here—the name's Will Morgan—and I say we ain't hiring."

"Well, Will Morgan, my name's Ord, and this here is Preacher. He makes the best son-of-a-bitch stew this side of the Mississippi; I can vouch for that myself. And we'll hang around awhile."

"Wait there, then." Morgan crooked his thumb toward the bunkhouse. "Outside. Like I say, I don't much care how you waste your time." The foreman spun on his heel and stalked back inside.

Neither Trace nor Preacher spoke until they'd rounded the corner toward the bunkhouse and were out of earshot. Horses were visible now, some ambling in a nearby paddock, some grazing in the pasture directly behind. Two riders were cutting several out of the herd to be branded.

Stolen or no, some fine horses were on the spread, judging from what Trace could see. But he needed to get closer. The pastureland stretched way back to the mountains. There were groves and valleys and outcroppings of rocks in the hazy distance that could conceal anything, and it stood to reason that rustled horses would be kept well out of view.

"What do you think?" Preacher asked.

"Not a very sociable welcome," Trace observed. "About what I expected, though. That fella needs taking down a peg."

"And you think you're just the man for the job? From the look of that thundercloud you're wearing for a face, I'll bet you're just itching."

"Not 'til I do what I've come for," Trace responded. "Personal feeling don't enter into it. All that can wait."

"Well, it don't appear that the wait'll be long," the old man replied.

A tall, lean rider was fast approaching on a black stallion. He was fair-complexioned and broad-shouldered, wore a gray Stetson and jeans too new to have seen much work, and a crisp white shirt billowing in the wind. His eyes were deep-set and dark, his mouth a thin, lipless line beneath a sandy mustache. Trace swallowed dry. His jaw muscle began to tick, and when he touched the brim of his hat in greeting, it was only with the tips of his rigid thumb and forefinger. The rest of his fingers were balled into a white-knuckled fist.

"What in the hell's the matter with you?" Preacher whispered, leaning toward him. "You've gone white as a cotton field! You know this hombre or something?"

"Not now," Trace gritted out through clenched teeth.

"You Ord?" the horseman asked.

Trace nodded. He didn't trust himself to speak.

"Jared Comstock," the rider announced. "I own this spread. My foreman tells me you're looking for work."

"That's right," Trace forced out.

"Well, I don't need any wranglers," Comstock explained. "We're full up. But I could use a good camp cook. Mine ran off, and we've been making do."

Preacher tensed. "Oh, now, I don't—"

"You won't find better than Preacher here," Trace interrupted, dosing the old man with a warning look. "And we're not a package deal. We've only been traveling together since Flat Springs, but I can sure vouch for his vittles."

Comstock grunted. "We'll see."

"You sure I can't give you a hand?" Trace offered coolly. "You can try me out for free."

"Sorry," Comstock said. He barked a harsh command to his horse, which had begun to snort and prance underneath him. Ignoring Trace, he turned narrowed eyes on Preacher. "You want a job, store your gear in the bunkhouse," he instructed. "You can show me what you can do at suppertime. The cookhouse is out back."

Trace spoke up. "Preacher's got some of my gear on his burro. I'll just collect that and switch it over to mine. Then I'll be on my way."

Comstock gave a dismissive nod, eyes cold and skeptical.

"If you change your mind," Trace remarked, "I'll be staying in town for a few days."

"Not likely," Comstock snapped. The horse underneath him began to dance, and he pulled back hard on his reins. The bit cut the animal's mouth, and blood began to leak from it. "Hold, you churn-head!" he snarled. The horse was rearing now, groans of protest rumbling in its throat, the animal's eyes wild.

Trace dismounted. Tossing his reins to Preacher, he approached the frenzied stallion, speaking soft commands.

"Get back, you fool!" Comstock bellowed. "This'un's a killer!"

Trace raised both hands in a gesture of compliance, and took a step back. "Just trying to help," he said. "I've gentled many an ornery mustang in my day. You've cut his mouth there. That's why he's fussing. Keep that up and you'll ruin his mouth, cause it to callus. You'll never get him to behave without gaining his trust first."

"I don't need your help, wrangler, I already told you that," Comstock snapped, "and I sure don't need you telling me how to handle my horse! You'd best be moving on. Now git!"

Trace touched the brim of his Stetson in silent farewell and moved off toward the burros, but his eyes never left Jared Comstock, who dug his spurs into the horse's sides and galloped off, raising a cloud of dust in the direction of the two men branding in the corral.

"Now what are we going to do?" Preacher complained. "I told you to watch that short fuse. You've got that fella mad as a peeled rattler."

"You're going to stay here and cook," Trace commanded, his lips scarcely moving. He stared after the horse and rider. "Yes, sir, you're going to cook like you never cooked before, and you're going to keep an eye out for a pretty lady who answers to the name of Mae, with big brown eyes and hair like sunset gold, and anything that smells of rustling. I'm going to do just what I said: hang around in town awhile. As soon as you can, I want you to meet me there with whatever you've learned. Don't raise suspicion, but don't take too long, neither. You ain't seen nothing like what'll happen when that short fuse of mine burns down to the powder."

"What makes you think I'll see your woman, stuck way out here in a cook shack?" the old man barked. "You plumb loco?"

"You wanted to tag along," Trace growled. "This is what tagging along gets you. Just do as I say."

"What's got you snakebit, Ord?" Preacher asked. "You look like you've seen a gosh-darned ghost."

"Worse," Trace gritted out. "That's my horse he's riding."

Chapter Five

"*Well*, you could have bowled me over with a feather that day," Preacher was saying.

Nearly two more had passed since they parted company. Two days of hell, of waiting. Trace had watched for the old man every hour from a nearby ridge. Finally he'd spotted the buckboard leaving the Lazy C, likely to pick up supplies, and Trace met his friend at a small, unseen grove just off the trail.

"What I don't get is why you didn't claim that mustang on the spot. Couldn't you prove he was yours?" Preacher fussed.

"I could've proven it. Diablo's hooves and shoes are notched."

"Then, why?"

"It wasn't the right time," Trace said. "Comstock wasn't packing, unless you want to call that mean-looking blacksnake on the pommel of his saddle a weapon. A coward's weapon. I'll bet he knows how to use it, too. But that foreman of his was. If I'd drawn on Comstock—and it would have come to that if I'd claimed back Diablo, believe me—who knows how many other riders would have drilled me from behind? You, too. He and a couple of boys were on the porch watching my every move as I rode out. I've no doubt they saw and heard it all."

"You don't make no sense, Ord," Preacher opined, lifting his dusty slouch hat to scratch his head. "Ever since we first met, you've been braying about getting that black devil stallion back. Well, you get the chance, you've got proof that he's yours, the poor animal was being abused something terrible and—cool as you please— you tip your hat and walk away. I take back what I said about you having a short fuse, but I still think you've been chewing on locoweed."

"That *woman* stole my horse," said Trace. "I need to find out if she's in cahoots with this outfit or a victim of it. Then I can do something."

"If Comstock don't kill that mustang first," the old man said. "That horse recognized you, Trace. I see that now. That's why he acted like he did."

"Don't you think that tears me up inside?" Trace's anger burned hot. "Do you have any idea what it took for me to turn my back and leave him there? If that gal is part of this gang, it's one thing. If she's here against her will, it's another. She was running from something, remember? If she's still alive, I have no idea what she's told Comstock, and I could get her hurt or killed. That's why I need you there. You have to find out the situation."

"You ain't going to cotton to a lot of what's going on," the old man said darkly.

"Spit it out!"

The old man gave him a sad smile. "I knew you'd be champing at the bit, but I couldn't get out here no quicker without rousing suspicion. You see, they ain't exactly welcomed me into the fold with open arms. They like my cooking well enough. I never was worried about that. But they ain't giving me rein to move free about the place. They keep me pretty close to the bunkhouse and the cook shack, and they're generally a tight-lipped bunch."

"How many riders?" Trace asked.

"Ten that I've seen, but I gather there are more. Some out on the range never come in—leastwise, they haven't since I've been there."

"What about the girl?" Trace urged.

The old man hedged. "You ain't going to like what I have to say."

Trace snapped. "Don't mess with me, old-timer. Is she there or not?"

Preacher frowned. "I didn't see no womenfolk at all, and I didn't hear no mention of any, neither. Nobody was saying much around me. A couple of times, when the wind was blowing just right, I thought I heard a woman's voice up to the main house. Once I might've heard crying. Another time it sounded like a man and woman arguing. Tried once to get up there, to see for myself. Made it to the back porch on the excuse I was wondering if they had a Dutch oven. Comstock comes out and chases me off. Even so, I spotted a shadow inside. A female shadow."

"Was it her?" Trace asked through clenched teeth.

"I'm getting there," the old man shot back. "I kept my eyes and ears open after that. Didn't see the woman again, but listened real good to what them riders was saying. There's a woman on the place all right, a woman named Mae. But . . ."

"But *what,* old man?" Trace prompted.

"Here's the part you ain't going to like. She's Comstock's wife."

Trace took a step backward. His mind reeled to the ring on her finger and what she'd said when he asked her name, how she'd stumbled over her answer. But why was she running through the canyon on foot like a mad, wild thing when she had a whole herd of horses at her command? Something wasn't right here. Mae hadn't been headed southwest to the Lazy C when she lit out; she'd been headed east. Those riders had caught up and turned her back toward the mountains. Back toward the Lazy C.

"I don't suppose there's any chance of Comstock changing his mind about me?" he asked.

"After the stunt with that horse?" The old man loosed a guttural chuckle. "Not likely."

"I was trying to settle Diablo down," Trace snapped.

"I know, *I* ain't holding it against you. I'm just saying you spoilt your chances of getting hired on, is all. Man seems none too trustful to begin with, and you're someone that horse respects. Set Comstock's hackles up."

"When are you coming into town again?"

Preacher shrugged. "Not for a week, maybe two."

"Doubt I can wait that long." Trace shook his head. "Riders are coming and going every day from the Lazy C. I'll be spotted sooner or later." He pointed to the northwest. "See that ridge?"

Preacher nodded.

"There's a little grove with a stream running through it. I'll camp there and keep watch from up top during the day. See if you can't get in good with the ranch's wranglers. Drink and play cards with them, find out what's going on. I need proof before I send for the ranchers who hired me, or for the marshal up north; the circuit judge is likely on Comstock's payroll. And . . . keep your eyes open for Mae. Something's not right here." After a moment Trace asked, "Is Diablo all right?"

"He ain't happy. That Comstock is running him into the ground. He's all cut up from whippings. Truth to tell, I've been trying to figure a way to set him loose. I would, too, except I didn't want to get caught before I found out something to help you."

"Don't—not yet. Leave Diablo to me. But before it's done I'm going to give that hombre a taste of his own bullwhip. You can count on that."

That night, Trace slept in the cul-de-sac. All day he'd haunted the ridge above, and at dusk he rode Duchess down the rocky trail of ragged steps to the outcropping of red rock where he'd hidden his gear and burro. It was the perfect seclusion, being tucked behind trees and far enough from the trail to risk a small campfire.

The air was sweet and clean, blowing down from the mountain peaks that still showed snow on their caps. Sage colored the distant foothills. New grass swayed in the breeze, and the stream ran cold and full from the melted snow from above. Spring was in full swing, but Trace couldn't enjoy it.

Early the next morning, he watched hawks and eagles sail on the wind, and he caught a glimpse of deer, elk, and once he could have sworn he saw a great black bear. He set snares for rabbits and kept himself busy. It was that or his temper would get the better of him and he'd charge, guns blasting, into the Lazy C Ranch. He usually was a patient man, but this waiting was awful.

The following day he rode to the Outpost. No one in the town seemed to know of anyone named Ahern. His casual questions met with stony stares, closed mouths, minimal answers. He assumed this was because it was a company town, and everyone was heedful that the company was Jared Comstock. Buying supplies, Trace made a lot of noise to spread the word that he was heading back to canyon country, searching for wild mustangs; then he rode out in that direction, inviting many curious stares. He left late in the day, which allowed him to double back under the cover of twilight and return unseen to his campsite.

Trace chafed to take action. This waiting wasn't getting him anyplace. It was all he could do not to immediately ride to the Lazy C, reclaim his horse and get to the bottom of the mystery of Mae. If she was Jared's wife, then so be it. He'd take his horse, ride away, and never spare her another thought. He'd find proof of Comstock's rustling, send for the ranchers who'd hired him, and tell them to fetch a U.S. marshal.

But he couldn't get that haunting face out of his mind. He knew animals well, and guessed people weren't much different. He'd seen fear in Mae's brown eyes. Something pretty bad had pushed her to run away in the middle of the night, with no gun, food, or proper clothing, and to become willing to risk being shot as a horse thief.

He hoped Preacher was being careful. The old man was smart but often talked too much. One slip, and Jared would be all over him. This was Trace's job. He was used to working alone, which had the benefit that he didn't have to worry about others. This time, if anything happened to Preacher it would be his fault.

"One more day, Duchess," he said, patting the sorrel's neck as he made his final evening check before turning in. "Then I've got to make some sort of move."

Out of the corner of his eye he caught a glimpse of motion: a horse and rider traveling at a gallop, as if the devil were on their heels. Not eastward toward the Outpost, though. And it didn't ride like Preacher.

His heart leapt. Was it Diablo? He didn't hesitate. He mounted Duchess and spurred her down the sloping trail through fallen rocks, finally breaking free into the grove below. Running his horse flat out at twilight was hazardous when he didn't know the land, and he prayed she didn't find a prairie dog hole. He leaned forward in his saddle, steering the mare to intercept the other rider.

Diablo ran like the wind. That had Trace worried. He had always said there was no match for his stallion. Of course, that had been before Diablo was abused by Jared Comstock. He had to give Duchess her due; she ran with her full heart. And she was gaining.

Trace grimaced. Could his mustang be so altered, or had he misjudged the sorrel beneath him? To ride a horse, you could either break or gentle him. He'd witnessed both methods. Gentled, Diablo had kept his spirit. He had a feeling Jared Comstock would break a horse, grinding him down until he lost all fight. But if Comstock had ruined his horse, Trace was going to kill him.

As Duchess pulled within range, Trace put two fingers in his mouth and let out a shrill whistle—a command he'd taught the horse to obey, a summons that had always worked in the past. This time, though there was a slight hesitation to the horse's gait, Diablo's rider slapped the end of his reins like a whip and once more the stallion sped ahead.

Trace leaned low over Duchess's lathered neck, driving her to her limit. Once more the mare nearly closed the distance. There was no moon; twilight was quickly shifting to full darkness. As his eyes adjusted, however, the rider came into focus and Trace loosed a string of oaths. Without hesitation, he ripped the lasso from his pommel, whirled it over his head, and threw it, the circle dropping over the mustang's long, muscular neck.

Diablo went wild, the encircling rope nearly pulling Trace from the saddle. Both horses almost stumbled and fell. The mustang's screams filled the night, reminding Trace of the first time he'd brought the horse down. Certainly, Diablo's rider was having a hard time keeping astride. What could be driving them to such acts of painful desperation?

"Hold, you black imp of Satan!" Trace commanded, winding the rope around his saddle horn to keep Diablo from pulling it out of his hand. The stallion puffed visible breath from flared nostrils, tossed his head, mane flying. He did not slow his flight, however.

Trace reeled in the horse until he could reach out and pull Diablo's rider out of the saddle and across his lap. He growled, staring into the face that had haunted his dreams. "Bitch. I ought to wring your pretty neck. You've got a lot of answering to do."

Chapter Six

Despite her struggling, which was about as wild as the stallion's, Trace held Mae fast. And, like when he'd gentled the stallion the first time, he allowed her to get the fight out of her system.

It wasn't easy. His blood ran hot because of the horse. Diablo has been abused, nearly driven mad, all because of Mae's selfish actions. Trace was having a hard time reining in his fury. Nonetheless, he gritted his teeth and allowed her to fight. But then holding her became harder for other reasons.

The feel of her in his arms, the heat of her body so close to his, plus that wiggling around on his lap, began a fiery ache in his loins. That sexual need was fed by his anger. Diablo's misuse made him heartsick, made him want to lash out in punishment, but the rest of him wanted to throw Mae down and worship her like a goddess. Such a terrible mix of emotions riddled him that he scarcely dared trust what he might do next.

"Quit that!" he snapped, shaking her. "I'm not going to hurt you, but you're going to hurt yourself, maybe us

both, if you don't stop struggling. Your damn willful-
ness has already cost my stallion. That wound in your
shoulder is too new to stand this strain. You're going to
open it again."

"Let go!" the woman raged.

"Enough! It's me, Trace Ord. You stole my horse,
remember? I can't say he's fared well because of it."

She whimpered, and her blows softened, shifting to
two stiff arms that kept him at a distance.

"That's better," he said. "This is your fault. You
wouldn't be having these troubles if you'd confided in
me when I asked you, instead of sneaking off with my
horse in the dead of night. You proud of what happened
to Diablo? Do you even give a damn?"

"I never harmed your horse," she sobbed.

"No, you just stole him for your rustler friend," he
retorted. "I'm going to use that damn bullwhip on him.
Bet on it, lady."

"I wouldn't harm any horse," she defended.

"Your actions caused my horse to suffer. He's near
mad from the treatment. But we'll get to that. Like I
said at our last meeting, you've got some explaining
to do. Now, I'm going to put you down. If you run, I'll
only catch you, so don't waste the effort. Run and I'll
lasso you like I would a heifer."

Trace slid her to the ground and swung out of his
saddle, but his feet had scarcely hit dirt before she bolted.
Quickly tying both horses to a dead cactus, Trace gave
chase. His long-legged stride ate up the distance, and
finally he grabbed her. They crashed to the ground with
a hard thud, damn near knocking the air from his lungs
as he bore the brunt of their fall. He rolled until he had

her pinned under him. She still struggled, but the fight was almost out of her.

"Don't you . . . get it, you hellcat . . . ?" he panted. "You're no match for me. Don't make me hog-tie you. I will if I have to. I'm fed up to the gills with this nonsense."

"Let me go!" she almost wailed.

"Where? Where will you go? There's nothing for miles except the Outpost. You really want to go there? You sure as hell aren't taking my horse again. You're loco if you think you can go wandering around the territory on foot. You won't last a day before something bites you or somebody catches you . . . or worse. So stop acting like a fool and actually think for a change."

She seemed to crumble. She fought tears, but he saw several drop from her lashes, streaking down her dusty cheeks. "I won't go back!" she snapped. "You can't make me go back. I saw you out at the ranch. I *saw* you. You're in league with them! I didn't recognize you at first, without the beard, and your hair is shorter, but then I heard your voice and I knew. You were with that old cook. You may as well kill me here and now if you're planning on taking me back to the Lazy C!"

Trace almost laughed, though he saw nothing funny in the situation. "*Now* she talks. I told you, I'm not going to hurt you, and Trace Ord never goes back on his word, even if some half-crazy, horse-thieving female drives him toward it. Now then, settle down. My camp is back up the trail in a grove. I'll take you there, and then you can tell me what the Sam Hill's going on."

"Not near the Outpost!" she cried.

"No, nowhere near. But I'm not giving you a choice,

Mae. I'll let you up, and then we're going back to the horses. Afterward, I will take you to my camp. You have a lot of explaining to do."

He eased off her, stood, and took her hand to pull her to her feet. Mae offered no resistance. Slapping at the dust on her clothes, she walked beside Trace to where Diablo and Duchess stood tied. Mae quickly reached for the mustang's bridle.

"Oh, no, you don't," Trace growled, grabbing her wrist. "My mother didn't raise a foolish child. You're going to ride before me on Duchess. The only place you'll get your hands on that black devil stallion of mine again is your dreams."

As promised, he rode them back to his campsite. He paused before stepping down from Duchess to draw a deep breath. With her practically sitting on his lap, the trip back had been torture. Each step the horse took shifted Mae, creating friction against his groin. He held her close, his hand on her belly. There was no other choice; give her an inch and she'd run again.

"Good thing my mama raised me to be a gentleman," he said under his breath.

Mae turned. "Beg pardon?"

"I was commenting that you're lucky my mama raised me to respect female folk. Now, here is how things go. I am going to step down off Duchess. Making my poor departed mama happy, I will offer you my hand in a genteel fashion. You, like a lady—no matter how hard that comes to you—will accept it, and you will climb down without trying to steal Duchess and run off. You try anything of the sort and I will run you down and truss you up. You can lie on the ground like a calf ready for branding while we have our discussion. Understand?"

She nodded.

"Despite your clear lack of concern about their condition, you are going to help me water these horses and rub them down. Then I will brew us some coffee and we will talk. So help me, Mae, don't run. You really don't want to push me that far again."

She surprised him by obeying. They cared for the horses and she sat watching him with big eyes while he built up the fire and fixed the coffee. He wasn't trying to delay the confrontation, but after he saw the condition of Diablo he figured he'd better get a good grip on his temper before dealing with her. He could barely stand to look at Diablo, tearing up whenever he saw the whip marks in the horse's hide.

Pouring water into a cup, he added herbs for the ointment he would brew for the stallion. Stirring the mixture, he glanced at Mae. She sat on a fallen log, both hands wrapped around her tin cup as if she were holding on for her life. How pale she looked in the firelight—like a ghost, except for the golden sunset of her hair shimmering in the firelight. Wavy and long, it was tamed at the nape of her slender neck by a thin bow.

Damn her! Mae wasn't going to get away this time, not until he'd gotten to the bottom of what the hell was going on.

"Are you warm enough?" he asked. "I don't dare add to the fire or I risk us being seen. If you're cold, take one of the blankets."

She shook her head. "I'm not cold."

"The old cook I rode in with?" Trace set the cup next to the fire to warm. "Is he still there?"

"Yes," she said.

"He's all right, then?"

She nodded. "I nearly died of fright that day," she confessed. "When Jared rode up on your horse, I . . . Why didn't you claim him?"

"He's your husband," Trace accused, ignoring her question.

"Yes, but that's not . . . that's not important."

"What a fool thing to say. Maybe you don't think so, but I'd say it's mighty important." Trace's temper rose again. "He was one of the riders who caught up with you by the stream?"

Mae stared, her tin cup raised to drink. "How did you—?"

"I tracked you." Trace reached into his pocket and produced the kerchief he'd fashioned into a sling for her, stained dark with her blood. "Four riders in all. One of them handled you pretty roughly by the look of this. You didn't seem eager to go with them. You mind explaining?"

Mae stared at the bandana. Tears once more welled in her eyes, but they didn't fall. She looked away, and Trace returned the bloodied kerchief to his pocket.

"You followed me to the Lazy C?" she asked.

"No. I followed your tracks 'til it got too dark to see. I was forced to return to camp. That's where I met up with Preacher. Next morning, we set out to pick up your trail, but the sandstorm wiped it out. I was headed for the Lazy C in the first place, so Preacher came on to the

Outpost and then the ranch. I had no idea that's where you were, 'til I saw Comstock ride up."

"On Diablo. And you didn't even try to claim him," she said again. "Why?"

"It would've been clear to a blind man that you were running from something. That being the case, I had no idea what you might have told Comstock to explain Diablo. I had to know how you figured into the goings-on at the Lazy C before I acted. I didn't want to get you into trouble—if you were innocent."

"Innocent of what?" Her eyes snapped up from the tin cup to pin him. "Don't talk to me of innocence! What was your business at the Lazy C? According to what you just said, you were headed there before we ever met. There's only one kind of man that looks for work at the Lazy C, and innocence is not one of that sort's characteristics."

"I think it best you answer my questions first. You level with me, and then, if I'm satisfied with what you've got to say, I'll fess up to you. Start from the beginning. What were you doing out in that canyon, alone and on foot? Where did you think you were going?"

Mae set her empty cup aside and hugged her knees. Trace reached for a blanket and tossed it into her lap, not trusting himself to be any closer. He needed to maintain a cool head around this hellcat, and that was damn hard to do.

She looked at him for a long moment, and then slid the blanket around her shoulders. "I was doing my best to head east until I picked up the railroad," she began. "I had money for a ticket . . . home."

"Where's home?"

"My grandfather owns a horse farm—Foxtail Farms in Kentucky, outside of Versailles. Not big like Almhurst, but he gives them a good run for their money with quality horseflesh. The farm was hit hard during the war. Both sides kept coming through trying to take horses for their armies. My grandfather had the boys dig a huge cellar under the manor house. Outriders would send word that soldiers were in the area, and they'd drive the horses down into the cellar and then cover the entrance with sod and park wagons and buggies atop that. We had to leave a few out for them to take every time, of course. It wouldn't look right, a horse farm with no horses. They were suspicious, but we held on, surviving when other farms collapsed." Her face softened. "It was so pretty, that farm. With its whitewashed fences and barns." Dropping her chin on her knees she added, "I wanna go home."

"Well, that explains how come you can ride better than any Indian I ever met." Trace swallowed hard the knot in his throat as he watched her staring into the fire. More than once over the years he had done the same thing, staring into the fire while wishing to go home. Only, for some, going home was only a dream. Home was long gone. All the people who mattered were long gone. Oh, the land was still there, but that was all.

"I could sit a horse before I could stand," Mae remarked wistfully.

Trace was softening, empathizing with her desperation in wanting to go back to a place where she felt safe, so he reminded himself that poor Diablo had suffered because of her. "Don't tell me you walked all the way from the Lazy C to that canyon?"

"N-no . . ." she replied.

"Well?" Trace reached for the ointment cup that was warming by the fire, and he stirred the herbs again.

"That cook friend of yours, Preacher. He replaced the cook that Jared told you ran off. The cook's name was Bill Coulter. I got him to take me. I paid him, but he . . . he took it the wrong way. He thought . . . He wanted . . ." She grabbed a blanket and pulled it tight around herself.

"I get the picture," Trace said, sparing her. "You ran off from him?"

She nodded. "I wasn't thinking about anything, just getting away from him. He was drunk, and foul. . . ." She shuddered. "I just ran. He couldn't go back to the Lazy C—not after running off with me like that. I'm guessing he's probably halfway to Texas by now, fearing Jared will catch up. I never looked back. I kept running and running 'til my sides ached and I could scarcely breathe. Then I saw your horse. He was like an answer to a prayer. I couldn't run anymore, I couldn't even walk, and then you . . . you . . ." Burying her face against her raised knees, she sobbed.

Trace grimaced. So much for keeping his distance. She was crying. She'd been alone and scared, had run just as his sister had run to escape the Yankees. Only, his sister hadn't gotten away. He couldn't go home and comfort her.

Going over, Trace laid a gentle hand on Mae's arm. "Hush now. Why couldn't you have told me all this back in the canyon? Do I look like the kind of man who would turn his back on a lady in distress?"

Her head snapped up, her wounded gaze accusatory.

"You have no idea what I'd just come from. Any man was the devil to me! I didn't know who you were, what kind of man . . . How could I? And you shot me! I had just nearly been raped by someone I thought I could trust. After that, how could I trust a perfect stranger? Then you reminded me that somebody would be coming after me. I knew you were right, and that's why I stole your horse again. I almost made it away, too. I almost made it!"

"Yeah, I saw that you were close to outrunning them." Trace wanted to hold her, to tell her it was all over, but after her confession about nearly being raped, he didn't want to spook her with an offer of comfort. He reached for her cup, poured it half-full, and handed it back. "I understand wanting to go home, but why didn't you just ask your husband to take you? Why put yourself in harm's way again and again?"

"I was running *from* Jared Comstock," she moaned. "And from that foreman of his, Will Morgan. He was no better than the cook. Of course, Will would never have taken me away. He would have used me right there, right under Jared's nose!"

"And your husband would have allowed that? Why did you marry him if that's the kind of man he is?"

"I didn't have much say in it," she said. "My mother and father—Allyce and Jack Ahern—lived on my grandfather's farm in Kentucky. I was born there. My father practically ran the farm and Grandfather treated him like a son. He even deeded him half the farm to keep him in Kentucky. After the war, things were tough; it was hard to hold on to what we had. Then gold fever struck. Word came back about a strike in the

Black Hills in South Dakota. My father was determined to make a quick fortune and help put Foxtail Hall back on the map. Mother stayed behind with me. He wanted a year to see if he could strike it rich. Only, he never came back. Oh, we got a letter now and then, from one place or another. Finally they stopped. We feared the worst. Mama died from a fever, but I really think it was a broken heart, and then it was just me and Grandfather. About six months ago I got a letter. Surprisingly, it was from my father. He said he'd hired on at the Lazy C doing odd jobs—mending fences, building corrals, and the like, but he was sick, and didn't know how long he could last at cowpunching. Said he was too old to be a wrangler any longer. I wanted my father home, so I came west to find him and bring him back to Kentucky."

"Did you find him?"

"Granddad didn't want me to come, but he knew he couldn't stop me. I finally found Dad, but he wasn't the same man who left Kentucky when I was a child. He was friends, after a fashion, with Jared's father, William. That's how he landed at the Lazy C after he left the Black Hills. Enough people were striking it rich; I think Old Man Comstock believed there was a lot of gold. After his first claim panned out, William loaned my father money to continue looking. One claim after another was a bust, however, which left Dad owing a lot of money. Foolishly, he made a grand gesture of signing over his half of the farm in Kentucky as payment. Jared's father, from what I learned, never intended to claim it—he wasn't even sure my father still had the right to sign it away, since he'd been gone so long. He just kept the paper to save my father's pride. But then William died and, well, Jared isn't the man his father was. . . ." Her voice trailed off, and she once more stared into the fire.

The anger Trace had felt toward Diablo's treatment was eclipsed by a different fury. In his travels he'd heard many such stories as Mae's, of families destroyed by the war, losing farms to carpetbaggers and taxes; there was no end to men like Jared Comstock, taking whatever they could and at whatever cost, honor be damned. That didn't make such stories any easier to hear.

Mae looked worn down. Defeat twisted the corners of her small mouth.

"You don't have to go on—" he started to suggest. Somehow he'd help her get back to Kentucky.

"No," she murmured. "You wanted to hear this, and I'd best get it said while I've mustered the courage. The day I arrived at the Outpost, I was directed to the Lazy C, where I found my father reeling drunk, being abused, and held up to ridicule. There's no law hereabouts. Everyone is beholden to Jared. He owns the Outpost and everyone in it. I walked straight into a trap. When I arrived, Jared told Father he'd cancel the debt and give him back the deed to the farm in exchange for me. When I refused, he said he'd put my father out of his misery right in front of me and take me anyway."

"And so you *married* him?" Trace asked through stiff lips.

"At gunpoint, yes. Only, the gun wasn't pointed at me; it was aimed at my father. Jared sent Morgan into town for a preacher. Once the marriage was performed, he tore up my father's markers, gave him the deed to the farm and his wages, and turned him loose. But he was found the next morning, shot to death behind the saloon. The deed to the farm was gone, along with all the money Jared had given him."

"You think Jared Comstock killed him?" Trace asked.

"No, not Jared. He never left the ranch that night. But Will Morgan did."

Trace shook his head. "When did all this happen, Mae?"

"A month, I think. I've lost track of time. It's been one big nightmare for me. I just want to go home to Kentucky. At first I tried to find the deed. I didn't want Jared to get his hands on Foxtail Hall. But then the situation became too dangerous. I had to get away."

"I asked about the name Ahern in town. Nobody seemed to know it."

She uttered a humorless laugh. "They know the name, all right. Everybody knew Jack Ahern. They just won't admit to it. Those who still have a conscience at the Outpost are too afraid of Jared to risk getting involved." Her poignant brown eyes fixed him. "Now you've heard my story. I think it's time for you to tell me—how do you fit into all this, Trace Ord?"

Trace answered her question with one of his own. "Is Jared Comstock a horse rustler?"

She shrugged. "I wouldn't put it past him. He does as he pleases. They're driving horses in all the time, but I can't say for certain from where. I'm not allowed near anything to do with his business. I've spent near a month locked in my room trying to avoid . . ." She bit her lip and flushed scarlet. "Why do you ask?"

Trace drew a ragged breath. For a moment he couldn't

speak. There was no doubt that she was sincere. His work, however, depended upon anonymity. He never disclosed his position, or his personal affairs, easily. He hadn't with Preacher, and he hesitated now with Mae. He usually trusted his instincts, but they were clouded by what he was beginning to feel for this girl. He wrestled with that for a good length of time before he spoke.

"Can you trust me, Mae?" he asked.

She hurled back at him, "I can't trust anybody out here!"

Trace sighed, taking her hand in his. "I can't say I blame you for that, after all you've told me. And with me shooting you—after you stole my horse, mind—we got off to a rocky start. Still, when I caught Diablo he was wild. It took me a long time—a couple cracked ribs and a broken wrist—but he finally trusted me. So I'll just have to earn your trust, too. I'm putting my life on the line telling you this, but . . . I'm a renegade rider. Do you know what that is?"

"No," she said.

"A renegade rider is a wrangler who goes about rounding up horses that have strayed or been rustled from their owners," he explained. "Right now, I'm working for two ranchers up north, who are pretty sure that I'm going to find a large part of their stock on the Lazy C. That's why I was in such an all-fired hurry to get there. It's why I tried to hire on, and why Preacher is out there now, hoping to dig up enough proof for me to send for those ranchers and the marshal."

Mae's eyes were wide as saucers.

"I'm a damn good wrangler," Trace went on. "I wouldn't have had one bit of trouble proving myself to

Comstock, one on one. That foreman, Will Morgan, jinxed it after he and I got off on the wrong foot. Some people are like that—they rub each other the wrong way before the first words are even spoke, and no fixing it."

He sighed and added, "I didn't want Preacher tagging along, but he convinced me that it would look less suspicious: a drifter and a tagalong cook. I figured Comstock would take me and turn him away. I never dreamed he'd send me packing and keep Preacher. I'm worried about that old codger. He's no match for the bunch you're describing. When I met him, the old fool was set on trying his hand at mining in Death Valley. I don't want his death on my hands. Already have too many on my conscience. No room for another."

"You've got to get him out of there," Mae said. "That place is a nest of rattlesnakes."

Trace nodded. "I'll figure something. Right now, it's you we've got to deal with."

"Our tracks!" she realized with a lurch. "Jared will follow them. He'll find us! He's an excellent tracker. We're boxed in here!"

"There's no moon tonight. No one'll be doing any tracking 'til morning." He broke several low-hanging branches off a nearby cedar and lashed them together with a strip of rawhide from his pack. "I can cover our trail with this"—he exhibited his handiwork—"by retracing our steps and then dragging this along behind Duchess. It's an old Indian trick I learned from the Navajos. But to do that, I've got to leave you here alone with Diablo. Can I trust you? Can I have your word that you won't run off again while I'm gone?"

"If you're so worried, why don't you just drag that thing behind Diablo? Use him instead," she snapped.

Trace rose and picked up the cup holding the horse's ointment. "Diablo needs care. Also, I might miss a few. Duchess's tracks could belong to almost any horse on the range. Diablo's hooves and shoes are marked, and Comstock surely knows that. If you take him out of this grove and run again, you might as well leave Comstock a map right to you. I don't think you want that. Now, I'll help you get back to Kentucky, Mae, but you've got to trust me for that to happen."

She tried to smile, but he saw her chin tremble a bit. "I suppose I don't have any choice, Trace Ord."

He shook his head. "No, you don't. Can you handle a Winchester?" he asked, holding out the rifle. "I won't be long. Try not to shoot me when I come back."

Finally she managed a small smile. "Not even once?"

Chapter Seven

*S*hivering more from fright than cold, Mae Comstock sat clutching the Winchester. Except for the occasional snap and crackle of the fire, there was no sound. No breeze stirred the trees in the grove around her. No woodland creatures spoke. The only other noise was the ragged rhythm of her heart, ticking off the minutes, reminding her of her grandfather's clock back home.

Would Trace Ord come back? Was he wrong; had Jared and his riders already picked up their trail despite the darkness? She grimaced. She hadn't told Trace everything. Now she almost wished that she had. But his eyes, piercing her with their hawklike sharpness, had been so dark and strange as she told her tale, how could she? If what she said had already produced such seething rage, what might the rest do? Murder, more than likely, and there'd been enough of that, Lord knew.

A renegade rider? She hadn't known what that was until he explained. She'd heard Jared Comstock make reference to renegade riders as men more dangerous than the law, however, to be avoided at all cost. And anything Comstock deemed a threat was likely to be Mae's ally. Trace had certainly acted like a gentleman tonight. Now that she knew he wasn't one of her husband's kind, the burden on her heart lightened. She'd prayed it was so, but she'd been confused ever since Trace turned his back and walked away from the Lazy C without his stallion. Had she finally met an honorable man in this damnable territory—one that her grandfather would welcome onto the front porch of the old Southern manor? Dared she hope? It was only a glimmer, but it was all she had and she clung to it the way she gripped the Winchester. It was more than she'd had for over a month.

There was no mistaking the shambles his closeness made of her poise. Her thoughts reeled back to the most recent occasion, his strong arm encircling her waist, holding her before him. And he'd plucked her from Diablo's back as though she were as light as a broom straw. She relived the pounding of his heart against her, recalled his raw male scent.

Mae pressed her fingers to her lips as she recalled the hardness of his muscular, corded body, the blistering heat radiating from his chest as he pinned her to the ground. Heat caused by the exertion of riding her down . . . and by something more. He *wanted* her. She had felt it, especially when she'd lain underneath him on the ground, helpless against the need evident in his lean length. There had been no mistaking the thick pressure of his arousal against her thigh through their clothing.

And yet he hadn't hurt her. Somehow she'd known he wouldn't—not the way Jared would have, or Will Morgan, or Bill Coulter. This man was different. But he was angry at her, and he had every right to be. She'd done him wrong, done his poor horse wrong. Maybe that was what instantly fixed him as a different breed of man. Jared used horses simply as a means to get richer. In contrast, Trace cared about Diablo. She'd seen the pain in his eyes, seen him care for the horse, speak with soothing tones to the terrified animal. She couldn't imagine Jared doing the same.

Maybe she wouldn't run tonight. Diablo was safe in Trace's care; perhaps she would be, too. Though she was terrified of staying, terrified of trusting the unsettling emotions Trace Ord had awakened in her, she was far more afraid of Jared. She hoped the two didn't run into each other tonight.

As the minutes ticked by, doubt crept in whether Trace would return. Mae waited, waited what seemed an eternity. Finally her decision was rewarded. Trace reappeared, moving with the stealth of an Indian, his tall, lean shadow materializing before her eyes. She lurched to her feet. Her grip tightened on the Winchester but then relaxed as her breath was siphoned off on a sigh of relief. She said, "I didn't . . . I mean, I wasn't . . . I . . . I was afraid—"

"That I wouldn't come back?" he laughed. "Did you think I was just going to ride off and leave you here with my horse?"

"I . . . was afraid you might be wrong." She faltered. "That Jared would come after me tonight, that is, and that . . ."

"Don't tell me you were worried about me?" he chided. Was that a twinkle in his eye?

There was absolutely no use trying to have a reasonable conversation with the man! "Well, how would I know what happened if you didn't come back?" she snapped.

"You can give me that now," he said, reaching for his rifle.

"Oh!" she cried, almost dropping it. As she gave it over, she winced. The wound in her shoulder was still tender.

"Pain?" he asked, his eyes narrowed.

"A little," she confessed. There was no use in lying. "It's nothing to bother over. I'll mend."

"Uh-huh. Well, maybe you better let me have a look," he suggested. "That tussle we just had didn't do it much good, I'll wager."

"It'll be fine," she assured him. "I'm just stiff from sitting here so long with that rifle."

Trace stared for a long moment, clearly making up his mind if he should pursue the issue. Mae held her breath. She couldn't meet his eyes. A rush of hot blood raced into her cheeks and she didn't need a mirror to prove that they were aflame; they always reddened when she was embarrassed. Like now, when all she could think was Dear God, he's seen me naked to the waist!

"Have it your way," he said at last. "I've covered our tracks. We should move on, get you to Kentucky . . . but we can't. Not 'til I see about Preacher. I can't just disappear and leave him in the middle of that nest of rattlers."

She moaned. "They'll find us! I know they will! You don't know Jared, he—"

"And you don't know me," Trace interrupted. "If Jared Comstock finds us, he's a dead man, plain and simple.

Is that clear enough for you? The minute I saw him ride in on Diablo at the Lazy C—spurring him raw, lashing him with his quirt—I promised Preacher I'd one day give him a dose of that blacksnake he wears on his saddle. That was before you told me your tale. The man deserves a horsewhipping for what he did to my horse. He deserves facing down and killing for the hell he's put *you* through. I'm a hard man, Mae. War and its aftermath made me that way. I'll kill if I have to—have killed before, and likely will again. Understand?"

Mae lowered her head and nodded.

"I'm glad." Trace removed his hat and knocked it against his thigh. "We're safe here. No one can find this place, and I've made sure nothing will lead anyone back here. Nobody's going to find us. Tomorrow, I'll climb the ridge and keep a lookout for Preacher. With luck he'll have some information on Comstock rustling horses, and I can bring in the law."

"And what if he doesn't come?" Mae asked. "Or what if someone follows him?"

"Don't be crossing bridges that aren't built," was Trace's reply. "Once word gets out that you've run off— and on my horse again, no less—he'll come along right quick. I'd stake my life on that. Why did you take Diablo, by the way? Comstock's got a whole corral full of horses."

"I didn't return to the Lazy C of my own free will," she defended. "They *dragged* me back. You said you saw the tracks. I was desperate to get away again before . . ." She bit back words she dared not speak. Not yet. "Jared and the riders were arguing in the bunkhouse. I couldn't hear about what," she said instead. "I saw my chance and fled. I took Diablo because I couldn't bear to see him abused anymore. I owed it to him to get him away from Jared."

Trace's expression hardened. She didn't blame him for his anger, but she'd been desperate when she first stole him. Desperate times called for desperate measures. Yet she regretted that the mustang was hurt. Tears swam in her eyes. Trace's handsome face blurred before them.

"Horses have more sense than humans," she said, through a terrible constriction in her throat.

Trace gave a soft laugh. "You won't get any argument from me."

Mae blinked back her tears, felt compelled to add, "Diablo hated Jared from the start. He tried to trample him when they caught up with me, and Jared beat him with that whip of his. It was my fault he fell into Jared's hands. I couldn't leave him there. . . ."

"How did you explain the horse?" Trace asked, heading over to his pack. "When Comstock first caught you."

"I told him the truth," Mae said. "Well, as close to the truth as I dared. That I stole him from someone's camp and got shot in the process, but it was just a graze that I'd doctored myself."

"And he believed that?" Trace was unfolding a blanket. He glanced up.

Mae nodded, avoiding his gaze, those eagle eyes, so deep-set and penetrating. They seemed to see right into her soul. Into her lies.

Shaking his head, Trace pressed, "You're sure he believed? All of it?"

"I don't think he believed that I took your shirt from the stockroom he keeps for his riders, but there was no way for him to prove that I didn't." Mae hesitated, then shook her head. "Jared wouldn't know one work shirt from another. I've never seen him wearing one. His riders do the work, and he struts around like the lord of the manor."

Trace nodded. After a moment he said, "You could have done anything: given him a description, set him on me to get him off your back. Why didn't you?"

"Because I knew you'd track that horse. Or I hoped. I hoped that sooner or later you'd find him. I *wanted* you to find him, and I thought that if I told the truth and our stories were the same, you might get Diablo back without getting killed, and I might not . . . Jared might not . . ." Mae couldn't stand to see Trace's expression, and before she even thought she spun on her heel, prepared to flee. A moment later she was in his arms.

"Easy," he commanded. His eyes roamed her face, but his thoughts were unreadable. "You're like a wild mustang," he murmured, "ready to bolt and run, mane flying. But running never solved anything. At some point you have to turn and make your stand. In the army you learn to pick the best place to fight. In life . . . well, it's not much different. I'm your high ground, woman. I'm the best you've got."

Her heart pounded against her ribs and she couldn't breathe right. "There's no one else," she whispered.

"That's right," he agreed. "I'm all there is. But I'll do right by you."

She didn't resist the strong hands that molded her to

him, nor did she shrug off the gentle fingers that brushed tendrils of hair from her face. She stood staring into his eyes, eyes gleaming with firelight and hooded with desire, and after a long, breathless moment he lowered his mouth over hers. The kiss was gentle, nothing more than a light brush of their lips, as if Trace feared doing more. Molten warmth bubbled up through Mae, burning her with desire. Still, Trace held back, giving her a chance to tell him to stop. She didn't want him to stop.

Pulling back, Trace paused, before the hint of a smile shaped his mouth. He looked younger, not the hard renegade rider that had shot her. Then the grin widened and he pulled Mae close. This time he tasted her deeply, igniting a blistering surge through her belly and thighs.

Her breath caught in a soft moan as his hands roamed the curve of her waist and down over her jean-covered hips. How tall he was, and yet how perfectly they fit together. There was no mistaking the pressure of his manhood thick and hard against her belly. It was a hardness that should have flagged danger, and would have done with any other man . . . but not this man. Somehow she knew Trace Ord would never harm her.

Their embrace lasted only seconds, but to Mae it seemed an eternity—a searing, throbbing, white-hot eternity, that left her weak and trembling. When their lips parted, hers followed his, and he tangled his hand in her hair and pressed her face to his heaving chest. Mae was surprised that beneath her hot cheek his heart beat out a ragged rhythm, and his breath came short. Then he groaned, lowering his lips to the top of her head, and groaned again as her hands fisted in the back of his shirt.

It was a long moment that they stood thus, as though one meant to absorb the other. When Trace finally broke the magical silence, his voice was husky and deep with a desire that resonated through Mae's body like thunder, though he spoke in a whisper.

"I've got to finish what I set out to do," he said, releasing her. It was not an apology or an explanation but a statement of fact, a statement of who this man was. He did not need to elaborate; Mae understood. Still, he went on. "I gave my word, and I won't go back on it. A man's word is the measure of his worth. There are two ranchers counting on me to get their horses back. I can't be clouding my mind with what's happening between us."

"So, what are you going to do?" Mae wasn't ready for the raw emotion he'd ignited in her soul. His scent was all over her, filling her nostrils, tampering with her senses and equilibrium. Stepping back, she sat on a fallen log, distancing herself from the force of him.

"There's a herd of wild mustangs in that canyon where you . . . where we met," he said. He ran a hand through his chestnut hair, clearly confounded. "I *was* going to cut one out of the herd and use him for bait to get myself hired on at the Lazy C. I figured once they saw my skills with taming horses, they'd give me a shot. Given the man's attitude now, hell has a better chance of freezing over than Jared Comstock hiring me on. . . ."

"I've spoiled your plans," Mae despaired. She vaulted off the log, her guilt getting the better of her. "Take me back!" she blurted. "You're resourceful. Hide Diablo somewhere and tell him you found me wandering in the desert. I'll say the horse threw me and ran off. He has no idea that horse is yours. I'll play my part, and once you tell him about the herd he'll take you on, Trace! He will. He won't be able to resist those horses. If you promise to get him those . . ."

She trailed off when she saw Trace's expression. He stared, his jaw muscle ticking. His eyes flashed in the firelight. Mae took a step back, but he bridged the distance in one giant stride, grabbed her arms in iron fists, and shook her gently. "You are never going back to the Lazy C, you got that?" he seethed through clenched teeth. "Never, Mae! And when I'm done with what I set out to do, I'm going to face Jared Comstock down for what he's done to you and yours. You have to know that."

"I owe you!" she argued. "I never meant—"

"You don't owe me anything," he returned, letting her go. "Are you crazy? Do you think for one minute I'd let you do a thing like that? And what would I do with Diablo, leave him out here to starve or run wild again? No. If Preacher hasn't found out anything, I'll take you up those mountains east of the Lazy C to a mesa I know where a small band of Hualapai Indians make camp this time of year. They're a renegade bunch with an outlaw chief. White Eagle's his name—an outcast, and one mean brave—but we're friends. He owes me. He'll keep you safe 'til I do what I came here to do. You can bank on that."

"If you can leave me with this White Eagle, you can just as easily leave Diablo there. He'd be safe, and we could do like I said—"

"No! Damn it, Mae, I said no. That's the end of it.

We wait for Preacher. Once I see what he's got to say, I'll know what to do next. If worse comes to worst, I'll take you up the mountain. We can't travel by day; it's too risky, and I'll have to tie burlap on Diablo's hooves until we leave this sandy clay and hit red rock, or they'll track us for sure. When we reach the Indian camp, I'll leave you and Diablo there and—"

"And what?" Mae countered. "You can't face Jared alone. What are you going to do, just ride on in like you did before? He kicked you off, remember."

"Nobody kicked me off, Mae. I left so he wouldn't suspect Preacher—so that the old codger would have a chance to find out something . . . and so as not to add to your troubles. I still hadn't found out which way the wind was blowing with you and that outfit, if you re-call."

"You're going to do this, aren't you?" she shrilled. "You're going to just . . . just . . ."

"You think I'm new at this—a greenhorn? Lady, you have a lot to learn about me. This is *what I do*, Mae." He sighed, a mix of exhaustion and frustration.

"But if you take me back, he'll never suspect you."

"No!" Trace thundered. "It's out of the question. Any man who'd do like Jared Comstock did to you is lower than a snake's underbelly. I'd be lower than that if I put you in his way again. Now get some sleep. We don't know what tomorrow will bring, or when we'll sleep again. You've got to trust me, Mae. Get some rest. I'll turn in shortly, once I've seen to Diablo."

She said no more. Trace was a stubborn man, used to dealing with life in his own fashion. There clearly wasn't any use in arguing.

Mae sat for a bit longer, then did as told. Snuggling down into the bedroll he'd prepared for her, she watched Trace tend the horses. Pretending to be asleep, she watched as he slathered the ointment he'd prepared onto Diablo's wounds. There was gentleness in his touch. It did her heart good to see the way he ministered to the horse, to know a man had such caring within him. She nearly spoke, watching Diablo respond, the mustang's muscular flesh rippling, his bobbing head turned back as if to caress his master in appreciation. She couldn't make out the words Trace whispered. She didn't have to, though; there was genuine affection in the sound.

How Granddad would love this man, she reflected. Wistfully, she envisioned Trace on Foxtail caring for the broodmares and the young foals with the same tenderness. The images were so strong she could almost feel the warm Kentucky sun on her face, smell the bluegrass. Was there a chance they could turn their backs on this horrible place and fine a way back East? With Diablo, naturally. Granddad would welcome that horse with open arms. Oh, what a bloodline would come from a crossing his stock with the Kentucky Thoroughbreds!

The hauntingly beautiful daydream faded to mist as a twinge of guilt assailed Mae. Trace had been entirely open, and she hadn't been totally honest. She shivered and pulled the blanket closer around herself. Should she throw caution to the winds and tell all? No. This was definitely not the time to share the rest of her story. She did trust Trace, but not with that. It would have to wait. She'd seen what was in his heart and eyes, felt it in his kiss and the pressure of his strong, corded body that molded so perfectly to hers. The ghost of his arousal still lingered, holding sleep at bay. But soon. Maybe she would tell him soon.

The dwindling campfire flared up, crackling with yellow and orange flames as Trace added a few dead cedar branches; he was feeding the fire carefully, so no smoke or sparks danced in the air, nothing to reveal their hideaway. Mae couldn't resist watching him. It was so easy to build castles in the air, dreams of them all together on a farm in Kentucky. Only, she had experienced too many disappointments this past month. It was better not to hope.

Her eyelids heavy, she closed them. Since she was a little girl, whenever she'd had a problem to solve, she always went to sleep with it on her mind and usually awoke with the answer. Once more, she drifted off praying for answers.

Chapter Eight

Trace woke well before dawn and built the fire back up before he approached Mae. He put on some coffee, and divvied up the last of his hardtack and jerky for breakfast. Wasn't much, but it was all he could offer. He couldn't take time to hunt fresh meat.

The minute she opened her eyes, he was sorry he hadn't just gone on and let her sleep.

He saw the fires of determination there; she wanted to help him by going back, the damn fool woman. Climbing the ridge was the only way he was going to keep her from pressing the case that he return with her to the Lazy C, which was the craziest plan ever hatched, as far as Trace was concerned, so he'd better hurry up and do it.

"Trace, I've been thinking. I have to go back. I am your only way back on the Lazy C. I have to find that deed to Foxtail. My granddad isn't a young man; I don't want him to have to face Jared trying to steal that farm from us. I mean, from him."

"No. I won't even discuss it, Mae." He ignored that hopeful expression becoming a frown. "Now eat up. I've got to get up on that ridge and keep an eye out for whatever's going on down in the valley."

"Trace, hear me out," Mae begged. She clasped her hands in front of her, clearly desperate to make him understand. "I need to go back for that deed. If I go home to Kentucky without it, Jared Comstock will come after me and—"

"No!" Trace set about gathering up several supplies.

"Then take me with you. Please."

"You're safe down here," he snapped.

She shook her head. "I'll go crazy with worry."

He sighed. "That fiery sunset of your hair would stand out for miles atop that ridge, shining in the sunlight, and you know it. Might as well wave a flag. No, you stay put, hang on to the Winchester, and shoot anything but Preacher that comes through that draw. Understood?"

"I'm afraid to stay down here alone," Mae remarked.

"Just do as I say. I have enough worries with Preacher down there in the path of that killer husband—"

Mae snarled, "Don't ever call him that. They spoke words over me, married me by putting a gun to my father's head, but that vulture is not my husband."

"Sorry," Trace said. "I've got worries on my mind, Mae, and no time for chat. I should never have allowed Preacher to go down there. He's doing my job while I'm standing around like a blamed fool. One misstep and that snake Comstock will kill him—which would ultimately be my fault for letting him talk me into his plan. I will *not* make the same mistake with you. Stay here. Put out the fire. Keep an eye peeled and the Winchester in reach, and stay away from Diablo. He needs to heal." Then, swinging himself up on Duchess's back, Trace didn't wait for a reply. He rode out through the sage and started the climb into the hills.

By the time he reached the flat table of rock below the summit, he was starting to feel bad for his shortness with Mae. She meant well. But that was the crux of the thing. She'd meant well in coming out to find her father, and look how that had ended! Fool woman had meant well when she stole away with some low-down, no-good varmint who only wanted to get his hands on her, and she'd meant well every time she'd stolen his horse. He needed to get her back to Kentucky. That farm she'd talked about sounded a little bit like heaven. She needed to be back there, sipping mint juleps on the veranda at sunset. Maybe with a kid or two at her knee. Talking about his sister, his mama said children always settled down high-spirited females. Poor Annelee had never had the chance. Trace would die to ensure that Mae did.

Feeling his belly grumble, he groped in his saddlebag. Jerky, that's all he had, and he'd foregone the simple delight of roast rabbit, pan biscuits, and a pot of fresh brew. Well, it wouldn't be the first time he'd made do. Wouldn't be the last, either.

Dropping Duchess's lead rein down, he left her to graze on the few tufts of grass. She was a well-trained mare. Cowboys tended to teach their animals to stay wherever a rein was dropped, nothing being more deadly than getting tossed and having one's fool horse run off with your weapons and grub. He patted her haunch. "Damn glad you're not in season, Miss Duchess, or Diablo would be kicking up a fuss."

Climbing to the summit, he flattened himself on a

rounded pinnacle of stone. His eyes trained on the dark S that was the trail winding through darker sage toward the Lazy C. The morning air was still cool, but he'd worked up a sweat. He stripped off his Stetson and wiped his brow. "Well, I don't expect to find no burning bush up here, like Moses did, but Lord, I wouldn't mind a few answers—just a little help," he said to the sky.

This wasn't the way it was supposed to be. He always worked alone. Instead, through no fault of his own, he was no closer to getting those wild horses, he'd gotten off on the wrong foot at the Lazy C, and he'd spoiled his chances of ever being hired. And he certainly wasn't *alone*. He was saddled with a fiery Kentucky woman who acted before thinking, and with a crusty old sourdough who was probably going to get himself killed.

"Not if I can help it," Trace muttered.

He was uneasy that Preacher was involved at all. Almost as uneasy as Mae made him.

He was in a quandary over what to do with her until he could get her back to Kentucky. To be honest, he was having a damn hard time even thinking straight. He was falling for this woman. Yes, they had only seen each other a couple of times, yet she touched him in a manner he couldn't explain—perhaps didn't *want* to explain. So much of who he was and what he wanted out of life had died in that waste of a war. No one had expected the nightmare Mr. Lincoln's army had unleashed. They talked bad about Nathan Bedford Forrest? Trace had nothing but respect for the man; he'd said what needed doing and got 'er done, as the saying went. And yet so many had died and suffered. The nation had been irrevocably changed.

Trace swallowed. That was a lifetime away. That was why he'd changed his name. Trevor Guilliard had died back there, five years ago; he'd been buried in the same grave as his sister. On that cold rainy day he'd returned from the prison camp and found his mother dead, his sister dying, Trace Ord had been born. And yet Mae reminded him that a bit of Trevor Guilliard still lived. She reminded him of a kinder time, of manners, of lace tablecloths and a mother telling him to keep his elbows off the table. He hadn't been there to save Alicia Guilliard. He hadn't been able to do more than hold his sister, Annelee, and cry, and then to offer her a proper burial. Scant comfort. But with Mae he had a second chance—a chance for atonement, redemption. Perhaps if he saved Mae, he might yet save himself.

Also . . . she awakened feelings in him, feelings the likes of which he'd believed himself unworthy to seek out for far too long. He'd never allowed himself to fall in love, never thought of planning a life with someone. For too long he'd just gone about being a renegade rider, no thoughts to a month ahead, or even a week. Mae was making him long for things he'd shunned. She made him remember he had a heart. He'd never been afraid of anything in his life, but he was afraid of this.

He imagined Mae below, clutching the Winchester, and considered the desperation that had driven her to risk fleeing the Lazy C a second time. There was no doubting her courage. But there was something else, too, and not just that she wanted back that deed to protect her grandfather. A couple of times he'd seen her biting the inside of her lip, as if trying to decide whether or not to tell him something. But what was it? What was she too afraid to confess?

While his brain was filled with images of how it felt to hold her in his arms, he couldn't dismiss the conviction that she hadn't been completely truthful with him. That hurt. But then, it had hurt to see Diablo jerk his head away several times last night when he cared for him. The horse no longer trusted him. Trace would have to earn that trust again, just as he would have to prove to Mae he was worthy of her. Time was running out, though. He sensed it. There was danger in whatever she was hiding, and he would have to probe her soon to find out what it was. His instincts were too strong to resist, as they'd saved his life many times in the past.

By damn, just thinking about Mae set his pulse racing and blood surging into his groin. It had been a long time since he'd been with a woman, but . . . she hit him like whiskey. Trace snatched up his canteen to swish some water in his mouth, spat at a nearby lizard—damn lizard probably thought this was his lucky day. He'd even *dreamt* last night, dreamt of the rolling hills of Kentucky, of broodmares lazily grazing in white-fenced pastures. He'd been riding down a long road wending toward the main house, and Mae was running out to greet him. But he wasn't sure he wanted such dreams. Wanting only opened him to hurt. And there was no question that whatever Mae was keeping to herself might sneak up and bite him. Nonetheless, he would do what he could to save her. She might be a horse thief and a bit of a liar, but she didn't deserve the coming storm. His eyes looked out at the horizon: clear, not a cloud in sight. But a storm was a-coming.

Trace's eyes narrowed as he held up a hand to shield them against the sun. "Well, by damn, maybe I got that sign from the Lord after all." A dust cloud was racing along the trail. Too much for a horse to kick up, it had to be a wagon raising it. Trace grinned happily. "Right timely, old man."

He scrambled down from his perch to the shelf below. Leaping upon Duchess, he and the horse descended the ridge, taking care not to come down in the same place where he'd made his ascent, not wanting to draw Mae's attention. . . . The last thing he needed just then was her showing up to press her case. Trace had a feeling Preacher would take one look at those doe eyes and storm back to the Lazy C singing "Marching Through Georgia." Whatever Mae wanted, the old man would do. Trace had trouble refusing her himself.

Preacher was traveling at such a breakneck speed that Trace had to drive his sorrel hard to catch up. The old man's lack of caution was unsettling. Riding hell-bent? That bespoke trouble.

He wheeled Duchess around in front of the wagon and shouted, "Slow down, old-timer!" As the contraption rolled to a halt, Trace added, "You're halfway to the Outpost already."

"She's lit out again," the old man gasped, "and on that damn horse of your'n, too!"

"I know," Trace said. "I've *got* her and my damn horse. We can't talk here." He grabbed the harness of the horse hitched to Preacher's wagon and led him off behind a stand of rocks where their conference wouldn't be in plain sight. It troubled Trace that other riders from the Lazy C hadn't already appeared in hot pursuit.

"Where have you got her?" Preacher asked.

"Tucked away behind a crack in the ridge. I covered our tracks."

"You better hope you did," the old man groused. "That husband of hers gathered a bunch of his riders, pulled them out of the south range when he found out she was gone. They were all in the bunkhouse at breakfast, chowing down on the biscuits and redeye gravy I made, when Comstock comes in looking for Morgan. Not sure why, but he grabs the man by the throat, jerks him up from the table, and half strangles the jackass before the crew could pull him off. He seemed to blame Morgan for letting her get away, even claimed Morgan took her for himself. Either way, he was plumb loco. Then one of the stable boys came in and said Diablo was gone. They were so busy gathering horses and getting saddled up, they seemed to forget about me, so I figured I'd come warn you. He sent outriders to pick up the trail, so unless you covered her tracks straight back to the Lazy C, they'll at least know which direction she headed."

"Where are they now?"

"Don't know. Comstock said she wouldn't head to the Outpost, since she knew no one would help her there. Now . . . no one saw me leave, but they will see the wagon tracks."

"We have to leave," agreed Trace. "And I've got to cover these tracks. That won't stop them, but it might slow them down long enough."

"What are we going to do?" the old man questioned.

"I'm going to take Mae up the plateau on the other side of the Lazy C. There's a mesa there, where a renegade band of Hualapai camp. I know their chief, White Eagle. He'll hide her. Then I'll come down and deal with Comstock and Morgan."

"Them Injuns might have come down out of there by now," Preacher mused. "They do in the spring when the snow starts melting."

"I'll just have to take that chance," Trace said. "I've got to hide her someplace safe while I settle the score with Comstock. Then I mean to see her safely home to Kentucky. Her granddad has a horse farm there she never should have left. Did you find anything out? Is Comstock rustling?"

"If he isn't, I'll eat this here wagon . . . but I've got no proof. Lord knows I tried, but they don't make me privy to their goings-on, and keep me close to the bunkhouse. Can't snoop around much. There's *something* shady going on, though. I'd stake my life on it, and you'd best find out what it is right quick. They're planning a drive in a couple weeks."

"That soon?" Trace erupted.

"Yep. He's hiring drovers in town. Was headed there when he found out Mae ran again."

"With her hidden away, maybe he'll hire me on. There ain't many drover types around these parts. If he's hard up for help, surely he'll hold his nose and give me work, if only for a few weeks."

Preacher shook his head. "Is that hellcat really going to stay put with old White Eagle? You can't go back in there on Diablo. You leave her and that horse up in the hills, I'd be worried she might take off again. What's she got to stick around for?"

"I trust her. She feels guilty. Hell, she even wants me

to take her back there. She wants me to tell Comstock I found her wandering out on the sage after Diablo threw her and took off. She wants to find a deed Comstock is holding."

Preacher mused for a moment. "You ain't going to like it, but I say she makes sense. It'd be a fine way to get on his good side. Comstock would be beholden to you for bringing her back, and you can bet he'd damn sure hire you. That's one pretty brave lady." He shook his head again. "But what would you do with that mustang of yours? You won't want to let Comstock lay hold of him again. One's sure to kill the other."

"Are you plum loco?" Trace thundered. "I'm not doing it. She isn't going back there!"

The old man seemed to accept Trace's word as final. All he asked was, "What do you want me to do?"

Trace sighed, trying to think up a plan. "If that wagon vanishes, they'll know you had something to do with all this. Just take it to the Outpost and get some supplies, act like nothing is wrong. I'll cover any tracks around here. Then I'm going back up the ridge. I'll watch from there 'til you come back. If you've seen Comstock or any of his riders, drive by with your hat off. I'll know they're in the area then. After dark, I'll burlap Diablo's feet and we'll head out for the Indian camp. Go about your cooking. No poking around. Keep your head down and give them no cause for suspicion. Once Mae's safe, you'll see me again, old-timer. Not until."

Chapter Nine

Praying he'd find Mae still there, Trace returned to the campsite at dusk. In the distance he'd seen Preacher drive by with a loaded wagon and wearing his hat, and Trace hadn't seen any sign of Comstock or his riders, either. That made him uneasy. They could be anywhere, and he had to tell Mae that they dared stay where they were no longer.

He breathed a sigh of relief when he spotted her sitting atop the fallen log, his Winchester across her lap. He'd been quietly fretting she'd take Diablo and run, not trusting him to keep her safe. But maybe she finally believed him that Diablo's prints were road markers for Comstock to follow, and maybe having reached this level of trust, the fool woman would tell him whatever else she was hiding. He rode into camp.

She rushed up with a dozen questions, and he smiled sadly. Annelee had been the same way. He handled Mae just as he had his sister, letting her get all the questions out before he spoke. "It's not safe here. Comstock has half his crew out looking for you. I am really surprised we haven't seen any of his riders yet."

She gave him a look. "I'm not stupid, Trace. I rode north for a spell, picked up a creek, and rode down the middle of that to cover my tracks. I came out on rocks, leaving no prints. Then I circled around and headed back this way. He thinks I won't go anywhere near the Outpost for help."

Trace nodded, impressed. "Smart thinking, but when they find nothing of you or the horse in that direction, they'll eventually come back to the Lazy C. In the morning, they'll fan out in a bunch of directions. Bet your pretty little behind on that."

She went back to the fire and dished up some stew. It didn't smell as good as Preacher's, but Trace was hungry enough to eat a snake, scales and all, so he figured this would taste mighty fine.

She said, "It's not much. Found some airtights. Beans, but they'll fill your belly."

"My belly thanks you," he replied. "Let's eat up, pack, and get out of here. I covered our trail as best I could, but Preacher's are different. Wagon tracks aren't as easy to hide as hoofprints. Comstock's men could easily get suspicious."

"Was Preacher all right?" Mae asked, picking at her pan of beans.

"I'm happy to say the bunkhouse was too busy raising a fuss over your leaving to do him any harm. Comstock and Morgan got into a fight at first light. Then your husband—"

Her eyes flashing, Mae growled, "Don't call him that."

"Sorry. The low-down, yellow-bellied sidewinder . . ." He stopped when she smiled, and his heart did a slow roll. Struggling to keep his mind on what needed doing, he stared down at the beans. "Preacher went on to the Outpost and got supplies after he met me; then he went back, so Comstock's men may not pay much heed to an old man's comings and goings. He didn't see any of Lazy C's riders going into or coming back from town. You evidently did a good enough job heading north. But they *will* ride back and look in other directions come morning. We have to be long gone by then. I want to ride slowly so I can cover our tracks until we reach the hills."

"What are we going to do?" she asked anxiously.

"We need to pack up and be on our way," was all he said. He kicked sand into the low-burning fire and began dismantling the camp.

When he was done, they approached the horses. Mae hestitated, clearly unsure what to do. She had ridden into camp sitting before him, and from her expression she was remembering that. Trace reached out and touched her face, stroking her cheek with his thumb.

"I want you to ride Diablo," he said.

Her face reflected shock. "You do?"

"Yes. For several reasons, sweetheart. I need to be free to handle Duchess and cover our tracks. I've wrapped the stallion's hooves, but if I miss tracks, those should be Duchess's. Also . . ." He took a deep breath, his whole body clenching against the possibility. "Also, if the worst happens and Comstock or Morgan catches up with us, you lean over that horse's neck and give him a slack rein. You're light on his back; he'll take off like he's got wings. He's wild, remember, but I saw how you handled him and he trusts you. There's nothing on this range that'll beat him, provided you don't let yourself get trapped. But don't look back, Mae. No matter what."

"But where are we *going*?" Her voice quavered.

"We can't go anywhere near the Outpost; that's suicide," he replied. "We both know that. Travelers could report spotting us. So what I plan is to cut across the sage to a high plateau on the other side, east of the mountains. Doubling back across the valley is the last thing your—Jared Comstock would expect you to do. You've already doubled back once. When he figures that out, he'll never expect you to do it again. He won't know Duchess's tracks, either; he's looking for Diablo's. Two days from now, we should reach a mesa where White Eagle camps, and you'll stay with his people 'til—"

"That's crazy!" she blurted. "We'll have to pass right above the Lazy C! Why can't you just take me southeast—to the railroad, where I can get a train home? I can wire my grandfather for money and—"

Trace interrupted. "For one thing, there's no time. Besides, that's the first thing Comstock would expect. You can bet he's sent riders to the stage line and every train stop for miles around. Someone will be waiting there for you, Mae. We've got to do what they don't expect. This isn't going to end 'til they've exhausted every option, but they won't go near the Indians. He's not *that* stupid." He wanted Mae to see this was the only option, but her face went pale and her eyes held terror. Something else occurred to him: "You're not scared of Indians, are you, Mae?"

Her mouth worked. Finally she admitted, "I've heard

some awful stories about them and what they do to white women."

Almost offended, he hefted her onto Diablo's back and handed her the stallion's reins, then wound the lead to his burro around the saddle horn. "Put that horse dung out of your mind. You think white men have treated you so well? The Indians are a noble people, abused, mistreated, lied about . . . You'll be a damn sight safer with them than Morgan or Comstock."

"We're right on the California border! Well, almost. But we're closer to it than your Indians. Why can't we—?"

"I thought of that," Trace interrupted, "but I don't know those parts, and I sure don't know anybody I could trust to look after you 'til I settle this."

"But I'm scared," Mae replied. She clearly hadn't been taking him seriously when he first suggested this plan. "When my great-aunt lived outside Louisville, they had a marker for victims of something they called Long Run. Whole families ran for miles trying to escape Indians. Many were killed"—she bit her lip—"and scalped."

"That was back some time, Mae. Those Indians picked up ways taught by white men—the *French*. Yep. Didn't you know scalping was a white man's creation? They paid Indians for scalps during the French and Indian Wars—English scalps. Outside of a few trappers, the Plains Indians never saw any Frenchmen or learned their 'civilized' ways. Thank God."

Mae sensed his annoyance and said, "I didn't mean—"

Trace gave a huff. "Question is, are you more afraid

of the Indians than you are of Comstock?" When Mae didn't answer, he nodded. "That settles it. Now come on. Ride in front of me, so I can use the drag to cover our tracks. But keep a close eye on me and do as I say. We've a lot of ground to cover before sunrise."

As Trace swung up in his saddle, Mae gave a nod and said no more. There wasn't any use; he wasn't going to listen, and going on without him was unthinkable. He knew the territory, she did not. Having him take her back to the Lazy C would be a living nightmare. She would have done it, hoping to get that deed back, but only with him by her side. Being caught alone and dragged back yet again would be another matter. She shuddered just imagining it. She felt safe in Trace's presence, and something else, something that quickened her pulse and pumped hot blood to her cheeks.

Twisting in the saddle, she watched him riding ramrod-rigid behind Diablo, every muscle tensed in the saddle. As she studied his strong profile, angular features, and that mouth, which was too damn sensual for a horse wrangler, it hit her: she was falling in love with this man of contradictions. A tough man, made tough by this ragged land and a war where there were few winners, yet despite all that, he was gentle with her and Diablo. He was a man very much like her grandfather, and she smiled, imagining introducing the two.

The shadow of a russet beard was just beginning on Trace's cheeks. There was silver at his temples, revealed in the half-light cast by stars winking down from the overhead vault of deepening indigo. She watched him without detection. He didn't even seem to be aware of her, busy as he was making sure the drag did its job. The terrain had his full and fierce attention; no crawling, buzzing, or jumping creature, no sound or shape of the land they traveled escaped him as they picked their way out of their hiding place and across the land. He was in his element. The sight of him so absorbed took her breath away.

The burro trailing behind slowed their progress somewhat, but they had to be careful as they traversed the open sage, headed for the plateau on the far side of the valley. Lights blinking in the distant north chilled Mae's blood. The Lazy C. They were so close—at least, it seemed that way. Night in the desert had a way of deceiving a traveler. She didn't speak her apprehension, yet Trace seemed to read it, though he wasn't looking at her. He nudged Duchess lightly with his knees, quickening their pace.

A thin string of clouds drifted over the distant mountaintops, tinting them a lighter shade of blue. Despite it being spring, there'd still be snow in the higher elevations. Strange night-blooming plants perfumed the air, their scents released when trampled beneath the animals' hooves. There was comfort in that mysterious perfume, as though no danger could exist in such an atmosphere.

She and Trace reached the plateau before midnight, after miles of heart-stopping openness. Mae felt exposed the whole time, as if a thousand eyes watched her progress. Now there were trees and springs and rocky washes that would flood when the snows higher up melted, and Trace stopped to give the animals a drink of the cool, clear water. Both riders stepped down to give their horses a breath, and Trace checked the burlap covers on Diablo's hooves to make sure they were holding up.

It was a brief respite. Trace was a stern taskmaster and insisted they push on; too much ground had yet to be spanned. Mae made no protest, agreeing, despite the pain in her shoulder throbbing worse with every step the horse took. Even though the air was cool and damp, she felt feverish, but they were nonetheless soon off again, threading their way through groves just burgeoning with spring foliage.

The cool green darkness of the forest was welcoming, soothing the heat burning her body. So tired, Mae felt her eyelids begin to droop. She hadn't rested while Trace watched from aloft throughout the day, had been too frightened to even close her eyes. She was paying for that now, swaying in her saddle and almost losing her grip on Diablo's reins before a shift in his stride caused her to jerk back awake.

Shaking her head to clear it, she rolled her shoulder, hoping to relieve the ache. Instead, a sharp pain racked her body. Her breath drew in on a sharp inhale. Surely, the wound should be healing. Today, the nagging pain was worse. Maybe she'd hurt it more than she thought when Trace wrestled her down to the ground? Something at the back of her mind warned it was more than a simple twinge.

They'd left the grove upon a narrow gravelly trail leading upward, gradually at first, then steeper. The mesa at last! In the minimal light, Mae could barely see.

"Let me go ahead of you here," said Trace, nudging Duchess around Diablo. "But follow me close," he charged. "If the burro balks, cut him loose. He won't go far. I'll come back after him once I've gotten you safely up this trail."

"It's so steep!" Mae worried, bending her head back to appraise the climb. It seemed like a wall or sheer rock face. "Trace, I don't think—"

"Don't think, just do like I say. Slacken Diablo's reins. Keep them loose. He was born on a mesa just like this one. Give him his head, and he'll scale this slope like a mountain goat. You don't know half the potential of that horse you've got beneath you."

Mae obeyed. There was no use protesting; the matter wasn't open for discussion. She didn't want to stay with the Indians, either. She wanted to head southeast to the railroad and home. Only, she worried about leaving that deed with Comstock. And worse, a new realization was starting to fill her heart: every clop of their mounts' hooves was taking her closer to a separation from this mysterious wrangler. He planned to leave her with strangers—Indians, no less!—while he returned to face every gun on the Lazy C. Her heart stuttered at the thought. She didn't want to be left behind. She didn't want to lose Trace just when he was coming to mean so much to her. Even from this distance, and in such nerve-racking circumstances, he set a swarm of butterflies loose in the pit of her belly. And yet what choice did she have?

Trace had almost reached the top, and Mae heard him leak a muffled string of expletives, turning her skin to gooseflesh. Her heart leapt as gravel began sliding from under Duchess's hooves—she'd heard of rock slides covering whole passes! But after a moment the falling rocks slowed to a trickle, attracting a notice only from Diablo. But no. A high-pitched *hee-haw* signaled the burro had noticed, too.

"Hell and damnation!" Trace thundered. Duchess's iron shoes clattered on the solid rock above.

Mae, growing dizzy, asked, "Wh-what is it?" She held her breath as Diablo cleared the rim.

"No fires. They've pulled up camp. They're gone." Trace glanced around the area, which held no signs of an intention to return. "We can't stay here. Not for long, but perhaps overnight. That rock formation *there*." He pointed. "We'll leave the horses behind it, out of sight."

Mae eyed him, incredulous. "You think we'll be followed to this mesa?"

"I don't know," said Trace, "but we can't be too careful. I saw no sign of anyone, but . . ."

"We're trapped up here!" Mae realized, in genuine terror at the thought.

"No, we're not," he replied. "There are a dozen ways down here, and a couple of ways up, too. See those crags?" He pointed up to where ragged outcroppings ascended from rocky steps to what seemed to be another level. "There's a cave up there. Tomorrow I'll figure out which way White Eagle went."

"You can't mean to follow them." Mae was incredulous.

"You got a better idea? I have to get back to the Lazy C before they drive those horses to market, and I can't until you're safe, Mae. Once Comstock disposes of that herd, I've got no way to prove he's rustling." He led both of their horses and the burro behind the rocks, and began to unsaddle and stake Duchess.

Mae dismounted. "You're not going to hobble them?" she asked.

"No," he answered. "If we need to make a fast get-away, we don't want to be fumbling with hobbles, and I can't leave them bridles-down. We don't want to have to go looking if we need them in a hurry."

"Take me back," Mae pleaded, laying a hand on his rock-hard arm despite her resolve to avoid physical contact. His taut, cordlike muscles rippled beneath her fingers, and her breath caught in a soft gasp she hoped he didn't hear.

"Y-you just said it yourself—there's no time for all this," she said after a moment. "Trace, I have to go back and get that deed. I can get you onto the Lazy C. Just take me back. I can help you get all the proof you need, and also the deed to Foxtail. I have to. You're wasting time dragging me all over the place. If we work together—"

"No, I told you! I'm not going to put you through something like that. There'll be gunplay before this is done. Comstock isn't one to give up anything without a fight. Are you trying to get me killed? If I have to worry about you getting in the way, that's exactly what's going to happen, guaranteed." He studied her for a moment. Those eyes—those quicksilver eyes bored into her so steadily that she couldn't meet them.

"Is there some other reason you want to go back?" he asked. "Makes no sense that you keep running from there and now you want to go back."

"Of course not," she protested, though she flushed. "I'm trying to help you!"

"You haven't told me everything," Trace asserted.

"That much I know for certain. What are you holding out?"

She was keeping the whole truth from Trace, to be honest, but this was definitely not the time to satisfy his curiosity. Actually, she was hoping she'd never have to tell. Not to this volatile man of honor.

After fighting waves of heat all day long, she suddenly shivered with a chill. She rubbed her arms briskly, hoping he'd forget his question.

"You cold?" He frowned, stripping a bedroll and blankets from the burro.

"Where are the dwellings?" she murmured, scanning the vacant mesa. "Once I get inside—"

"There are none," he interrupted. "They take their dwellings apart and pack them on their backs when they migrate. They haven't been gone long—two or maybe three days. We will catch up."

"How do you know that?" she wondered.

"Their tracks are still fresh. We're lucky we didn't get snow down here, like they probably did up in the mountains. Late spring squalls can be ripsnorters." He shrugged. "We'll know where they went soon enough."

"We're wasting time chasing these Indians," Mae cried, fighting dizziness. "You won't take the time to see me south to the railroad, but you've got plenty of time to waste tracking this . . . this White Eagle? Why didn't you let me go? I was nearly away. Why did you have to stop me?"

"You were riding my horse, or have you forgotten that?"

"Oh!" she said in disgust. "You and that animal! He's only a horse. One would think that I kidnapped your child, your flesh and blood. I was riding for my life, for my hon—never mind. It doesn't matter."

" 'Only a horse'? All this from a horse breeder's grand-daughter," Trace teased. "I'd be willing to bet my six-shooter your grandpappy would understand my upset at having Diablo stolen."

Mae heaved a depressed sigh. "My granddad and you could certainly spend hours talking horses."

"I wish you could have been there to see what I went through to get him," Trace mused. "I wish you could have seen how I stalked him for two years, was humiliated by him time and time again until I finally separated him from his herd and tricked him into a blind canyon, one on one. Yeah, he's like my flesh and blood all right. Our blood mingled on that day I broke him, so you might say we've been blood brothers ever since."

Mae fought the shudder of another chill, but she barely noticed, so caught up was she in his eyes. He seemed so *alive* as he spoke of Diablo. She wondered if they would flash with the same passion because of her.

"Why didn't you take one of Comstock's damn horses?" Trace asked.

"I told you why," Mae sobbed. "I couldn't bear to see him mistreated." She couldn't bring herself to tell him how cruelly Jared Comstock had abused Diablo, though she knew he had a pretty good idea. "And because . . ."

"Because what?" he prompted, his passion palpable, the cords in his neck standing out in bold relief.

"Because we're alike," she murmured. "We both needed our freedom."

That tied his tongue, she thought. For a longer

moment he stood staring down at her, his eyes dark, gleaming pinpoints beneath the ledge of his sun-bleached brows. He was so close. His body heat warmed her, riding the sexual stream that linked them. It was beyond bearing. She couldn't trust herself to his close-ness, yet she was helpless, rooted to the spot. If he hadn't broken the spell, she would have fallen into his arms.

"Follow me," he said hoarsely. Slinging a canteen and blanket rolls over his shoulder, he led her toward the outcropping of overhanging rocks he'd pointed out.

"You can't mean to go way up there?" she cried, dig-ging in her heels. She wasn't sure she could make the climb.

"We can't stay down here. There's no shelter."

"You're serious."

"Go ahead of me. Feel your way. I'll be right behind you. You won't fall. The rock is cut out like steps. The Indians did that so that they could get to the cave and post a lookout easier."

Mae balked again, incredulous. "You expect me to sleep in a . . . a cave up there? With you?"

"Yes," he replied, nudging her forward. "We can't light a fire down here and risk the chance of being spot-ted. That loco husband of yours is fool enough to track you no matter what time of day, so who knows where he's at?"

She snapped, "I told you not to call him my hus-band."

Trace ignored that. "It's only fair to warn you that White Eagle and his band make it a practice of sharing this mesa with animals. They pay for the privilege by offering the furry devils a few morsels now and then. If they come looking and don't find anything else . . ."

"All right, all right, you've made your point," Mae conceded.

The upper level rose to a height of fifty feet above the mesa floor, but as Trace promised it was a fairly easy climb, even in the dark. Mae only slipped once, but quick hands shot out and grabbed her almost before she lost her balance and steadied her against him for longer than she thought necessary. There was great strength in him, but no roughness. No man had ever held her from behind in that way, and her heart leapt with the strange sensations such an intimacy set loose. His hot breath on her neck sent waves of icy fire coursing through her veins and prickled her scalp with gooseflesh. These things alone threatened her balance more than any slippery, frost-glazed stair of rock.

Once she stood on solid ground at the top, he let her go and strode to the cave where he disappeared into the blackness within. It was only for a moment to drop the blankets, but her heart hammered in her breast, thundered in her ears until he appeared again.

"You're shivering. Go in out of the wind," he commanded. Until that moment, she wasn't even aware that the wind had risen.

"It's dark in there," she lamented, taking a cautious step toward the entrance.

Trace laughed. It was a deep, throaty, baritone rumble that resonated through her entire body. "It's a cave," he said. "Caves are supposed to be dark."

"Wh-where are you going?" she murmured, feeling weak and scared.

"Not far, to gather some scrub for our beds—unless you want to sleep on hard red rock?"

Mae approached the mouth of the cave with caution. She looked up. The sky was clear, and the stars winked down innocently, shedding more light than she would have thought possible. How was it that she'd never noticed such things in Kentucky? What was it about the West that revealed Mother Nature's true intent? The vastness, perhaps, uncluttered by man's mundane distractions. Or perhaps it was something infinitely more: was she seeing it all through this man's unjaded eyes?

The entrance of the cave loomed before her, a different, more ominous shade of black than the velvety heavens overhead. But the sound of Trace rustling in the brush and snapping twigs from nearby was a comfort; he had kept his word and not gone far in his pursuit of scrub. Squaring her shoulders, she stepped inside. Though damp, it was slightly warmer out of the wind, and she'd almost begun to relax when a strange whirring stopped her in her tracks. It was coming from deep within the cavern. She had never heard the like: a buzzing, clacking whoosh. It grew louder, amplified by the cave. Mae took a step back, and then another as the wind picked up.

Wind, inside the cave? It couldn't be, but it was. No, not wind, a sudden rush of stagnant air displaced by the flapping of wings—hundreds of wings, *thousands* of wings! And then she saw them: a swarm of bats soaring past, over, and around her. Their wings grazed her hair, her face, her body in their haste to flee the cave.

Some of them struck her and dropped at her feet, stunned, causing her to stumble and slide on the damp rocks. Mae screamed. Fending them off with her arms raised to protect her face, she reeled out on the rocky ledge, surrounded by a veritable cloud of the flying creatures. They carried her along as they soared over the edge of the precipice in a flapping, shrieking stream, a frenzied river toward the plateau. Blood trickled into her eye from a wound on her forehead where one of the bats had grazed her with his talons.

She had no sense of direction, only that she must escape her attackers. The last sound she heard before she fell over the edge of the cliff was Trace shouting her name.

Chapter Ten

*T*race dropped the dead scrub in his arms and dove through the swarm of bats toward Mae. Her name spilled from his throat in a voice he scarcely recognized, mingling with her bloodcurdling scream, and in that one terrible, heart-stopping instant he realized what it would mean to lose her. His mind refused to accept such a possibility.

He threw himself down on the brink of the overhang and with frantic eyes scanned the darkness below. That he still heard her screams, and they were close, gave him hope, but it wasn't until the last of the bats funneled out of the cave and past him that he saw her. She was clinging to a clump of roots and branches protruding from a crevice in the rock face.

"Mae! Listen to me," he called, reaching down. She was close enough—just barely—but he didn't want to frighten her with any sudden move. It was clear that she was hysterical and in pain. "Don't be afraid," he added. "I'm going to grip your arm. Once I've got you, let go of the branch and hang on to me with both hands. I'll pull you up. I won't let you fall."

"I can't!" she shrilled. "My shoulder . . . Owwww!"

"Mae, don't think about the pain. You can *do* this. No! Look at me! Stay as still as you can. Those roots and branches are dead. If you put a strain on them, they'll pull loose from the rock. Keep looking at me and do exactly as I say."

Leaning over as far as he dared, Trace extended his arm downward and grasped her wrist. A soft cry escaped her throat as his fingers tightened in a deathlike grip, but she didn't let go of the branch.

"I've got you!" he crowed. "I've got you, Mae. You're safe." She was far from it, but he had to make her believe, make her trust that enough to help him save her from a fall that would mean certain death. "Let go of the branch and grab my arm, and I can pull you up."

"I . . . I'm afraid," she whimpered.

"Damn it, you promised to do as I say. Now let that go."

It was a long moment, but she finally responded to his command. With a desperate groan she let go of the branch and grabbed frantically on to his forearm. Once more, a pule came from her lips, and she stared up at him with terrified eyes.

"Mae, you've done the hard part. The rest is easy, but you've got to help me."

"I'm going to fall!" she wailed, glancing down. "My shoulder . . . I can't hold on."

"You can! Don't look down! Look up at me. That's it. Now, Mae, there's a small ledge a hair to your right, enough for you to get your foot on. Reach out to your right with your foot."

She nodded and then tried to follow instructions. If

the situation hadn't been so desperate, he might have laughed.

"Your other right, you silly goose." He gave her a reassuring smile, one he didn't feel. "Come on, woman. Reach."

She half turned as she tried to seek the small ledge with her booted foot. Trace gritted his teeth. A second swing of her leg and she had it, but rocks and dirt dislodged, causing her to panic again.

"It's no use. It's no use!" she sobbed.

He thundered, "Do as I say!"

She gave a desperate grunt, and Mae's bad arm jerked as her fisted fingers crawled around his arm. Finally, groping the rock with the toe of her boot, she found the solid part of the tiny shelf.

"Good girl. Now get the other foot on it, and then I can get a better grip on you."

Her feet almost slipped off, but her back arched like a scared cat's and she finally had a solid toehold. Seconds later, he hauled her up and over the edge, into his arms.

Trace rolled with her away from the edge. She clung to him fiercely. For a long moment he stared into her misty doe eyes to reassure himself that she was really there holding him, but that wasn't enough; he needed more proof. He tangled his hand in her hair and took her lips with a hungry, bruising mouth. He swallowed the moan in her throat. It resonated through his body, covering him with gooseflesh, setting his loins afire.

It was a brief kiss, although volatile, a reaffirmation they were alive. Her heart was hammering against his chest. He sat and pulled her onto his lap. Brushing back a lock of hair, he noticed the scrape on her brow and hugged her again. "You hesitated a couple times. That could be bad news in these parts. You've got to learn to trust me, Mae."

"It wasn't you!" she choked out in a sob. "It was me. I was afraid I would get you killed."

He finally laughed. "And it didn't bother you that you might die instead?"

The sane part of him wanted to keep her at arm's length, to immediately take her to the railroad and see her safely on a train for Kentucky. Let that be the end of it. There was no place in his life for such a complication as she presented. She didn't belong in the West; she came from a gentler life. The West had a way of making men hard and of aging women before their time. The West was too hot, too cold, and too damn dry out here most of the time; it took impossible adaptations to survive.

He'd survived, of course. But he was a renegade rider, and his daily work meant he could expect to be dry-gulched, faced off in a gunfight, back-shot, and murdered. Someday he wanted to find a place where he could set down roots, but that was still a vague dream, as much as Mae made him want more. Such a life as his was not for Mae. He had nothing to offer her. Mae needed to be back home in Kentucky as soon as possible. That part of him long dead—Trevor Guilliard—had suddenly awoken with an ache, but while he wanted this woman, wanted a life with her, there were too many problems reminding him that his dreams were far-fetched. He didn't even know if she felt the same way. And there was a husband to deal with.

Dismissing his silly hunger for what could never be, he stood, knees shaking, as he gathered Mae up and carried her back toward the cave. For an instant she seemed captivated by his eyes and was too shaken to speak, but when she realized where he was taking her, she stiffened and began thrashing in his arms.

"No! Oh, no! You're not taking me back in there!" Her voice was shrill. "There were millions of those dreadful things. Put me down. They'll be back!"

"Mae, those critters are halfway to Mexico by now. They're wearing sombreros, I promise you. We scared them just as much as they scared us. They're not coming back as long as we're camped out inside here. Besides, I'm going to light a fire. Even if they did return, that'd keep them away." He set her down on one of the blankets. "I'm going to get the fire started. Don't you move a muscle, hear? I don't care what else crawls out of this cave, you stay put!"

He gathered more brush, and a rock to heat; then he built a fire close to the entrance. Mae flatly refused to go farther in. Trace couldn't blame her, and he certainly didn't want a repeat of her tumbling off the cliff—he wouldn't admit it to her, but there was no telling what else they might be sharing that cave with.

Trace didn't realize the extent of Mae's injuries until he saw her in the firelight. Her cheek and forehead were scratched. One cut, at her hairline, was deep and matted with blood. Her clothes were torn, her sleeves having seen the worst of things. Fortunately, there were no significant wounds on her arms. Her hands were another matter. Several cuts on her palms and fingers were fairly deep and still oozing. And there was no doubt that she'd done damage to her wounded shoulder. She'd been favoring that arm.

He decided to start with the wound on her brow. "Take a swig," he said, offering her his canteen. "I've got to go down for our packs. You need doctoring. When I get back I will fix you up and then set about making us some beans and biscuits."

"I'm not hungry," she replied.

"You stay by the fire and I'll be right back." When she didn't respond, he said her name. She glanced up, unshed tears in her eyes, and he knelt before her, taking her hand. "I know all this has been very rough on you—a nightmare, I guess. But I promise you, Mae. Believe me: I *will* see you get back to Kentucky."

Not looking up, she gave a brief nod. That was all.

Trace hesitated, worried about her silence. He'd seen people after a shock; many got cold and distant, and you had to take special care of them. Turning on his heel, he hurried down the rocky steps, coming back with his arms full. Dropping the packs near the fire, he rummaged around until he found his pot. He poured some water into it from his canteen, setting it on the flames. Mae needed something hot to warm her insides, and he also needed water to cleanse her wounds.

When it heated enough, he poured a small amount onto a kerchief and then knelt beside her, gently bathing her face. She accepted his ablutions without comment. That worried him. Her cheeks were bright crimson. But was that from her closeness to the fire, from the harrowing experience, or from something else? He didn't dare speculate, not when his mind was distracted by that petal-soft skin in his hands. Rose petals.

That's what her flesh reminded him of: velvety smooth rose petals. Roses like his mama grew.

Poor Mae. She wasn't cut out for the harshness of this land. He could envision her in soft gowns, servants attending her. She was too fine, too gentle for the West. He needed to get her home where she belonged. She'd been through too much already.

He wet the neckerchief again and cleaned the wounds on her hands. Only one was troublesome, between her thumb and forefinger, and she winced when he touched it. He apologized just to break the silence. "I'm sorry. This one is deep, and it's in a bad place for healing. I have to get it clean to stop infection."

Her haunted eyes fixed on his hands, and at last she spoke. "You have a gentle touch for someone with such big hands. Like a doctor."

He smiled, pleased. "It's a common talent among horsemen. If you're not born with it, you sure acquire it quick. I'll bet your granddad's just as good."

A faraway look came into her eyes. Her lips parted, as if she were about to speak; then they closed again and she stared absently into the fire.

"Mae, I've got to look at your shoulder," he informed her. "I've got to see how much damage you've done to it. Take off that jacket and let me see to the wound. Make sure it's held. You look flushed. I am hoping it's not inflamed."

Mae did as bidden, unbuttoned her jacket, the flannel shirt. He had to help her slide them both off, for she winced when she tried to lift that arm. She loosened the top of her camisole and tugged the wide strap off her shoulder. Trace frowned. She hadn't opened the wound, but it was swollen, red, and angry-looking.

"It needs another poultice to bring the swelling down," he said. Pouring warm water from the coffeepot over his bandana, he bathed the wound. "My herbs are in my pack."

Working quickly, he mixed ground herbs to pack into the wound, which would be held in place by his kerchief. He reached out to press the poultice to the shoulder, and the warmth of her opalescent skin under his fingers excited him. Glancing down, he saw the water from where he'd bathed the wound had wet the front of her camisole. The material was nearly transparent. Swallowing hard, he stared at the clearly revealed dark nipple.

The hand holding the poultice dropped, and Trace tried to remind himself he was only caring for her; he had no right to look at Mae in this manner. Tried and failed. Her nipples strained against the cloth with her every breath. Even scuffed up, tired, and shaken, Mae was still a beautiful woman. He had to get her back to Kentucky where she belonged. She didn't belong out here, no matter how he might want her.

Though he attempted to swallow his desire, it only increased. Waves of warmth surged through his loins. Over and over he told himself the hundred reasons to keep his emotional distance from this woman, not the least of which was that his life was too damn empty now. When she went back to Kentucky . . . Well, he didn't want to contemplate the bleakness of a future without her. It would destroy him.

He started to turn away, but Mae reached out,

catching his face with her hand, guiding it around until their eyes met. He shook his head.

"Trace, don't turn from me. Please."

His whole body clenched as he fought both the emotional and physical pain of wanting her. Touching her as a man who wanted a woman would be wrong. Worse, it would destroy him.

She leaned close and brushed her lips against his. They were soft, moving against his mouth, warm, seeking. "Please," she whispered, and then bestowed upon him another kiss.

He was undone by her plea. Laying her back against the bedroll, he kissed her, tasting her deeply. How sweet she was, like honey. Her heady wild clover scent intoxicated him. She was another man's wife, but that didn't matter. Nothing mattered but them. Here. Now. She would go back to Kentucky and his life would once again be empty, but for this small space of time it would be filled with magic.

Every fiber of his body was suddenly obsessed with the notion of showing Mae how a man should make love to a woman, how a man should revere and pleasure her above and beyond himself. He couldn't imagine Jared Comstock had done as much. He opened the buttons on her camisole and spread it wide, moving with caution and gentleness since at any moment he fully expected to have his face slapped. But she didn't slap his face. Her breath caught in a strangled gasp as his lips grazed her throat, the swell of her breast, and then closed around the puckered rim of her tawny nipple.

A raw, guttural moan escaped him as that tiny bud hardened against his tongue. The sound mingled with something similar coming from deep inside her, as she fisted her hands in his hair and held him there, arching her body against him. Caught up in the eagerness of her response, he teased first one and then the other nipple with his tongue, tugged with his lips, and nipped lightly with his teeth. She shuddered with pleasure.

Trace rolled onto his hip, tugged off his boots, and stripped naked. Mae's gaze raked his naked body. Another gasp escaped her parted lips, and those dark eyes settled on his engorged sex. He almost laughed. It seemed almost as though she had never seen a naked, fully aroused male. How embarrassing for her husband.

Dropping down beside her, he helped unfasten her jeans. His eyes feasted upon her silky, translucent skin, the gentle curves of her body, and mound of red-gold hair curling between her thighs.

"You're beautiful, Mae," he murmured, gathering her against him.

His heavy sex bobbed against her belly. The flesh-to-flesh contact struck him like forked lightning, and he shut his eyes, threw back his head, and prayed—a defense mechanism he'd developed to delay climax. After a moment, he found her lips again and teased her tongue into his mouth, murmuring assurances that mingled with the compulsive moans leaking from her throat. She began to shake violently in his arms, and he showered her face, her eyes, and her arched white throat with kisses before drawing her closer still.

When his hand traveled over her breast to her belly and approached the silken curls beneath, she leaned her lips against his ear and murmured, "There's something that I must tell you." She was caressing his back with her tiny fingers. "I've never . . . That is, I haven't . . . ever . . ."

Trace froze. His heart seemed to tumble to a halt. His breath was short as he leaned back and looked her in the eyes, those incredible, limpid doe eyes. But she couldn't mean . . . ? Good God, that was exactly what she did mean!

"You once accused me of holding something back," she said. "This is what I've kept from you, Trace. I didn't think I'd ever have to tell you. I didn't expect to fall . . . But I have—oh, I have—and I don't know . . . what to do."

Trace began to breathe again, and his breath left his lungs on a groan.

"I don't want you to stop," she went on through a tremor. "I want you to make love to me. I've dreamed of this moment, fantasized about it. It's just . . . I don't know what's expected. How to . . . You know."

Of all the words she might've spoken, this was the last thing he'd expected. His mind swam. While he was experienced in the art of making love, he had no experience with virgins. Once again, he fought the urge to laugh. Mae would not understand.

"H-how . . . ?" was all he could get out. "Comstock married you. You can't expect me to believe—"

"It's the truth." She took his hand and put it against his face. "He seems to want to genuinely win my favor. I begged him for a few weeks of time to grieve for my father, to come to know him, and then I said I would accept him as my husband. I didn't think he would agree, but he did. Only, Morgan wasn't scared of Jared for some reason. You'd think he would be, with Jared being the boss, but he's not. His hands were all over me whenever Jared's back was turned. That's why I ran away. After Jared dragged me back, he was . . . cold. I cannot explain it. He scared me. That's the reason I took Diablo and ran again. We're kindred spirits, that horse and I—both captives of a cruel master." There was a tear in her eye, though she stared at him with quiet awe.

Trace drew a ragged breath and pulled her into his arms. His heart was beating like a blacksmith's hammer; hard, irregular, heavy thumps against her smooth breast. The muscle in his jaw began to tick. He had to force the words out. "A woman's first time should be special, not on the floor of some dingy cave." He couldn't even begin to think with her in his arms, but this had changed things. "And . . . if I take you here, you could go home with child. I can't allow you to do that, to face that alone."

He shifted her weight off him, despite her hands clinging to his shoulders, and got to his feet. Grabbing his trousers, he jerked them on.

"Wait. There's more," she said. "Remember when I told you that Jared brought a preacher from the village to marry us?"

Unable to speak, Trace nodded, his eyes riveted to her flushed face.

"He . . . wasn't."

"Who wasn't what?"

"The man," she said, raising herself to a sitting position, drawing her camisole close with a tiny shiver. "He wasn't a preacher. I saw him afterward. He came to the ranch to gamble with Jared's men after the first time I was brought back. I overheard them making sport of what they'd done, how they'd fooled me, tricked me into believing a seedy saddle tramp was a man of the cloth. They don't know I heard."

Trace rocked back on his heels. Blind rage starred his vision. After a moment, he reached out with trembling fingers and closed the camisole over her breasts. It was a display of painstaking control for a madman, which was what he certainly had become. "And you wanted me to take you back there?"

"I would have been safe with you and Preacher close by. I was trying to help you. If it wasn't for me, you wouldn't be in this predicament. And I really want to find the letter my father signed. I know they said whoever killed and robbed him must've taken that. But I *know* either Jared or Morgan did it. That deed to the farm is back there. If Jared were to show up with it . . . it could kill my granddad."

Taking up his boots from the floor of the cave, Trace tugged them on and then snatched up his shirt and jacket.

"What are you going to do?" she breathed.

"I don't know," he replied.

"Where are you going? No! Don't leave me!"

"I'm not going to leave you, Mae," he assured her. "I'm going outside, where I can think. I can't do that here with you. Not now, not like this."

"Trace—"

"Go to sleep, Mae," he said, stalking past her into the frosty night. "There's not much night left before dawn."

Of course, he already knew what had to be done. What he needed was the strength and the courage to do it. He had to let Mae go.

Chapter Eleven

$\mathcal{M}ae$ woke before dawn, her heart heavy with a dread of facing Trace. Not even the tantalizing aroma of coffee in her nostrils could coax her to leave the cave. How could she look him in the eye after what had almost happened between them? She was still so confused. Trace was a gentleman all right. Only, she hadn't wanted him to be a gentleman.

"Fool man," she muttered, rubbing the sleep from her eyes. At the back of her mind she also felt a modicum of guilt. Oh, she wanted Trace to make love her, but she also hoped that if he did so, he would follow her back to Kentucky. Maybe that wasn't an honest way to deal with a man, but then, men these days weren't dealing too straight with her.

Hot blood raced through her at the recollection of his naked body, the hard, well-muscled length of him standing over her, burnished by firelight. Her breath caught, and she relived the intimacy of their kisses, of his lips on her eyes, her throat, her breasts, awakening her to pleasures between a man and a woman she'd never dreamed existed.

She dreaded the mortification to come, facing his steel gaze. She dreaded the climb back down to the mesa, and the prospect of tracking his Indian friends. Still, she was no coward. Determined to emerge head high, as though nothing had occurred between them, she made herself presentable and stepped out into the misty predawn gray. Trace was nowhere in sight.

She sank down on a flat rock near the fire to compose herself, muttering, "Well, fie on him." Not finding him was a bit anticlimactic. She'd polished her aloof bearing and mustered the courage to employ it, but now that courage was fading fast. It was like swallowing a dose of castor oil; such a confrontation had to be done quickly if at all.

"Here," he said, appearing and handing her a plate of frijoles. "Eat up. We need to hurry."

Startled, she jumped. He'd approached with the stealth of an Indian. Where had he come from? It wasn't a very big ledge. He must have been crouching in the shadows. Or was it that he'd been standing in plain view all the while and she'd been too preoccupied to notice? Her hands shook helplessly. The spoon rattled against the plate she balanced on her knees while he poured her a cup of coffee and put it beside her on a rock.

"We need to move on as soon as you're done," he said. "Can you climb down by yourself, or do you want help?"

"I beg your pardon?"

"If you don't think you can manage on your own, I'll tie a rope harness onto you and lower you down."

Cheeks burning, she studied him. There was no trace of the passion he'd shown the night before in that expressionless face. No tenderness or caring. Instead, there was an angular hardness about his flushed features, as though they were carved of the same rock as the mesa. His rigid posture was unnatural and alarming. Trace was steeling himself against something.

Whatever it was, clearly he wasn't about to share it, and she wasn't about to probe him.

"I can manage without being hog-tied," she answered frostily. "The poultice helped. Thank you for waking me last night and making sure I put it on my shoulder." Sadly Mae recalled him awaking her, caring for her wound. It was obvious that he wanted no more physical contact. He'd been distant, but nothing like this.

He gave a short nod.

They ate in silence. She had scarcely swallowed the last mouthful on her plate when he doused the fire with the remainder of the coffee, collected the bedroll and gear, and strode stiffly to the ledge. "I'll go first," he said. "You come after me."

She had never been particularly fond of heights, but Mae wasn't about to let him know that approaching the cliff so soon after careening off it all but paralyzed her with fear. A cold, metallic, bloodlike taste was building at the back of her throat.

The first step was the hardest. Trace was right behind her, and she was certain he could hear her heart pounding. She didn't look over her shoulder, she wouldn't give him the satisfaction, and when she came to the dead scrub she'd clung to so desperately the night before, she looked away quickly, reliving her climb to safety: his strong hands pulling her up, her feet slipping on the wet rocks. How passionately he had kissed her when they rolled away from the edge.

"To the left!" Trace called.

Preoccupied, Mae stepped in a pile of loose rocks created from the debacle the night before. She regained her footing, but her heart jumped and she had a hard time catching a breath. A shower of rock dust and grit rained down upon him, and a spate of muttered expletives followed that he tried but failed to disguise.

Fortunately, the rest of the descent was accomplished without incident. The horses were saddled and waiting; Trace had clearly been working early. A diamond hitch secured their packs to the burro, and Trace now added the bedrolls and the last of their gear.

"How are you going to track your Indian friends in this?" she asked. "Shouldn't we wait until full light?"

"We aren't tracking them," Trace replied, jamming his Winchester in its saddle sheath.

"I don't understand. . . ."

"I'm taking you south—to the railroad," he said, swinging himself up on Duchess's back. "Stay behind me and do like you did coming up. Give Diablo his head and a loose rein. He'll do the rest."

"Wait!" she cried. "Trace, wait—"

He was already in motion. "Mae, I've been thinking on it all night. You're going back to Kentucky just as fast as I can put you on a train."

"Have I no say in this?" she snapped. She was panicked. He meant to put her on the train—alone.

"You're going home. It's where you belong."

"And where do *you* belong, Trace Ord? Don't tell me you don't feel something for me. You'd be lying. You think to put me on that train and then go back there and face Jared Comstock and Bill Morgan? You're going to get yourself killed, that's what."

"I won't lie to you, Mae," he said. "I'm going after Comstock. I've got to. That was my plan, what I was hired to do. It was in the works before I ever met you. What that bastard did to you and Diablo . . . well, he doesn't deserve to draw air, and I aim to see that stops. It was set in stone the minute I clapped eyes on what he did to my horse. As to me getting killed . . . I keep telling you to trust me."

"What about Diablo?" Mae pressed.

Trace hesitated.

"Well?" she prompted. "Trace, *take* me back to Kentucky. Bring Diablo. Come with me. Please."

Trace made no reply. He looked away, his steely-eyed gaze fixed on some point along the eastern horizon; then he tipped back his Stetson, gave a crisp nod, and eased himself out of the saddle. Removing his gloves, he wedged them under his saddle.

He walked to Diablo in slow, measured steps and looked at Mae, his face unreadable. All at once he reached up, dragged her out of the saddle, and pulled her hard against him. Her breath caught again, the wind knocked out of her. Her upper arms were locked in his grasp, and he pulled her closer still, until every inch of their bodies was touching.

"Last night never should have happened," he stated.

She jutted out her chin, challenging him. "But it *did* happen—or at least would've if you'd allowed it. You think you alone can decide my future? Then you don't know me, Trace Ord."

His face was etched with grief for a love he was going to kill before he ever gave it a chance to survive; she could read that in his eyes. He said, "We don't know each other. But one thing's for sure: I'm going to do right by you even if it kills us both. Now get up on Duchess and follow me down. That's the sun shining on those mountaintops. We've wasted enough time already."

"Duchess?" she repeated, confused.

"Duchess," he agreed. "I don't trust you with Diablo. Not anymore. And if I have to give chase again, I want that black devil underneath *me*."

"Chase me? Where would I run to, Trace?" she asked. "Afraid I'll ride this stallion all the way back to Kentucky? Then you'd have to come after us. . . ." She smiled, suddenly feeling the upper hand. "You're a coward, Trace Ord. Oh, you'll face down Jared, guns blazing, but you're afraid of what you feel, afraid to reach out for the future we could have together."

He was so close. His body heat scorched her, and his raw male scent was dizzying. His hot breath puffed in her face and she narrowed her eyes. For a moment she thought he was going to kiss her. How she longed for that! The mere thought of it, and she was aroused. So was he. Her heart leapt. His hardness leaned heavily against her belly, and his eyes were dark and dilated. If he would only kiss her . . .

But he didn't. Instead, he scooped her up in his arms and plopped her down on Duchess. Mounting Diablo, he pointed her down off the mesa toward the valley below and rode off.

"You're a coward, Trace. But I'm strong enough for both of us," she called after him.

* * *

Trace kept up a steady pace, glancing briefly behind him from time to time. The sun rose higher, crowning the mountains with a halo of flaming gold, while the plateau they traveled remained steeped in dusky shadow. Not until the sun turned lemon-colored and cleared the mountains altogether would the valley flood with light. He hoped to be some distance from the mesa and the Lazy C by then. It wasn't safe to travel by day, but the sooner he settled Mae on a train for home, the better.

Her perception both impressed and infuriated him. With Mae out of Jared's reach, he planned to go back to the Lazy C, federal marshal in tow. Somehow he would get the horses back he'd been hired to find and simultaneously whip the hide off Comstock for what he'd done to Diablo and Mae. Maybe in the aftermath he'd find that deed. But then what? Where was he headed? He had no more roots here in the West than a blasted tumbleweed. He had no wife, no children, no home, just a heartache from the past, demons of what-if eating at his heart and soul.

Mae had grown silent behind him, but he took little comfort in that. She meant to defy him; he was certain of that. It was only a matter of time. But she'd met her match. Through the whole long night he'd hardened himself for their parting, convincing himself it was the only solution. Of course, his heart didn't buy that.

Her doe eyes troubled him, and her plea to come with her to Kentucky was a knife in his soul. Images threatened his resolve: of touching her last night, of her soft flesh, so smooth and fragrant, of her so willing in his arms. The only saving grace was that he hadn't declared his love. She could suspect all she wanted, but once those words were out, there would be no controlling her.

He did love her. Mae made him think about living again. He feared it was too late for him, though. There had been too many hard years of being eaten alive with guilt. He had nothing to offer her. He was a nobody now, not some well-to-do planter's son. He had the clothes on his back, a spare set, and Diablo.

Pain twisted inside him. Some idiotic part of his soul could almost see him back in Kentucky. Likely, her grandfather and he would have a meeting of the minds, with horseflesh being the commonality between them. Horse breeders were a strange lot, perhaps not too very different from wranglers themselves.

Trace bit the inside of his lip, allowed the coppery taste of blood to fill his mouth, to remind him of the fire and blood that had destroyed Trevor Guilliard. The sad truth? Trevor and Mae might have made a good match years ago. But never Mae and Trace Ord. He wasn't fit for the likes of her.

The sun was high in the sky by the time they reached a narrow draw that opened onto a sandy-bottom wash where a small tributary fed a rushing stream. Rocks at its mouth made a good blind. To the east, the pass opened into foothills. To the south lay a stretch of red clay sand grizzled with sage, monuments standing in distant muted purple silhouette against a cloudless sky.

Prairie chickens and the occasional wild turkey strutted in and out among the rocks, observing the human interlopers with little interest and no fear. Trace watched the birds longingly. He salivated, imagining the juices from their succulent meat dripping into the flames of a sage and mesquite fire. On any other occasion, he would have bagged at least two. But there wasn't time for that now. He swallowed emptily and swung himself out of the saddle. He would have to settle for jerky and stale biscuits that would be hard as rocks, since they couldn't be soaked in coffee. He wouldn't risk a fire.

He glanced around, almost feeling Comstock breathing down his neck. The nagging sensation wouldn't leave him, and it grew, an animalistic warning that he was heading for a trap. But that was silly. Pushing the sense of dread to the back of his mind, he smiled. There would be a treat for Mae. He had an airtight tin of peaches in his pack.

What remained of the burlap on Diablo's hooves was all but tatters. Confident that they had covered enough ground to elude pursuit if it was possible, Trace stripped the cloth away and led both horses and the burro to the stream, where he left them, bridles down. There was plenty of new spring grass beside the bank to keep them occupied without fear they'd roam, and while they drank and grazed, he saw to Mae's needs. She groaned, wiping sweat from her brow.

"You all right? Shoulder bothering you?" he asked, handing her some hardtack and jerky. "We can't stay long. We've got a hard ride to cross those sand flats to the south. If we keep up the pace, we'll reach the railroad yard in Prescott tomorrow."

"And if there's no train when we get there?" Mae asked. "You said Jared would be watching the train stops."

"I'll stay with you until you're aboard."

"Trace, come with me." She stared at him, pleading. "Just put Duchess and Diablo on the train and come back with me. They'd have a good life on my grand-dad's farm. My father's dead; there is no hope he will ever return. There's no one for my granddad but me. You could carve out a place there. Help him with the horses. It's almost like fate, our meeting. You're right—I don't belong out here; this land is too cruel for me. But come back. My granddad fought so hard to build up the farm, struggled through the years of the war not to lose everything. There is a place for you there . . . a place with *me*."

"There once was a man named Trevor Guilliard," Trace began, opening his can of peaches with his knife. "He would have fit in the life you paint. That man died one rainy night back in 'sixty-five. There's nothing left of him. I have nothing to offer someone like you, so stop building castles in the sky, Mae."

Handing her the can, Trace turned his back. It was the hardest thing he'd ever had to do. He didn't have to see her haunting gaze to know it followed him as he strode off toward the horses; the hairs on the back of his neck were standing up the way they did whenever a wild horse was near. She was that, by God: a wild filly, with the power to stand up to the evils of men; no whin-ing, squeamish, milk-and-water miss, she. And raised among horses to boot. If only they had met under any other circumstances.

He snatched Diablo's reins and stalked east, down-stream, to where Duchess wandered in search of tastier grass, and then he collected the burro that hadn't budged an inch. Trace took his time returning to Mae. When he did, she had finished her meal and most of the peaches.

"I saved you one, Trace. It's no good unless we share."

Her sad-eyed look had vanished, and in its place was something dangerous: determination. Damn fool woman hadn't heard a single word he'd said. He hesitated, but she stood holding out the spoon and the open airtight. Only Mae would turn a canned peach into a battle of wills. He thought about taking the can and flinging the peach away, but he couldn't. The act would hurt her. He'd hurt her too much already.

With a frown he took the can. "This doesn't mean anything, Mae. I'm eating a damn peach. Nothing more."

She pressed her lips together and nodded. "Absolutely. It's only a peach. Nothing more."

Trace almost growled. Stubborn woman! He had to admit, the peach tasted good. You didn't get many treats like this in the West. Airtights were around, but peaches always sold quickly. He glanced up in time to see Mae's tongue poke out and wet her lips, licking away the last drops of juice. His whole body bucked, and he closed his eyes to fight the intense waves of lust racking him.

"Let me ride Diablo," she pleaded, laying a hand on his arm. "Just once more, Trace."

It took him several breaths to focus. Then he understood Mae was plotting again. "No," he answered firmly. "I'm on to that. I don't know exactly what you're up to, but—"

"I'm not going to run from you, Trace," she insisted,

but something in her mood was changed. There was something akin to panic in her voice. "Please . . . just that. Let me ride Diablo. It's little enough to ask, since you're going to stick me on a train and turn your back on me. I won't see him again. Please . . . ?"

She seemed so sincere. Trace still hesitated. Something didn't sit right. Every instinct in him cried caution, and he worked Diablo's bridle in his gloved hand considering her request.

She shrugged. "If you don't trust me, you can hold Diablo's bridle and lead me. Just let me ride him, Trace. I'll never ask you for anything again. I won't have the chance."

Against his better judgment, he let her mount the stallion. He also took her up on the offer to hold Diablo's reins. Atop Duchess, he turned them back the way they'd come and led the way out of the draw.

He'd scarcely settled in the saddle when he spotted four riders heading out of the sage, all driving their horses hard. Comstock was leading them.

Mae saw them, too. "I'm sorry, Trace," she said, "but you've had it your way long enough. Now it's my turn. It's four to one. You haven't got a chance. Get into a skirmish here and you'll get us both killed. Pretend you don't see them and head north—toward the Lazy C. It's our only hope."

"Hell and damnation," he growled through clenched teeth. He couldn't tell if that was triumph or fear in her voice. "You little fool. So that's why you let me hold Diablo's bridle."

"You recognized the horse, caught me running away, and were bringing me back to the Lazy C," she pressed.

"That's the only way. It's what you should have done from the start, like I told you. I can take care of myself. I have so far, haven't I? You'll be near to protect me."

"Damn it, Mae—"

She cut him off. "I'd rather die right here, right now, than face the prospect of never seeing you again, Trace Ord. It's too late for 'why.' I'll play my part. You just follow my lead and play yours." She gave him a sad smile. "I love you, Trace. I trust you. Now you trust me."

Chapter Twelve

The plan turned out to be a little more work than she suggested, as Mae had a moment of inspiration and broke away from Trace, holding Diablo back so that he could rope and capture her in full view of Comstock's riders. That exhibition turned the trick and called for very little acting, since Trace was mad enough at that point to kill her, but the episode earned Trace a job. Mae spent the trip back gloating over her victory—until, locked again in her room at the Lazy C, she began to realize the chilling ramifications of her actions. The steps on the stairs were a wake-up call.

She lifted a heavy candlestick as the door opened, and Jared came inside. He'd changed his dirty trail clothes. He wore a pristine white shirt and meticulous attire. He was hatless, he'd shaved, and his blond hair was wet, curling about his earlobes. But the comely appearance was a direct contradiction of the man himself. Oh, he was a handsome man, with the looks of an angel. Most women would be flattered he wanted them—until they got close enough to see that any spark of humanity missing.

His steps were slow and sure, those of a drunk trying to appear sober. He reeked of whiskey.

"Don't come near me, Jared Comstock," Mae warned, brandishing the candlestick. "Or—"

"Or what?" he drawled, still advancing, clearly not frightened. "Why did you run again, Mae? You know I'll only bring you back. Every damn time."

"Why did I run?" she retorted. "For the same reason I ran before. Because I'm tired of being held captive, tired of your games of deceit, tired of Morgan pawing me when he thinks your back is turned."

"What are you talking about?" Comstock asked, hand on hip.

"We made a bargain," she continued. "I told you I needed time. You agreed, and then you left that watchdog Morgan to guard me. Don't tell me you're blind, Jared. I wondered if this was some sort of game the two of you played, that he's the real boss around here, for he does as he damn well pleases, making free with your whiskey, your help . . . your woman." She knew just how far she could go, and she'd reached that point and crossed it. Retreat was no longer an option.

"Are you saying he put his hands on you?" Comstock looked furious.

"Put? I told you before. He was all over me— squeezing, pinching, trying to get his hand between my legs. Is this how you earn my love, by letting your men manhandle me like a whore? Am I to be used and passed around? Put him near me again and I'll run all right, the first chance I get. And the next time, you won't find me, I promise you that. What does he have on you? He acts like he can do as he wants around here and you'll do nothing to stop him. Why?"

Comstock jeered. "I suppose you'd like that drifter, Ord, to keep an eye on you? Something's going on there. I'd bet my last nugget on it. Don't think I won't find out what that something is."

"Don't you dare bring that varmint here to guard me!" she replied. "He's no better than you are. You're two of a kind."

"That remains to be seen," Comstock said. "I saw how he hog-tied you, Mae. Very impressive. But he's going to have to prove himself if he wants to wrangle for me, and I'm going to ride him like a bucking bronco 'til I know his story. You better be telling me the truth about Morgan, Mae—for your sake, and for his. But I *do* know somebody I can trust to keep his hands off you 'til I sort this out."

"Good. Look into Morgan. But you think he's just going to *tell* you he was all over me? Use your brain, Jared. The man is a snake. You can bet he's the one that killed my father. But I'm not the poor, sick drunk my father was, and I won't let him near me. You'd think a husband would protect a wife—especially one trying to earn her respect so that she can finally be in the right mind to fulfill her marital duties."

Comstock's manner changed. "You know I'm crazy about you, Mae. And I told you I never had anything to do with the death of your old man. Why would I do that? I already had what I wanted: you."

"If you're innocent, Morgan did it. I'll bet you could make him admit it, too," she pressed. "If you really cared about me."

"All right, all right, simmer down. You got no proof Morgan's involved. I don't even know why you think it." He threw up his hands in a gesture of truce. "Look, sugar," he added, "I don't want to fight with you. I promised you some time. Ain't I been good and stuck by that? I've given you plenty of time, despite what you done. Still, I'm losing patience. I've got better things to do than to go chasing you all over the territory. I could claim my right as a husband any time. It's best you know that."

He ripped the brass candlestick from her hand and threw it across the room. "You think that thing would stop me if I was of a mind to have you? Think on that, Mae. Think on it hard." He wheeled around then and stalked from the room, locking the door after him.

Her heart hammered in Mae's ears, hot blood thrumming at her temples. What had she done? What had she led Trace into? She'd told him she could take care of herself, but she was no longer sure that was entirely true.

She sank down on the bed, suddenly full of regret. Though she was grateful, she didn't understand why Jared permitted her to keep putting him off; it wasn't in keeping with the man's vile nature. Bullies loved hurting those weaker than themselves, loved taking what they wanted. One might think he was enamored of her, but she just couldn't buy that he had tender feelings of any kind. That didn't make any more sense than Jared letting Morgan strut around pretending he was the boss. There had to be more to this situation she just wasn't seeing. Still, whatever the reason, she was damn glad something was keeping Jared in check.

Shaking, she got to her feet, dragged a chair to the door, and propped it under the knob. Whomever he sent to guard her, they weren't going to get in. Then, sinking back down on the bed, she succumbed to exhaustion, praying that Trace was equal to whatever Jared Comstock was planning.

At sundown, Trace Ord was in a blind rage as he arranged his gear in the bunkhouse. One by one the others straggled in. Jared Comstock was not among them; the boss had herded Mae into the main house when they arrived and had not emerged since. Worry over what might be happening between them at that very moment all but paralyzed Trace's mind with fear. He dared not show it, though.

Trace hadn't seen Preacher, but that wasn't unusual since the old man had a cot in the cookhouse. No matter the temptation, it wouldn't do to arouse suspicion by running straight to the old man. Instead, he stretched out on his bunk in the corner, pulled his Stetson down over his eyes, and listened to the hands talk. He felt as if he were dozing in a nest of rattlers.

Damn her! Mae had sacrificed herself. Of course, though he hated to admit it, she'd been right. Once they were spotted, there was no way he could stand and fight with her in the line of fire. But he had to find a way to get her out of there quick. And then . . . well, the only way she would ever be safe from Comstock was if Trace saw him and his rustling outfit in jail—or dead. He favored the latter option.

"Has a nice ring of finality to it," he muttered to himself.

A poker game was forming in the corner of the bunkhouse. Feigning sleep, Trace wasn't invited to participate. A rider called Ben watched from his cot. Will Morgan, Chip McVey, and three others were at the table. One was a tall, lanky rider named Wally. There was an older ranch hand with a handlebar mustache and grizzled forearms who walked with a limp and answered to the name of Jeb, and lastly came a mean-looking youth known as Michael Slade—the only one Trace knew by reputation.

Slade's face was deeply lined, his skin like tanned leather. Clean-shaven and fierce-eyed, and the only thing people knew about him was the rumored notches on his Colts. He was reputed to be one of the fastest gunslingers in the territory. He sported an air of casual regard, but Trace recognized that mask for what it was. The youngster's guns were tied down, slung low on his hips and within easy reach. Those eyes moved about alertly, as quick as his hands.

Trace took great care not to attract any notice. He had a bit of a reputation himself. Gunslingers made it their business to know who was a threat, who was competition. He was fast enough for word to have reached Michael, and that possibility made him uncomfortable. He had to ignore the nagging feeling that things were falling apart.

He hadn't lain there long before the bunkhouse door came crashing in. Jared Comstock's tall, lanky figure appeared, blacksnake in hand. With a flick of his wrist, he lashed out the whip with a blood-chilling crack. It wrapped around Will Morgan's neck twice and yanked him backward onto the floor, chair and all.

Cards, coins, and bills went flying. Michael Slade leapt out of his chair, guns drawn, until he saw who was meting out justice; then he jammed them back in their holsters. The others sat slack-jawed, their eyes trained on Will Morgan writhing at their feet, clawing at the whip wrapped around the neckerchief he wore.

There would be no credibility to sleeping through this. The foreman's strangled cries and Comstock's bellowing voice were loud enough to wake the dead. Trace eased back his Stetson and slowly swung his feet to the floor, frowned, and faked a yawn.

"Lay hands on my wife, will you?" Comstock shouted. He turned to the others. "Wally, Chip, stand him on his feet. Ben, get up from there and fetch a rope. Jeb, stay out of the way! The rest of you, get him outside— you, too, Ord. You're new here. I want you to see right off what happens to any man who crosses me."

Without question or hesitation, the others dragged Morgan outside. Trace followed, his thumbs hooked in the waist of his jeans, and he leaned against the frame of the bunkhouse door, watching Comstock's men haul the foreman down the steps.

"Bring that rope here, Ben," Jared barked.

"You're making a mistake," Morgan was saying. "You fool! You know I didn't break my orders—no more than you did, eh? If she said different, she's a damn liar. Nobody could get near enough to that she-cat to lay a finger on—" The handle of Comstock's blacksnake caught him across the lower jaw, cutting him off. "You don't dare cross—"

Jared struck him across the mouth, this time with a

backhand. "Lash the son of a bitch to the hitching rail," he commanded the others.

Jeb and Wally carried out the order and quickly stepped away. Comstock grabbed the foreman's shirt in a white-knuckled fist and ripped it open down the back. Then, despite Morgan's screams of protest, he used his blacksnake.

Slade hovered nearby, watching, hands seemingly lazy but close to his holsters. Trace glanced around. More men were gathering, coming from the barn and the corral. But where was Preacher? That racket should have brought him. Not that Trace wanted him to see. Morgan deserved this and more, but it wasn't a pretty sight. At ten lashes, he grimaced and stopped counting. The flesh on Morgan's back was a bloody mess. Trace couldn't help but remember the whip marks on Diablo's sleek, black hide.

Comstock's men had begun to mumble among themselves, saying enough was enough. That only fueled their boss's rage and earned them a warning glare. Mercifully, the foreman had lost consciousness. He was hanging from the rail by his wrists.

"Cut him down," Jared commanded at last, to no one in particular.

Wally responded, shuffling over and fisting his hand in Morgan's blood-matted hair. He pulled the foreman's head back and squinted down at him. "By damn, he's dead, boss," he said.

Comstock shrugged. "Dig a hole and plant him. Let this be a lesson to you—to *all* of you. I'm in charge here. You do as I say. No questions asked," he added, addressing the entire gathering though his eyes were riveted on Trace. "That corpse there was my right hand, my *best* hand, before he crossed me. None of you stands on firmer ground. Now clean this mess up.

"Not you, Ord," he rumbled when Trace moved to help. "You get some shut-eye. Come dawn tomorrow, you're going to show me your stuff. It'd better be good. You're going to have to do your job and Morgan's, too. We're shorthanded, and there isn't time to find a replacement. I need someone I can trust."

Mae hadn't dozed long when a sharp knock at the door wrenched her bolt upright. It took her a moment to remember where she was, and another to accustom her eyes to the darkness and make her way to the door.

"Missy," said a gruff voice from the other side, "it's Preacher, the cook. Ord's friend."

"Is he all right?" she asked.

"I won't lie to you, I ain't seen him," he replied.

"What are you doing here? If Jared catches you—"

"Easy, now, it was Comstock who put me in charge of guarding you. Guess after Morgan he figured a crusty old man was safer. Maybe I can carry messages between you and Ord 'til he can figure something out."

"Oh, Preacher. Will you tell him I'm all right? He probably doesn't care anymore, though. Not after . . . after . . ."

"Now, now, none of that," came the old man's voice. "I knew how much he cared for you before he did."

Tears welled in her eyes. If only it were true that he cared. Even if it had been true once, she couldn't see how it possibly could be now. Still, it was something to hope for, and she grasped at hope with every fiber of her being.

"Morgan's in for it. Comstock's after blood over something he done. That's why he give the job of watching you to me," Preacher was saying.

"Oh, God, that's my fault!" Mae realized. "I told Jared how Morgan . . . tried to attack me. I had to do something to put him off Trace. He doesn't trust Trace, Preacher. You've got to warn him. He's going to make him 'prove himself.' Trace has such a temper, I'm afraid he'll—"

"Don't you worry, missy, just leave all of that to me. And don't worry about Morgan, neither. He's one mean hombre; I can vouch for that. Whatever he gets, he deserves. Get some sleep. I'm moving away from the door, just in case. The minute it's safe to talk again, I'll come back."

Mae stumbled away from the door and sank back down on the bed, comforted by Preacher's words. She heard the floorboards creak under his receding steps. She hoped he returned quickly.

Chapter Thirteen

*W*hen Trace Ord strode into the cookhouse before dawn with the others, he breathed a sigh of relief. Preacher was pouring coffee, which meant at least one burden weighing down his conscience was lifted.

The sly wink the old man directed his way had Trace suppressing a smile. They had to talk, but not while all the shifty-eyed wranglers were monitoring his every move. Comstock was watching with not a little interest, either. Of course, it wouldn't do to ignore the old man; they were all aware that Trace and Preacher knew each other.

"Hey, old-timer," he sang out. "You still here? I figured you'd be mining the dunes in Death Valley by now."

"Nope, heeded your advice about the desert being a killer. Ain't no tenderfoot, but figured it was safer here. 'Sides, I sort of like having something besides beans to eat." Preacher piled bacon on a platter. "I'm settled in right nicely. The boss pays a good wage, and the grub is good. You should like it here."

"Good news for me," Trace returned. "I haven't had

a decent meal since we parted company." He turned to Comstock. "I told you he was a damn good cook. Did I lie?"

"You surely did not," Comstock drawled. "If everything else about you is straight-shooting, we'll rub along just fine."

The words were cordial enough, but the sarcastic delivery gave Trace gooseflesh. Especially when all through the meal he sensed that Preacher wanted to tell him something but couldn't. It threatened to affect his demeanor as he went out with the hands to the corral afterward, where a number of horses were milling. Chip and Wally straddled the corral fence, while Michael Slade sat atop it, the heels of his boots braced on the second rail. Ben watched from the other side.

Trace leaned his arms on the top rail and watched the horses, taking note of each beast's individual potential and also the brands on their rumps. Close scrutiny showed him nothing but a sideways C, the Lazy-C brand. He hadn't expected anything else. Finding proof wasn't going to be *that* easy; otherwise Preacher might already have done it.

Comstock was strolling toward him. Trace had to be careful. He couldn't tip his hand this early in the game, no matter how anxious he was. Hoping the test to come would lead him one step closer to his goal, he adjusted his posture and put on his poker face. "Fine-looking horseflesh. If the rest of your herd is as fine, you should do very well at market. You might want to consider adding a mustang stallion or two if you're thinking about breeding."

"These are only a few examples," Comstock replied. "I've got a full range of superior horseflesh."

"I surely would like to see that," said Trace.

"Maybe you will," Comstock drawled.

"Do you breed your own?"

"I breed some, buy some . . ." Comstock answered. "Only a few are wild. Take that bay there." He pointed. "The boys I got here are the finest bronc stompers in the territory."

Trace scrutinized the horse in question: a well-muscled, reddish brown stallion with a sweeping black mane and tail, two hands to the withers above any of the other horses in the corral. The beast showed a proud head, and his dark eyes had a wild darting glare. Trace noticed that he led with his right shoulder, then followed up with flying forefeet. It was clear that on the open range he'd been a herd leader, and that he was trying to lead the mares corralled with him now. Trace had seen many like him, Diablo among them. So, this was to be his test.

He gave Comstock a lazy smile. "The bay's a biter. Notice how the others give him a wide birth. He'll take a plug out of anyone who comes near. Does he have a name?" he asked, pushing back his hat.

"Wally calls him Lucifer. He's a devil all right, but it's too fine a name for him. He needs taking down a peg, to be shown who's master. Once he's broke, I'll find a proper name for him."

"I guess you expect me to break him for you?"

"For starters."

Trace took off his spurs and handed them over. "Hold these," he said.

"Are you loco?" Comstock chortled. "You can't hope to break that horse without spurs."

"Won't need a quirt, either," Trace replied.

The men on the fence began to hoot with laughter and making bets on the outcome. Only Michael Slade, spinning his guns, made Trace uneasy. A corral full of nervous horses was no place for gun work.

"Suit yourself," Comstock drawled. "It's your funeral. Hey, boys, if we'd known all this last night, while you was at it you could have dug two holes."

Trace ignored the brays of mirth, monitoring Comstock's narrowed slate gray eyes and lopsided smirk. The man leaned on the corral gate, watching and chewing on a piece of hay, clearly confident he had the upper hand—which promised all too clearly that Trace needed to be on his guard. They were going to toy with him, likely intending the fool horse to kill him. But Trace was ready for that.

Stripping off his bandana, he soaked it in the horse trough and tied it back around his neck with a loose knot. Wally brought a saddle and bridle meant for the bay, and draped them over the corral fence. A flicker at the window of the house caught his attention. Mae? He swept that concern to the back of his mind. Right now, he needed to concentrate on the task at hand.

Comstock could have made it easier by separating Lucifer from the others. Putting the horses together served only one purpose: to work up the horses and keep them edgy, making the job all the harder. Trace would have to rope the bay, bridle and saddle him, then mount him and stay on his back until the defeated animal yielded.

"Throw a rope on him," Comstock said. "Show me how you cut a horse out of others in close quarters. Then we'll open the gate so you can run him into the little corral to wear him down and break him."

Trace didn't reply. He snaked the bay's bridle from the corral fence and entered the pen. Wally handed him a rope, and Trace formed it into a lasso. Jeb swung the corral gate open. Trace walked through, the gate snapping shut behind him.

The bay was clearly trying to re-create the role as lead stallion he'd played in the wild; Comstock had made Trace's task as difficult as possible. It was a large corral, but too many horses occupied it to safely single out and rope one wild stallion from such an agitated press. First he had to get them all running in one direction. Having observed that the bay charged with his right shoulder, Trace stayed on the beast's left, edging closer until he'd displaced the horses in between them. The object was to wear the bay down as much as possible beforehand. But the bay had a gaze that was almost human, bespeaking great cunning.

Trace made ready to throw the lasso. The whoops and hollers from the corral rail weren't helping matters, and his first two attempts failed. The first rope closed too low on the horse's head and he shook free; the second try was again too shallow. Trace adjusted his distance and, whirling the lasso, hurled it again. This time it landed just right, far enough back on the horse's head that the bay couldn't shake free. Trace gave the line a jerk, and it slipped down and tightened around the horse's neck. The bay reared, pawing the dusty air, stomped the ground, bucked and kicked like a mule. It took some fancy footwork to say out from under those killer hooves.

"Open the gate!" Trace bellowed, hanging on. His shoulder, which had borne the brunt of keeping Mae from falling the other night, was hurting like the devil.

None of the men made a move. Instead, Michael Slade's gun replied, and several whoops and shouts. The following screams, snorts, and terrified cries of the animals made an earsplitting din.

Trace loosed a string of oaths as more rounds boomed from Slade's smoking Colts. The bay writhed and twisted on the end of his lasso, making a desperate effort to free himself, dragging Trace into the middle of the milling herd. Trace swung around and kicked the gate with all his force, Comstock standing on the other side. The man jumped back and several hands hopped off the fence. The gate opened, and the bay stallion flew through, tail arched high, again dragging Trace in his wake. Comstock's men leapt for the gate to close it before the mares could follow.

Yet another volley sounded from Slade's Colts. Trace paid them no mind. He was gradually reeling the bay in, shortening the distance between them by inching along the rope. The horse was lathered, snorting with exhaustion, when Trace edged close enough to reach out and touch his rippling flesh. Crooning softly, he soothed the horse while stroking his twitching withers, each caress moving a little higher along the horse's neck and, finally, face.

The bay danced and then snorted, bobbing his magnificent head. With a gentle hand Trace fit the bit and bridle into place, then slipped the rope off him. There was some resistance, but nothing Trace couldn't handle. He just had to keep dodging the nips. "Bite me, horse, and I will bite you back," he said softly. "You wouldn't want those fillies over there to witness that, now, would you?"

Comstock's men had transferred to places on the little corral rail, perched in much the same positions as they were earlier. A saddle came crashing to the ground at Trace's feet. He didn't see or care who threw it; he was blind with rage. Nonetheless, he led the bay over and gentled it with more soothing sounds and restful strokes. He dropped a blanket over the horse's back. Once the bay held still, he gently eased on the saddle.

The bay pranced in place, snorting and tossing his tangled mane while Trace tightened the cinch and eased down the stirrups. He wanted to end this here and now. He would leave the corral, strap on his irons, and deal with Comstock and his henchmen one by one in face-offs. Then, if he were still standing, he would send for the northern ranchers and let them sort out their own horses. He'd skip the marshal. Rustler or not, Jared Comstock needed to die.

But no. Mae stood between him and that fantasy. Before he acted, he needed to get her away from the bastard. And yet a plan formed in his mind that just might work.

"Easy, fella," he crooned in the horse's ear. "We're almost done." He scrutinized the bay's side, where the cruel rowels of a Spanish spur had gouged him more than once and left permanent scars. "I won't spur you, and I won't whip you, but I will break you. How long that takes is up to you."

With the words scarcely spoken, he swung himself into the saddle. More shots rang out, still aimed at the ground. Trace ignored them—*expected* them—but the bay did not. It bucked high and wheeled in circles, kicking the corral rails, lunging and whirling and shrieking protest into the wind. Trace soothed the bay all the while, holding on to the leather pommel and the horse's mane with an iron fist. He leaned forward, crooning into the animal's ear, promising that it soon would be over, praising and comforting the horse as it leapt into the air again and again in a vain attempt to free itself of its burden. Charging at the rail, the bay turned sharply with the intent to crush Trace against it, but Trace held on, even as the horse fell on his side—not once, but twice.

Exhaustion was Trace's ally. The horse's chest heaving to draw breath, all fight left him. Trace was finally able to coax him up on all fours. Riding the bay around the corral, Trace eased him into a loose trot and a slow canter. Finally he walked him around the corral twice and then swung himself down.

"Good boy," he murmured. "You're no devil. Your owner is." And with that, he walked the bay to the corral fence and handed the bridle to Comstock.

Without a word, he strode next to the rail fence where Slade sat smirking. Trace just stared at him, meeting the gunslinger's cold, empty gaze. Then, before Slade could blink, Trace grabbed him by both ankles and jerked him off the fence. Straddling the bastard, he grabbed the front of his shirt and planted a rock-hard fist full in his face. A nose-breaking crunch sounded, but Trace hit him again, and blood gushed from the gunman's nose and split lip. A third blow closed Slade's right eye.

When Trace drew back his arm a fourth time, the youth held up his hands in defeat.

"If I was packing, you'd be dead," Trace seethed, putting his face right in the gunman's. "The next time you take one of those irons out of your belt within a mile of me, you better be prepared to use it." With no more commentary, Trace got to his feet and stomped out of the corral.

The curtain at the window flapped again. Mae, watching. He wondered what she thought about the violence in him. Well, too damn bad if it offended her. It was going to take a wagonload of violence to save either of them now.

Chapter Fourteen

Preacher wasn't in the cookhouse as Trace hoped when he stormed past. He went to the bunkhouse and was strapping on his guns when Comstock arrived.

"There's no need for that, Ord," the ranch owner said. "You've gone and messed up his pretty face. That's enough."

"So you say," Trace erupted. "I say different."

"I'll handle Slade," Comstock assured him. "He's young and reckless, but he was only funning."

Trace glowered. "Well, you've had your fun and you got your horse broke. Now it's my turn."

"What's that supposed to mean?"

"I offered you a sweet deal, Comstock, and I agreed to let you try me for free. If you want to have any more 'fun,' you're going to have to pay for it—one way or another."

Comstock's jaw muscle clenched. "I don't take kindly to threats, Ord."

"It isn't a threat. It's a fact," Trace replied, tying up his bedroll.

"Where are you going?"

Trace shrugged. "Never did take to bunkhouse living. Reckon I'll camp under the stars from now on."

"Look, I know you're all horns and rattles right now, and I can't say as I blame you. But no harm's been done. I appreciate you're breaking the bay."

"He's broke, but he's still a killer. I'm thinking he's killed before."

Comstock nodded. "You've got the right of it. There's more than one notch in his tail."

"Breaking him won't change that. Nothing ever will."

"You've got a peculiar way of handling horses," Comstock observed, playing with his mustache. "I did hear tell of an hombre once who broke horses like you. The Indians called him the Whisperer—a renegade rider out of Texas. Nobody seems to know his name. Bad business, messing with renegade riders. Worse than Texas Rangers in their doggedness. You're from Texas, isn't that so, Ord?"

"Texas is a big place, Comstock. Been through there. Been through a lot of places since the war. I'm from Louisiana."

"They say this Whisperer has a gentle hand—like you. I figure you might have run up against him somewhere in your travels, and maybe he gave you a pointer or two."

"My daddy taught me how to break horses," Trace said smoothly. "He owned a breeding farm in northern Louisiana. Lost everything because of the war. He taught me horses respond better to a gentle hand than a heavy one. Just like women."

Comstock grunted. He handed Trace back his spurs. "Don't know how you ever did it without those Spanish rowels," he admitted. "I'm curious . . . What was it you said to the bay?"

On the verge of losing his temper, Trace looked the man in the eye while jamming the spurs into his pack. White dots of rage starred his vision, and his hands balled into fists. But there was too much at stake to act upon his instincts. "I just let him know who was boss," he said, in the same soft yet unequivocal tone he'd used with the horse.

"Hmmm," Comstock responded. "You mentioned going after a heard of 'stangs in the canyon. How many riders you figure we'll need to collect them? I can count on Wally, Ben, and Chip. Jeb's too sore in the joints to wrangle wild horses anymore, but I can bring a few boys in off the range. And we've got Slade."

"You've got Slade. . . ." Trace gave him a deadly smile. His first instinct was to say no to Michael Slade, but that would mean leaving him behind with access to Mae. "You won't need to call in your stringers. Wally, Ben, and Chip will be enough—and Slade. Just keep him out of my way."

Comstock scoffed. "We can't capture a herd of wild horses with five riders!"

"Won't need more," Trace promised. "I was going to hook up with White Eagle and his horse hunters. They know where Standing Thunder is, and they'll help us bring him and his herd in cheap for trade."

"I don't like messing with Injuns," Comstock said.

"Well, that's the deal," Trace said, slinging his gear over his shoulder. "Take it or leave it. I could do it on my own and keep all the profits if I was of a mind. And this isn't the only horse ranch in the territory. You saw what I can do; I won't have any trouble finding another employer."

"Now, let's not be so hasty," Comstock cajoled. "I didn't say no. Them Injuns up on the mesa still?"

"Nope. I just came down from there before I ran into your wife. They're down in the valley most likely. We won't have any trouble picking up their tracks."

"I don't know," Comstock hedged. "I don't like those thieving Hualapai."

"White Eagle owes me," said Trace, "and I'd trust him and his with my life—unlike your crew."

"I guess I had that coming," Comstock conceded. He looked pensive.

"Uh-huh. You need time to think about it?"

"Nope," Comstock decided. "We'll leave at dawn tomorrow, and if those horses are half as fine as you say, we're both going to be rich men."

Trace hesitated when Comstock offered his hand. The last thing he wanted to do was shake, but he did just the same. He'd already gained one point: with the Indians watching his back, it wouldn't be quite so easy for Comstock and his men to bury him in that canyon. If the rest of his plan worked half as well, the risk involved would be a small price to pay for Mae's safety.

Risking Comstock's anger, he tended Diablo. Once the healing wounds were salved, Trace threw a blanket over the horse and led him into a stall. Diablo's grateful nuzzling both touched his heart and stirred his anger. It was clear that the animal didn't understand why he'd been abandoned and mistreated, and that he looked to Trace to liberate him. Trace couldn't look him in the eye.

Speaking to the horse in soothing tones, stroking his sleek neck, he didn't hear Preacher approach. Sensing a presence, he spun on his heel, his Colt free of its holster and aimed before the pivot was completed. The rapid movement spooked Diablo. Eyes wide with fright, the horse began backing into his stall.

"You two simmer down," the old man said.

"Mae?" Trace urged. "Is she all right?"

"She is," said Preacher. "Put that damn thing away. With that short fuse you're going to get yourself killed. Then you'll be no use to the gal, no use to the horse. I seen what you done to Slade. . . ." He clicked his tongue, shaking his head. "Busted his nose and spoiled his pretty face. What'd you hit him with?"

"My fists," Trace snapped, "and he's lucky that's all I busted. What are you doing out here? What if Comstock comes in on us?"

"He isn't going to. He's up at the house eating. I come out here when I get a chance to sneak this black devil a treat." He held up a bunch of carrots, and Diablo whinnied.

Trace shoved his Colt back in its holster and took a carrot, which he held out. Thrilled by the treat, the horse settled down.

"What the Sam Hill happened to Morgan last night? You pop him, too?" Preacher fussed. "We heard the ruckus. Then he wasn't in for breakfast, and nobody's talking."

"Comstock beat him to death with his blacksnake. They buried him out in the sage."

"The hell you say! Damn, Mae said *she* turned Comstock on Morgan. Don't guess we need to tell her the result."

"How come you got to her without Comstock knowing?" Trace asked.

Preacher laughed. "He knew all right. He put me in charge of guarding her before he lit out after Morgan. Guess he figured an old cuss like me would treat her nice and he wouldn't have to worry no more. What went on at the corral? We heard shooting."

"A bit of a shivaree, you might say. Comstock had no intention of me surviving the tussle with that bay—or at least he had no intention of letting me out of there in one piece. They were playing with me, like a cat plays with a mouse. They figured I'd never be able to get near the bay. When I did, Slade shot off his guns trying to get me trampled. I beat the holy hell out of him."

"Musta made that temper feel better to rearrange his features, but not a smart move, Trace. He's a sidewinder, one that don't shake his rattle before he strikes. He ain't going to take too kindly to you ruining his smile. So now what are you aiming to do?"

"I'm going to take Comstock after those wild horses."

"You'll never come back alive—not in that company."

Trace didn't need to be told. "I won't be alone. We're going to meet up with White Eagle and his hunters. They'll watch my back. Comstock didn't much like the idea, but I said the Indians work cheap—for barter—and that we need them because they know right where the horses are, and that'll save us time. He's itching to start that drive to market, but he's drooling over that herd more. We leave at dawn. I've cleared out of the bunkhouse. I told Comstock I'm camping under the stars from now on. I need your help, old-timer."

"Anything. Just name it."

"I'm camping out in the sage tonight—at least it's going to look that way. As soon as the lights go out in this compound here, I'm going to check out some of Comstock's herd—in the paddock, and out on the range—looking for Bar O and Double Bar T brands, or at least for brands that have been messed with."

"You'll get caught."

Trace reached inside his shirt and produced an envelope. "Hang on to this," he said, handing it over, "and don't get caught with it. It's the addresses of the ranchers I'm working for up north. Also . . . as soon as you can manage it after we leave for the canyons, I need you to get Mae out of here."

"She'll never leave without you. That gal's in love with you, Trace."

"I don't care what you have to tell her, or how you have to manage it. Rope her if you have to. Help her find that deed or letter or whatever Comstock has, and put her on a train for Kentucky. Then get to a telegraph office and send word to the ranchers to fetch a marshal and get down here pronto."

"You ain't got proof yet."

"I will before the night is out. The only reason I'm going after those horses is to give you time to get her on that damn train. Just do like I say, and tell her . . . tell her I said if she ever wants to see me again she's got to do exactly what you say. Period."

* * *

Trace's message for Mae troubled his conscience, since he didn't intend to see her again. It was better this way, though. She deserved so much more than he had to offer. She belonged on her grandfather's horse farm in Kentucky, not tagging along after a renegade rider with no roots to put down and death riding on his flank. It was only a matter of time before bad luck caught up with him. Perhaps that's even what he'd hoped for during the past five years.

He hadn't declared his love. That would only complicate things. She loved him now, but love and hate were two horns on the same steer. She'd never forgive him for his lie. She'd get over him. She'd meet some decent, upstanding young Kentuckian who would sweep her off her feet and worship her for the rest of her life, and she'd forget Trace. Just the thought caused him physical pain, but he knew it was the kindest solution for them both.

Yet his body remembered how perfectly their bodies molded. The one thing his flesh, mind, and spirit had in common was pain. His heart was breaking.

There was a cottonwood tree at his campsite that gave him some cover while he monitored the Comstock compound. He'd left his burro at the ranch. They would use packhorses on the trail, which were faster. Unsaddling Duchess, he laid out his bedroll with his saddle as a pillow, then bunched up the extra blankets in the shape of a body and topped that with his Stetson. He then wedged his Winchester between the blankets in such a way that it appeared he was holding it at the ready while he slept and waited.

When the compound went dark, Trace mounted Duchess bareback and moved stealthily through the sage toward the paddock behind the corrals. Passing the ranch house, he strained for any sound that might mean Mae was in danger. All was still. No lights showed in the windows or from the bunkhouse or cook shack. All hands were turning in early, most preparing for the hard ride at first light.

Trace gave the buildings a wide berth. Clouds hid the moon, abetting his mission. Ahead, the foothills were visible, a dark fringe at the base of the mountains. He wouldn't face a problem here, only out there in the darkness where the rest of Comstock's wranglers camped. The ones he hadn't seen. So far, no campfires showed. It was well past midnight, so he hoped that the stringers were asleep.

When he came within reasonable walking distance, he slid off Duchess's back and left her grazing, bridle down, on a patch of new spring grass. He dropped and crawled toward a string of horses silhouetted against a rocky wall in the foothills, but took no comfort in the fact that he saw no sign of riders among them. They would hardly have left the beasts unattended; the look-out had probably fallen asleep.

Had he gone in mounted, he would have been spotted easily. Instead, feeling his way along, he soothed the string of horses toward quiet with soft murmurs and gentle hands. Luckily, he seemed to have happened upon broken stock, not a wild horse among them. They were used to humans—although, considering their abused appearance and response to affection, he imagined they were unaccustomed to humane handling. By the time he'd threaded his way through the lot, he'd found not only Bar O and Double Bar T stock, but a number of horses with other altered brands. And that was after examining less than a hundred head.

Trace was thankful that the moon was hidden, grateful that he couldn't see the horses' wounds clearly. As it was, he realized that more than one had met with Comstock's blacksnake. With a refreshed and passionate disdain for the rancher and his operation, he crept back through the sage, swung himself up on Duchess, and returned to his camp. He could sleep now. He'd done the job he'd set out to do. His instincts were correct, the wheels were set in motion and word would be sent to the ranchers, who would bring the marshal and see justice done. That was no longer his priority. Come dawn, he would occupy Comstock far enough away to give Mae the only thing he ever could: her freedom. Even if the cost was his life.

Chapter Fifteen

Trace broke camp and rode back to the Lazy C well before dawn. Lights in the bunkhouse drew him. The riders had already gathered for breakfast—Chip, Wally, Ben, along with others—and Slade, whose dark, swollen glower menaced him the minute Trace crossed the threshold. But it was the look on Preacher's face that froze his heart and stopped him in his tracks. Something was wrong.

It didn't take long for Trace to find out what that something was. A voice from behind spun him around, and he faced Jared Comstock with Mae on his arm.

"Better sit down and dig in, Ord," he said. "Preacher's got to clean up and outfit the chuck wagon before we can head out."

The cold fingers of a crawling chill crept up Trace's spine. Three telling scratches on Comstock's cheek and a puffy bruise on Mae's lip spoke for themselves. She was dressed for the trail, in a split-skirt riding outfit. The look in her eye was pleading, but Trace turned away and took his seat with the others and let Preacher fill his plate.

"Steady," the old man whispered, leaning over him.

"We've already eaten," Comstock drawled, seating Mae at the table, "but we'll take some coffee before we head out."

Trace glanced at Mae. Again, she flashed him a pleading look. That, coupled with Preacher's one-word caution, stayed his hand against every instinct. He picked up his fork and stabbed a piece of bacon instead.

Comstock was watching him closely. Quick sidelong glances at the others while he ate revealed that all the riders—Jared included—were packing guns. Now Trace understood Mae's pleading glances. He could take one of them out, or two, or maybe even three; he was that fast. But he couldn't get them all, and then she'd be left with no one to defend her.

Trace's mind was racing. The food tasted like straw; the muscles in his jaw began to tick as he tried to force it down. The only reason for taking Comstock to the canyons to capture this herd was to get the man and his crew away from the Lazy C, so Preacher could take Mae to safety. That wouldn't happen if Preacher and Mae were going along. That also meant there wouldn't be any way to get word to any northern rancher or the U.S. marshal. Trace considered. Should he press for Mae to be left behind or accept the situation without question? Or was Comstock waiting for him to do precisely that? Trace had no choice. He would have to go along with whatever Comstock was planning in order to stay alive and protect her.

One man at that table was itching for revenge; that was certain. Slade's enmity was palpable. By the look of the rest, they were too afraid of Comstock and his blacksnake to go against him. If Trace only had himself to consider, he would have made an end of this immediately, one way or another. But there was Mae. She had to get back to Kentucky. And, by damn, despite all his feelings that he wasn't good enough, he wished he'd taken her back there himself.

Perhaps fate was stepping in, he allowed himself to think. Everything seemed so perfectly planned. He hadn't wanted to see her again, as parting would be easier for them both that way. Now all his fine resolve and noble intent fell away. He would never be able to leave her again. If they survived the coming storm, he'd take her back to that farm in bluegrass country and spend the rest of his life trying to help her forget the West ever existed. He just hoped he lived to accomplish it.

But she didn't need to know his plan. Determined to keep her at a distance, for her own sake and for the sake of his sanity, he employed a different strategy.

"You sure you want to drag her along?" he asked, crooking his finger toward Mae. "This isn't a Sunday picnic we're going on, you know. A wild horse roundup is no place for a woman. She'll only slow us down."

"My wife was raised among horses, Ord," Comstock remarked. "She can handle herself. Besides, I'm sure we can keep an eye on her."

"You'll keep an eye on her," Trace retorted. "You can count me out."

"I fully intend to," said Comstock. "And she goes. That's decided."

Trace decided to use this to his advantage. "If that's the case, I get to ride the black," he said. "I haven't forgotten what happened the last time I was in your wife's company. If I'm going to have to rope her again, I want the advantage."

Comstock hooted, erupting in laughter. "Deal!" The others followed suit.

Trace gave a crisp nod. "I'll need the black underneath me when we get to the canyons anyway. Unless I miss my guess, he isn't long this side of a wild horse herd himself. He's got that look about him. Where'd you get him anyway?"

"He belongs to my wife," said Comstock smoothly.

Trace avoided Mae's eyes, but his peripheral vision showed him her clenched posture. "He got a name?"

"Not yet. I'll leave that up to her."

Trace scooted his chair away from the table and got to his feet. "Well, she isn't going to ride him this trip," he drawled, tipping his hat to Mae. Then, without a backward glance, he swaggered out to saddle Diablo.

Mae climbed into the chuck wagon, where Preacher had made a comfortable place for her among the paraphernalia. She'd hoped to ride horseback—counted upon it—but Comstock was too clever for that.

Preacher had made her a nook so that they could converse unobserved. Mae was of the opinion that his effort was a waste. She had no words for him then; she was too scared for Trace. Jared's attitude bothered her. He laughed too much and seemed excited. That scared her more than his bullying. It was almost as if he sensed he'd won.

"Buck up," Preacher whispered, in reply to her dry sob. "I never seen a man's face go so gray as Trace's did when he seen you with that purple lip. How bad was that tussle you had with Comstock anyway? He's going to be asking me first thing."

"I found the note my father made, giving over his share of my grandfather's farm. Jared caught me in his study with it. I had my hands on it! Now it's in his safe. Says he's protecting it for me, keeping it from falling into the wrong hands. Bastard! I demanded he tell me how he got it, since the last anyone saw of it was when my father left for the Outpost.

"I guess I was a little pointed in my suggestion. I accused him of killing my father. He grew angry and hit me. Then he turned remorseful, begging me to forgive him. He explained he'd found the deed in Morgan's belongings. Tried to make out that he was shocked. He figured, I guess, that if he could distract me with his advances I might forget about Morgan and the deed. That's when he got the scratches. He scares me, Preacher. He actually thinks I can come to love a man who killed my father."

Preacher flicked the reins, setting the wagon in motion. "Ever consider that Comstock ain't right in the head? If that's the case, all this heading out to the middle of nowhere on some fool errand to hunt horses is mighty dangerous."

"He's evil, Preacher," Mae agreed. "In its purest form. There's some ugly things, ugly people in this world, but Jared's something else."

She thought about Trace. She'd seen the white knuckles of his hand poised at his side, inches from the gun slung on his hip. Their eyes had locked, and in that instant her heart stopped. Preacher was right. If Trace had drawn that gun, he would be dead. He probably would have drilled Comstock, but Slade was the fastest gun around. Trace would have died because of her—because of the grudge he bore against the man who'd wronged her. She could never live with that. And the terrible reality was, Trace and Comstock would clash before this drive was over. Lead would fly.

Dread gripped her heart in an icy fist and she murmured, "Trace is going to kill Jared, isn't he, Preacher?" she murmured.

"Uh-huh," the old man replied. "I reckon one of 'em will die, shot full of bullet holes. Let's just pray it's not Trace."

They made camp an hour before sunset by the mesa where Mae and Trace spent a night.

When Mae attempted to exit the chuck wagon, Comstock's firm hand prevented her. "I have a little present for you, Mae," he said. By the expression in his eyes, it was clearly going to be one she wouldn't like.

Reaching into his pocket, he withdrew something that looked like a dog collar. It tinkled. Bells? Mae glared, not knowing what he was up to but repulsed by his proximity.

"What the hell is that thing?"

"My version of a hobble. You will wear this around your boot. I'm belling the cat, you might say. That way, Preacher and I will know where you are at all times."

As he reached down for her ankle, she jerked it away. "If you think I am going to wear that, you've taken leave of your senses," she snapped. Not that she didn't already think that.

His face hardened. Reaching out, he grabbed her booted ankle and yanked her off her feet to fall back against a sack of flour. Holding her ankle in a viselike grip, he fastened the insulting thing around her boot. "I'll pitch you a tent by Preacher's bedroll. I want you out of the men's view. I've seen Slade and Chip eyeing you, and I don't trust this Ord fella any farther than I can throw this wagon. But that won't matter long. Once I get my hands on those horses, he won't . . . have a job. I don't cotton to insolent hired hands."

"What? You'll whip him to death, too?"

Comstock looked her up and down, clearly not liking the growing rebellion in her. "Well, you have yourself to thank for that. I was defending your honor."

"Are you *insane*?" The instant the words were out of her mouth, she knew they were a mistake. His face flushed red with anger, and his hand flexed about the hilt of the whip tied at his waist. She continued anyway, needing to set things straight. "I had nothing to do with you killing Morgan. Yes, I complained. I had a right to. If you were paying closer attention, defending my honor in the first place, it would never have happened. You bear the blame of Morgan's death alone, not me."

For a moment she feared she had pushed him too far, but then he nodded. "I suppose that's true."

"You know it is. You could have simply fired him."

"Let's say I just got rid of a thorn in both our sides. Sometimes, Mae, things out here appear one way when they are really another. You know, like those mirages I told you about, seeing water where there isn't any. A person meddles in matters that she doesn't understand . . . well, it's like sticking your hand into a nest of rattlers. By the time you hear the rattling, it's too damn late." She read the veiled threat in his words. "Anyway, Preacher will feed you here in the wagon, out of the way of the men's ogling eyes. I don't want you anywhere near them. He's to take you to the under-brush whenever you need to do the necessary. But don't try to run, Mae. I'll only catch you. I'm getting tired of these little games of yours—of *everyone's*. Think on it. I'll sleep in the open with the riders."

Mae frowned. Once again Jared was keeping her pris-oner and yet allowing her to keep him at arm's length. It was baffling. Men like Jared Comstock—bullies—didn't sit and wait or say pretty please. They just took what they wanted. They enjoyed hurting people weaker than themselves. From the very start this had puzzled her about Jared. But then, every aspect of the situation bothered her. Comstock's comments about rattlers made her realize just how little made sense here. As she watched him stalk off, she wondered what demons were really driving and controlling Jared Comstock.

Out of the corner of her eye, she caught Trace watch-ing her. It was a brief glance as he adjusted the cinch on Diablo. That gaze met hers, then dropped—Jared was headed in his direction—and Trace didn't look her way again. He swung himself up on Diablo and rode off without ever glancing back.

Fear returned. What if he didn't come back? Jared clearly didn't trust him, and the man's pause before predicting Trace would soon be without a job sent a chill up her spine. One thing was for certain: while a lot of things out here were a mirage, Trace was not one of them. He was honest and true. He was a gentleman, someone she could stake her life on.

She supposed she already had.

Not long after dark, Mae watched Comstock put up a small tent on the far side of the chuck wagon. Preacher eventually brought her a plate of beans and two biscuits. His bedroll was between the tent and the campfire, effectively creating a barrier between her and the men, who ate in sullen silence. Once their meals were consumed, nearly everyone crawled into a bedroll, knowing dawn would come all too soon.

Tired herself, Mae closed her eyes and allowed the sounds of the prairie to lull her toward sleep. Exhaustion allowed dreams, however: swirling blue mists, a figure moving through the haze. Someone was calling her name—a man's voice, resonant and deep, but a voice she'd never heard. She could almost see this man. He was a man of power, someone who had been controlling everything that happened since she'd arrived—

"Mae. *Mae!*"

It finally registered that this second voice was not part of her dream. She struggled to awaken, but fatigue kept trying to pull her back into the black.

"Mae! It's me!" the voice whispered, giving her good shoulder a shake.

She blinked, wondering if this was still merely her dream. Reaching out, she touched his face. Her fingers trembled as they slid lower, touching his broad, angular jaw, the cleft in his chin, and his lips, which her thumb at last caressed. His raw male scent rose in her nostrils. Trace. He'd come back.

He said quietly, "I've found the Indians. They're east of the mesa. When I return, be ready to move if I say."

He stood for a moment, hardly more than a shadow in the inky night. Then he was gone.

Chapter Sixteen

Trace smiled as he rode into the Indian camp, which was positioned on the mesa south of the entrance to the valley. A narrow trail forked down from both the rock walls, emptying into a draw. Alert to his presence, the men were waiting, almost as if they'd been posted specifically for him. But while the group, outcast from the Walapai tribe, kept to themselves and trusted no one, White Eagle was the leader of this rogue band. Minutes after exchanging greetings, Trace was seated in a crudely constructed summer dwelling, one of the several well concealed by nature behind the foothills.

White Eagle, wrapped in a buffalo robe, his shoulder-length hair adorned with three eagle feathers, was past his prime. His demeanor didn't evidence this. A dignified bearing bespoke his greatness as a warrior, and also a bone-chilling aura of ruthless cunning that always made Trace glad he numbered among the few white men the Indian called a friend.

"Many days have passed since the Whisperer has shared our camp," White Eagle said. "For this past moon, you travel back and forth through the land, going in circles. Now you ride with the enemy of White Eagle. The Whisperer would like to tell me his purpose?"

"I need your help," said Trace, speaking in a mix of English and the Walapai dialect. "Your enemy is my enemy. I ride with him only to protect two others who are in danger."

The Indian nodded. His eyes, as black as onyx, hadn't left Trace since his entrance to the makeshift dwelling. That scrutiny, however, didn't faze Trace. White Eagle appeared to have the power to see the truth in men's souls, and he had nothing to hide.

"The woman you brought to the mesa—she is your woman?"

"You knew I was up there?" Trace blurted. The Indian's knowledge never ceased to amaze him. "Yes, she is my woman . . . or soon will be. It's why I need your help. The leader of the men below means her harm, just as he likely means to kill me after I round up the wild mustangs near—"

The conversation stopped as a slender Walapai woman placed bowls before them. She flashed Trace a look that could kill.

"Pay her no need," said White Eagle, dismissing the female. "My daughter has been tempted by the white man's world but belongs here with her people. You did my bidding and brought her back to me. I told her to choose a brave for a husband. Foolishly she voiced that she wants you, Whisperer. Fury resides in her heart since she heard you have taken a white woman. But she is young. She will fix her mind elsewhere. So be it. Now, come, tell me of this trouble that has brought you to us."

Trace explained over the bowls of food what had happened and what he feared would happen. When he finished, there was silence while the Indian pondered what he'd learned. Trace's life, and those of Mae and Preacher, could well depend upon what the other man said.

"This Comstock has stolen ponies from White Eagle," the Indian said at length.

"He has stolen mine, too, and those of my rancher friends in the north. I am trying to prove that, and put a stop to this theft."

"Still, you plan to give this man Standing Thunder and his herd—"

"I never intended to give Comstock the herd. I used it as bait to draw him away from the Lazy C, so my friend could take my woman to safety and send for the ranchers in the north. Only, Comstock changed things. He brought the woman along as a weapon to control me. I need to spirit her away and send for the marshal."

"This I cannot do," White Eagle said. "We cannot visit the towns. No white man would give ear to our words."

"I wouldn't expect you to," Trace agreed. "I'll figure a way to get word to them, probably north from Flat Springs, if we can get there. I am hoping to use the horses to draw Jared's group in that direction. Do you know where Standing Thunder and his herd are hiding?"

"Echo Canyon," said the Indian.

Trace hesitated. "If trouble comes, can I bring my woman to you until I settle the score with these rustlers? I don't know that it will be necessary, but . . . well, it's just good to know all one's options."

White Eagle closed his eyes and thought, then gave a single nod. "You once fought for the honor of my daughter, brought her back to me. I owe the Whisperer the same. Ride to Echo Canyon. In two days, White Eagle will join with you. We will help keep you and your woman safe." He flashed a hard smile that wrinkled his leathered face. "It is good to see my old friend the Whisperer, and even better to learn he is still friend and not enemy."

Trace smiled. "I want Standing Thunder for my own," he pointed out. "I have stalked him through the canyons for four summers. Once we settle this, however, you are welcome to all the remaining horses." He offered his hand. "And don't call me Whisperer. These men know of my skill but don't know anything else about me. They know the Whisperer is a renegade rider. It could get me killed."

White Eagle nodded again. "It will be as you wish, my friend. We meet at Echo Canyon in two days."

Trace left the camp and headed back to where he'd tied Diablo. He pulled up short when he saw the horse, Breath Feather sitting astride him. Aside from her glossy black hair falling from a center part to her waist, she was naked. Trace was glad no Walapai braves were nearby.

He didn't miss a step. It was plain that she meant to disarm him with her nudity. Her breasts were only partly covered, the nipples hard in the cool evening air and protruding provocatively through the dusky curtain of hair. When he drew near, she flicked the hair back, proudly flaunting her breasts.

"Is she as beautiful as Breath Feather, your woman?" she asked in the Walapai tongue, sliding her hands over her breasts, down along the curve of her waist and hips. "I see your eyes tasting what you see."

"I see a spoiled child who will catch her death in the cold," Trace responded, snatching up her buckskin shift from the ground where she'd discarded it. He tossed it over to her.

She allowed it to fall. "I scratch her eyes out if you bring her here!" Hunching forward, she struck at him like a rattler, spooking Diablo, who danced on his hooves and whinnied. "I will pull the hairs out of her head! I will gouge her white skin until it bleeds!"

Trace reached out and grabbed her around the waist, yanking her from the horse and dropping her onto her feet, hard. He picked up her shift and thrust it at her. "Stop this. Now. You always knew there was nothing between us. I did your father a favor in bringing you back; that was the end of it. I owed him. There are plenty of fine braves for you to choose from right here in camp."

Her dark eyes flashed. "They all shun, turn their faces away from me. None among them will have me now. 'White man's leavings,' they say, 'unclean to the Walapai nation.' There is no one left to me but Whites."

"Whose fault is that?" Trace snapped.

She wilted. "I begged you to take me. On my knees, I begged you! But you would have none of me. I have waited for you. I knew one day you would come back. You have no woman! *I* am your woman!" She moved to throw her arms around his neck, but he dodged the embrace. He took her hands and crimped them around her shift.

"You are wrong. I love this woman you have heard of. I hope to marry her once I get her back to her home." He paused and looked Breath Feather in the eye. "And if you *ever* threaten her in any way, you will wish to God you never laid eyes on me. Your time will come. You will find a man who loves you, just as Mae has."

Breath Feather stared up at him, tears gleaming in her eyes. Her fingers worked, punishing the fringed buckskin of her clothes, clenching and flexing in an angry rhythm. For a moment Trace thought she was going to throw the garment at him, but she didn't. Instead she spat in his face as a snake spits venom, spun on her heel, and ran off, her long hair streaming behind her.

Trace stripped off his bandana and wiped away her spittle. Then, without a backward glance, he swung up on Diablo's back and headed off toward Comstock's camp.

He dismounted when he reached the stream and wrung out his kerchief. The icy water was melted snow from the mountains above the foothills, and Trace bathed his hot face and soothed his parched throat. Finally he tied the damp kerchief around his neck and mounted Diablo again. The whole incident with Breath Feather left a bad taste in his mouth. His words to her had surprised him. He'd always planned on seeing Mae home safely, of course, but everything else had been a little vaguer. Only, now the words were out. He intended Mae for his wife, and damn any man or woman who stood in his way.

He wished he could find someone to make Breath Feather happy, though. He knew she just needed someone with a firm hand and the smarts to gentle her. To some degree, everyone needed someone to gentle them. Sadly for her, it would never be him.

Chapter Seventeen

*B*oy, you do seem to just dig that hole deeper and deeper. Keep at it, and it'll be deep enough for a grave, if'n you ain't careful." Preacher gave Trace a dark stare. "How'd you get involved with them Injuns anyway?"

"Hunting horses," Trace answered, helping Preacher refill their barrels with fresh spring water. "A few years ago I was up on the mesa tracking Standing Thunder—had an idea of capturing him and starting a herd, stopping being a renegade rider. Almost had him, too, but the rope snapped and the fool stallion came at me. Got me pretty good. The Indians took me in, healed me. I owed them for saving me, healing me, and for a number of other things. In return, Wild Eagle asked my help. His daughter was gone, taken by white men. Frankly, I think the girl went willingly. She has hungry eyes, wants more than a nomadic life. White Eagle couldn't go after her, so he asked me. I had to say yes. The girl apparently set her sights on me."

"Poor girl," the old man mused, pouring another bucket into a half-full barrel. "You going to tell Mae about her?"

"There's nothing to tell. I did a job for a friend, nothing more." Trace shrugged, not needing this new complication.

Preacher shook his head. "Seems to me that keeping things from Mae is more dangerous than not, likely to cause more trouble just when you don't need it. Like the snake that strikes without rattling, might bite you in the rear end. Aren't you thinking of marrying the girl?"

"Well, Ord!" Comstock's booming voice interrupted their conversation. The man strode through the camp, kicked a couple of hands to wake them up, and moved toward Trace. "Did you find those Injuns?"

"I did," said Trace, reaching for the coffeepot. "White Eagle agreed to meet us at Echo Canyon."

"That's where the horses are, eh?" There was calculation in Comstock's eyes; the man was clearly considering dispensing with Trace and the Indians now that he knew the location of the herd.

Trace shrugged. "They won't be sitting there waiting, that's for sure. Echo Canyon is just our meeting place with White Eagle. He'll help us track the herd from there."

"How much does he want?" Comstock asked.

"Three horses. *Good* ones. Still, I told you they would work cheap," Trace returned. "White Eagle owes me a heavy debt. So you're benefiting from that."

Comstock took the coffeepot from the nearby fire and poured some into his cup. "Lucky you. Lucky me. You sure he won't go back on his word?"

"Once White Eagle gives his word, it's law."

"You better be dealing straight with me, Ord," Comstock warned, his demeanor having suddenly soured.

"Something don't sit right about you. I've had a queer feeling since the first time I clapped eyes on you, and a man who ignores his feelings is a fool apt to get killed."

Trace sipped some coffee himself. "I can pack and leave right now. Then you can go on to Echo Canyon on your own. Of course, White Eagle won't even show himself, let alone aid you."

All talk stopped as Mae appeared. She paused, her eyes locking on Trace, seeing him conversing with her husband. Not speaking, she approached. Trace gritted his teeth as the little bells around her ankle jingled. And if he was riled by the bell, Trace's blood actually boiled when he caught Slade leering at Mae.

Preacher's eyes flashed to Trace; then the old man picked up a tin cup and filled it. He made to pass the cup to Slade, but as he did, coffee splashed onto the gunman's hand. Slade howled in pain and grabbed at Preacher, but the old-timer deftly sidestepped.

"You clumsy old bastard," the gunslinger thundered. "You did that on purpose!"

"I did not!" Preacher said, bristling. "I was just giving you coffee to help you wake up. If'n your eyes hadn't been glued where they shouldn't be, you wouldn't have missed taking it."

Slade's gun was out of its low-slung holster and in his hand, cocked and aimed at Preacher, before anyone had a chance to blink. Trace's gun followed suit, only it was aimed at Slade.

"Don't think you really want to do that, boy."

Comstock flushed red along his neck. "Both of you put those hog legs away. Now! And, Slade, you keep your eyes where they belong. Understand?"

The youngster swung his gun so that it pointed at Jared. "Oh, I understand things. The question is, do you? Remember, you don't give me orders. Ever. I don't think I need to spell the situation out any plainer."

All eyes were trained on the pair, waiting for the first person to blink. Trace stood quietly, ready to kill one man or both.

Mae's white face haunted his peripheral vision. Her hand went to her mouth, and she was clearly terrified everything was about to erupt in deadly violence. Her gasp caused Slade's eyes to shift to her for a heartbeat. That was a mistake. One someone like Slade should never make.

A loud crack broke the silence. Comstock stepped forward, his blacksnake whip unfurled and ready to snap again. "I'm boss around here. And don't anyone forget it. All of you—get about your business. Eat up, we've a hard ride ahead."

Slade sneered at the word *boss* but eased his gun back into his holster. He was a hothead, like all gunslingers, but this attitude toward Comstock seemed beyond a young man's natural arrogance. Something just wasn't right in all this, but Trace was damned if he could figure out what.

Trace holstered his Colt, meeting Slade's eyes. The bastard had taken notice of how fast he was and wouldn't forget; cockiness would surely push the youngster to find out which of them was faster. Trace sighed. He was going to have to kill the boy before this was all through.

Mae wanted into the back of the wagon for a good hard cry. She'd been terrified that Trace and Slade were going to shoot it out, and that Trace would be the loser. Her heart had pounded like a terrified jackrabbit's, especially as Slade, who was supposed to be in Comstock's pay, made it clear he wasn't answerable to the man.

"Remember, you don't give me orders. Ever. I don't think I need to spell the situation out any plainer," the gunslinger said.

What situation? Was Jared working with someone else, maybe someone on the receiving end of the horses they were going to sell? Could Slade and Morgan both be working for this unknown man, riding herd on Jared to make sure he lived up to whatever bargain he'd made? That was the only thing that came to mind. But who? No one had ever come to the ranch who fit that bill—and of course the situation hadn't seemed to help Morgan in the end. Still, Mae quivered at the idea of a new person being introduced to this mix. She didn't doubt that whomever Jared Comstock dealt with would be evil.

Preacher came and offered his hand to help her to climb up into the wagon. Their eyes met, and he gave her a smile. It was forced. The old man, too, had seen how Slade openly stared at her, not fearing Jared's reaction. That was why he'd deliberately spilled coffee on Slade: it both blistered the gunslinger's hand, maybe giving Trace a tiny advantage should things come to a shoot-out, and drew attention to the young man's impropriety.

"Chin up, missy. They say it's darkest before the dawn." Preacher lifted his shaggy eyebrows as he gave her a boost.

Sadly, Preacher's words did little to disquiet her growing apprehension.

Chapter Eighteen

*T*race sat atop Diablo that evening, surveying the land. Everything had passed quietly since the incident with the spilled coffee, but the whole outfit still seemed to be walking on eggshells, waiting for something to happen. Everyone knew Slade would only wait so long before calling him out. Especially since he was fast.

He'd erred in letting everyone see just how fast he was, Trace knew. Now it was gnawing at the gunslinger, which of them was faster. Trace had seen it before: every young buck trying to earn a name glommed onto another gunman as the means. Like the way gold fever struck some men, making them blind to anything else, being top draw infected the mind of many a gunslinger, became an all-out obsession.

This was a damn nightmare. He hadn't truly intended to trap the horses with Comstock; he'd just wanted to lure him away from the ranch long enough for Preacher to get Mae safely headed back to Kentucky. Now he was forced to continue the farce, waiting for an opportunity to escape.

"How far is Flat Springs from here?" Comstock asked,

coming up alongside Trace. "I figure it best we stock up on supplies. You think they'd have barbwire in supply? Would making cornering those horses in a box canyon a damn sight easier. We could drive them down the coulee. Once they reach the end, we could draw the makeshift fence of barbed wire over the opening and have them trapped. What do you think?"

Trace hated such a strategy. Cattlemen and horsemen alike detested the wire, preferring free-range grazing and the use of branding to maintain one's herd. Animals were cut up or often died in the tangle. The use had caused many feuds and range wars to break out. That Comstock would want to use it didn't surprise Trace one bit.

Still, it was a legitimate excuse to make the side trip to Flat Springs. Trying to avoid suspicion, Trace tried not to appear too anxious. "Sound idea. Though you better be prepared for some cut-up horses. You could detour there alone while the drive heads north and meets up with White Eagle and his tribe. Shouldn't take you a day, maybe a day and a half to catch up."

Comstock barked, eyes moving over him to judge Trace's suggestion. "And leave my wife here with the lot of you? You must think I'm a damn fool."

Trace shrugged. "You're the one who brought her. There's no place for a woman on a drive, in my opinion. You already see how Slade's forgetting his place. Sticking a woman in a camp of men is like dragging a mare in season before a herd of stallions. Men get loco, edgy. Edgy men do stupid things."

Comstock didn't say more about the wire until they stopped for supper. Taking the plate piled with stew and biscuits Preacher handed him, he sat down on a fallen tree. After a few bites he asked, "Any of you boys know the way?" He lifted his fork while awaiting a reply.

"I've been there once—a while back," Chip drawled. "Not much of a town, as I recall. Of course, they rarely are. General store, trading post, livery, and saloon. Had a dirtier saloon gal than I've seen anywhere else. She was named Rose as I recall. Had this rose tattoo on her fat as—"

All the men broke in to howls of laughter, cutting him off.

"Heard ol' Rose set her cap on marrying you, Chip," Ben joked. "Wanted you to make an honest woman of her—and to scrub her back on Saturday night."

Comstock kicked Chip's booted feet. "I didn't ask about your whoring. Will they have what we need? I am hoping they'll have barbed wire."

The cowpoke shrugged. "They might. Hard to say. Only, you'll need a wagon to fetch enough of it. Maybe you can buy one there."

"How about you, Ben?" Comstock asked. "You up to the ride?"

"I reckon I could, if'n that's what you want," the hand replied.

Comstock finished off the food on his plate. Once he was done, he wiped his mouth and ordered, "Make tracks in the morning, boys. Get what we need and meet up with us at Echo Canyon."

As the man stood and started back to the chuck wagon, probably for more food, Trace's heart began to pound. This, he couldn't allow. He needed to be the

one to go to Flat Springs. Then he could send a telegraph to the men who'd hired him and tell them where
they were headed and that he'd found their rustled
stock. It was imperative either he or Preacher go, and
Preacher wouldn't be sent because he was needed to
cook.

Jared sat down with another plate of Preacher's stew.
Trace waited until Ben and Chip emptied their plates
and went about several last-minute chores, paused before biting into his biscuit. "Not telling you your business or anything," he said, "but you must like to toss
your money around. Supplies, wires, cutters, a wagon,
and a mule? Big wad of bills you're going to hand those
two. Bet Chip'll be glad to see Rose and her tattoo." He
smirked, as if pondering how the trail hands would
spend Comstock's dough.

Jared glanced around the campfire, his expression
revealing that he really didn't trust any of the crooks
he'd hired. "I'm not leaving Mae—not after what went
on with that bastard, Morgan." His jaw clenched as his
eyes found Slade. The gunslinger lounged on his side
while eating his food, but he could've been chewing
sawdust and he wouldn't have noticed; his eyes were
fixed on Mae. She sat beside the tent, eating her meal.
Slade's cold black stare never left her.

Comstock tossed his fork down on his plate. He stared
at Trace. "Why don't *you* go? You're wanting to catch
those horses as much as I. At least I can trust you to get
there and back with what we need and not waste my
money on some fat whore."

Trace frowned. "I hoped to ride on ahead of you all,
meet up with White Eagle. We could start tracking

them horses a mite early . . ." His eyes flicked past Comstock toward the wagon, as if checking if there were any biscuits left, but really he was eyeing Mae. Her face was ashen and her eyes wide with worry at the prospect of him riding off and leaving her alone. But there seemed no help for it, not if he wanted to call in the law. Since Comstock was keeping his distance from her, he was less concerned about leaving Mae behind with him.

Of course, there was also Slade. The gunslinger wanted her. And he wanted Trace dead. Trace would have to trust Comstock to keep her safe, with Preacher watching over her as well, until he could return.

But he still couldn't let his enthusiasm show. "I'm no grip, handling supplies. I'm a wrangler, a broncobuster." Trace got up and snatched another biscuit from the nearly empty pan.

Comstock held up his own plate and addressed Preacher. "Pass me that last biscuit, old-timer. You might be a sourpuss to look at, but you sure can cook. And you follow orders." He waited until Preacher obliged him. "I'm boss of this outfit and I'm tired of people forgetting that. Trace, I'll give you the money and list of what I need. Ride hard. Get the supplies and catch up with us at Echo Canyon. You need to be there to deal with that Indian friend of yours. He doesn't owe me anything."

"I'm taking the black," Trace warned.

"You're mighty partial to him, ain'tcha, Ord?" Comstock observed. He was staring holes through Trace. "You wouldn't be getting *too* attached to him, now, would you? My wife's horse?"

"You just ordered me to get to the Springs and then up to Echo Canyon before you meet up with the Walapai. I need a fast set of legs under me," Trace drawled. "And a horse like that needs riding every day. If I go, no one will be doing that. Mae certainly won't."

"Awww, take him," Comstock consented. "But you better be at that canyon before those Indians show or there'll be hell to pay. In fact, you'd better get going right away."

Sighing, Trace said, "You're the boss." He tipped his hat and went to pack up.

Behind him he heard Comstock grumble, "Damn glad someone around here remembers that."

Every step Diablo took away from the group increased Trace's sinking sensation that he shouldn't have left Mae behind. Only, there was nothing for it. What, Preacher and he would just up and shoot their way out, praying Mae would be okay? Or maybe he could talk White Eagle and his braves into slaughtering Comstock and his men in front of her. That'd be just peachy.

No, the law had to get involved. They had plenty of proof now. As much as he wanted to kill Comstock, it was likely better and safer to see things done properly—especially since Jared was now allowing Mae to maintain her distance. She was safe there with Preacher. The only drawback was Slade. The old man was no match for the gunslinger, and Trace was fearful that neither was Jared. But he was trapped into this plan.

Cursing every second away from her, Trace made the trip to Flat Springs in record speed. He was saddle-tired and dusty as he rode into town. Once there, he sent wires to Sam Overton of the Bar O and Bret Thorne of the Double Bar T, giving them the facts: their horses had been found and indeed could be collected at the Lazy C. He also gave the direction of where the outfit was headed, just in case. Thorne's ranch was just north of the canyons. He had a feeling the man might ride to intercept them and make sure Jared was taken into custody before going on to the Lazy C to round up his missing stock. He might even bring the marshal and some of Overton's men.

Not bothering with the barbed wire or the wagon, he bought the other supplies and made good time on the return trip. He planned to give Jared back his money and say they were out of stock on the wire.

It was dusk when he spotted Echo Canyon, and a shimmer of golden flame painted the mountaintops behind him. Below, steeped in purple shadow where twilight had already fallen, the red clay canyon floor stretched out, walled in red rock and fringed at the bottom with a line of cedars that hemmed a shallow stream. The canyon took its name from the echo of the wind off the vast amphitheater of weather-sculptured rock on both sides.

Preacher's campfire beckoned, its flickering light suggesting that things were all right, that preparations for supper had begun. Riding slowly, Trace stayed vigilant, alert to anything out of the ordinary. There was no sign of the Walapai, which surprised Trace, since he'd expected them to reach the valley before Comstock.

The aroma of Preacher's beans and meat roasting over the campfire greeted him as he tied up Diablo in

the remuda. His belly had begun to growl, reminding
Trace he hadn't eaten anything since breakfast. His
mouth was watering by the time he'd unsaddled the
horse, but his first thought was of Mae. A quick glance
in Preacher's direction earned him a faint nod, but
Trace didn't relax until he caught a glimpse of her face
inside her tent near the chuck wagon.

He gave her credit. She did a good job of hiding her
emotions. Though she watched him coming into the
camp and going to the wagon to take a plate, he could
have been any other drover.

"So, where's the wagon and the wire?" Comstock finally asked.

Trace shrugged. "No wire. No need for a wagon since
they didn't have the wire. I got the other stuff, though.
And they had a couple airtights of peaches. Thought
you might want to give them to your missus as a treat.
I'm sure this ride ain't too pleasurable for a female.
Never hurts to give a lady nice things."

Comstock nodded, smirking. "Fine idea. She might
like them." After a moment he said, "We haven't seen
hide nor hair of your Indian friends. You sure they'll
show up?"

"White Eagle is a man of his word," Trace said. "I'll
ride out after I eat, see if I can spot them coming."

"You do that," Comstock grunted. "While you're at
it, figure out a good way to pin those broncs once we
get them herded into the canyon. I can't believe Flat
Springs didn't have that wire. . . ." He shook his head
and wandered off to get some grub.

After he ate, Trace rode up onto the ridge. No one
followed. The night was clear; stars winked down from

the indigo vault overhead, and a first-quarter moon had just cleared the canyon wall. Squinting, Trace swept the land below with his gaze, searching the cedars and the rocky wash that edged the stream for any sign of the Walapai. Then he scanned the ridge opposite, first toward the west but eventually to the less likely direction, the east.

Where the rocky edge sloped back from various outcroppings into a dense wood, a short line of mounted braves seemed to materialize, standing mute at the edge of the timberline. White Eagle, at the head of the column, walked his dapple gray forward, while the others faded back among the trees. Trace raised his hand in greeting, and White Eagle did the same.

"You've found the herd," Trace said, seeing the Indian's smug expression.

The chief nodded. "Beyond the draw"—he made a sweeping gesture—"in the little canyon north of here. Build your corral below in the narrow place between. Separate them from Standing Thunder, and then you can drive them through the gap."

"How many braves are with you?"

"Enough," White Eagle replied.

Trace stared out over the ridge to the campfire below, then turned north. His sharp eyes spotted Standing Thunder high on a hill, and the other wild horses grazing just below.

The Indian read him so clearly: "You worry over your woman. That is why you find yourself beset with so many problems. You do not think straight because your mind is on this female with the hair of flame. Say to me that this is not so." The Indian laughed softly. "Chasing wild horses is no place for a white woman. Worse with these men. They are horse thieves, killers. If we did not fear trouble with the white law, we would take care of them ourselves . . . but that is not to be. They will see justice, though, as you intend. They will trouble this area no more. As for your woman . . . she sounds like a lot of trouble, my friend. You will need to marry her and give her many babies. Then *she* will trouble you no more."

Trace hesitated, turning back and staring out over the precipice as though seeking to divine the answer to all his problems from the tufts of aromatic mesquite smoke wafting up from Comstock's campfire below. There was another problem he had, one he hated to speak of. "There is something else," he confessed. "Breath Feather . . . We locked horns after I left your campfire."

"She spoke to you?"

Trace sighed. "She had a lot to say, yes. She threatened Mae. She's your daughter, and I respect you . . . but I won't stand for her trying to hurt the woman I'm going to marry. I figure you need to watch her."

"Breath Feather has not lived up to her name," White Eagle said sadly. "She is called so after the soft down on an eagle's underbelly. There is no softness in her. My daughter has brought shame upon her father and our people. My heart is heavy from the path she walks, and I know of no man with the strength to gentle her."

"Well, it won't be me," Trace admitted. "You know someone else has my heart, and I'm hoping those two never meet. If things go right, riders from the north will be here soon. A day, maybe two at the most. So . . . I guess we should start rounding up the horses in the meantime."

"We will meet you below when the sun rises," said the aging warrior, straightening his posture in an unmistakable show of pride and strength. "You will ride with White Eagle and his horse hunters. Do not fear. Your woman will be watched by my braves whenever it is possible. If only I could find someone to do the same for my daughter."

Before Trace could reply, the Indian was gone, vanished into the shadowy trees.

An unease filled Trace as he walked Diablo back to Comstock's camp. He hoped the man was sound asleep, that he wouldn't ask about the Indians until first light. Trace was bone weary after the hard ride to Flat Springs and back, and he wanted rest—and maybe to talk to Mae. Only, Comstock was wide-awake. The rustler's lean, dapper figure was all too visible in his blinding white shirt and jeans that didn't look as though they'd ever seen a day's honest work. There would be no rendezvous, however brief, for Trace and Mae.

On the surface, the night didn't seem much like any other. Mae was in her tent, and Preacher was bedded down not far away, snoring heavily, Trace's Winchester at his side. A couple of riders played cards while Chips was honing his knife. The men were apparently too keyed up over the roundup in the morning to drink themselves blind as they had the other two nights; that would have been too much to hope for.

"Well, you were gone long enough. Did you find this White Eagle?" Comstock asked as Trace strolled up to the campfire.

Trace ignored him for a bit, taking a cup from the side of the wagon and pouring some coffee. He knew it aggravated Comstock. Good. Men who were too emotional were dangerous, but they were often controlled by their tempers and easier to prod in one direction or another.

"Well, did you find them or not?" Comstock repeated.

"Yeah, I did," Trace responded, sipping his coffee. "They're up there all right. They beat us here. They were just waiting to talk to me."

"So, where's the herd?"

Trace rolled his shoulder, which was stiff, and decided to lie. Just to play it safe. "White Eagle's men are still tracking them. He and his riders will meet up with us at sunup."

Comstock looked uneasy, and Trace wondered if he was scared of Indians. A moment later, the man settled any doubt. "I don't trust them thieving Walapai."

Trace gave a tired laugh. "Since I met you, Comstock, I cannot say I've noticed you trust much anyone or anything. You don't trust the men you hire. You don't trust the Indians. You don't seem to trust your wife, belling her like you would a cat. . . . Just who do you trust? A man who cannot trust must feel mighty alone."

Jared was alone, that was clear. He was also the biggest puzzle Trace had ever seen. He was a bully and, like most bullies, a coward at heart. But usually bullies surrounded themselves with slimy stooges who scurried around both fearing and worshipping them. He didn't see that happening with Jared. The man had two strong-willed employees that totally disregarded him, and also a bunch of drifters who gave him no more allegiance than a snake would a coyote. The man seemed desperate and weaker all the time. Trace hoped Slade didn't pick up on that and try to take advantage.

Tossing the dregs of his coffee into the fire, Trace spat out the rest of what was in his mouth. Steam hissed up at him, and his nostrils flared against the aroma of bitter coffee and mesquite. "Don't tell Preacher," he groused, "but that brew tastes like horse piss."

Comstock laughed. "Drink much horse piss, do you? I made it. Preacher faded long ago. Get some shut-eye yourself. Morning is going to come quick, and then we will see if you're as good as you say with wild horses. For your sake, I sure hope so."

"A threat if I ever heard one," Trace muttered under his breath. "A stupid threat from a stupid man." He gave a crisp nod and went to settle himself apart from the others, though close enough to keep an eye on Mae.

As he always did in a difficult situation, he tried to just rest, one eye half cracked. He managed to stay awake until Comstock bedded down for the night, but finally both eyelids began to droop, heavy with sleep; he'd been too long in the saddle. Propped uncomfortably against the trunk of an old cedar, he shook himself awake several times, but the effort was in vain. Despite his resolve, he fell into a deep, dreamless sleep.

Chapter Nineteen

There would be no roundup today. The corrals had to be built first. Not that Trace was in a hurry; the northern ranchers needed time to come with the law. Just past dawn they set out: Trace, White Eagle, and half the Walapai riders. The rest of the Indians remained out of sight, keeping an eye on Mae and Comstock, as their chief promised. Despite Trace's hope, there was no opportunity to speak with Mae. Comstock stayed too near the camp, watching everything like a hawk. No, there was nothing to do but trust Preacher to take her in hand while they all played out their hands.

They followed the timberline north-northeast to a gap in the rocks that would soon form the funnel-shaped makeshift corral they'd devised, emptying into a larger makeshift corral of wood that they were set to build. The landscape was made for such a horse trap, sheer-faced rock on one side, chest-high split rails they'd build on the other. The horses—there were fifty to a hundred they'd counted—would have no choice but to run the narrow gantlet and then be forced through a gate admitting no more than five abreast.

His mind's eye saw the great herd stampeding through the canyon, and he could almost hear their frenzied cries. He shuddered, imagining the noble beasts in the hands of Comstock and his crew. But with luck, the northern ranchers would arrive in time. Standing Thunder could never survive in the power of a man like Comstock. He was like Diablo and Mae, too wild to be broken. He needed to be gentled instead.

"The Whisperer is not happy he must capture these horses for others," White Eagle observed, as though he read Trace's mind.

"No, I'm not." Trace glanced at him. "And remember, these men do not know that Trace Ord is called Whisperer. It might mean my death, White Eagle."

The Indian shrugged. "I understand. But they and their chief keep their distance. He fears me and my kind, I think." After a moment the Walapai added, "My riders watch your woman."

"Tell them to beware especially of one called Slade," Trace cautioned. "They will spot him instantly. Dressed all in black, he wears his guns strapped low on his hips. He's fast," Trace warned.

The Indian seemed surprised. "As fast as you, my friend?"

Trace shrugged. "Maybe."

"That is not good. If you do not know . . . He will be wondering. He will want an answer."

Trace had certainly considered the possibility.

His attention was caught by Standing Thunder, who stood poised on a mesa on the eastern fringe of the little canyon, a noble statue carved of the same red rock upon which he stood. Trace's heart leapt at the sight. Admiring the slanted shoulders, the deep, powerful chest, and the long, sleek neck—the mark of a long-reaching stride—he could scarcely draw breath.

As though in salute, the stallion reared, forefeet churning, jet-black broomtail sweeping this way and that. Trace patted Diablo's neck to soothe the restlessness in the horse's spirit. When White Eagle laid a hand on his arm, Trace's muscles tensed beneath the Indian's wrinkled fingers.

"He sees you," the Walapai leader said. "He tastes you on the wind. Many years he has roamed these canyons, riding with the wind. He is a clever spirit. I have passed through his lands many times and never once tried to claim him. Perhaps I felt that as long as he ran free, then I would remain free. We have understood each other . . . until now. The time of the wild horses draws to an end, much like the time of my people."

Trace glanced at the Indian, unable to speak.

White Eagle shrugged. "The days to come are not clear, my friend. I dream on this, seeking the path to lead my tribe. I must make choices soon. Nothing stays the same, no matter how much we want that. These ending days seem fated for both the stallion and me and my kind. I would rather see the great broomtail in the Whisperer's hands than in the power of one such as Comstock."

A shiver ran up Trace's spine. He certainly didn't want this horse in Jared Comstock's power. Nor did he want Mae to end up 'there. Everything was coming to a head. Standing Thunder, White Eagle, Comstock, Slade. . . . Bad medicine was brewing. A storm was coming, and it would soon break. Trace just hoped he could hold tight to what he loved.

Now he had to go back and get the people together to build the corral.

Something was wrong—terribly wrong. Mae felt more a prisoner than she had while locked in the ranch house. She saw Trace only at a distance. For the three days of the trip, Jared Comstock hadn't let her out of his sight. This last day was the worst, while the men were out building the corral. He would no longer leave her in Preacher's charge, he said, was keeping her confined to her tent and the chuck wagon, giving her no chance to speak to the old man. Preacher wouldn't keep watch outside her tent at night anymore, either. Comstock himself would do that, and Mae was terrified by the thought.

He approached and handed her a plate of food. "Ever see a wild horse roundup, Mae?" he asked, sitting down to eat beside her.

"N-no," she said. "I'm from Kentucky, remember? Horses are bred and raised on the farm there, not taken from the wild."

"You'll have to tell me all about your grandfather's farm," he suggested.

Mae paused, the food untouched on the plate. Every hair on her body was standing on end. "Why would you be interested in that?"

"No reason, I suppose." Comstock shrugged. "But I'm hoping that, as things settle down between us . . . well, as your husband I'm sure your grandfather will want to get to know me. He can't be a young man."

The deed in his safe was gnawing at Mae's mind. She told herself to ignore that. Picking up a biscuit, she went through the motions of eating, barely tasting what she put in her mouth.

Evidently sensing he'd pushed too far, Comstock switched directions. "Well, eat up and get ready to ride. Come tomorrow, you'll have an adventure to tell your grandfather."

"You're going to let me go along?" Mae was shocked, considering his recent protective behavior.

"Yep. Can't leave you behind. It's not safe." He exhaled. "Don't get any harebrained ideas about running off again, though. You don't want to rile me. Once this roundup is over and things settle down, I'll have plenty of time to court you right proper, like we talked about. Maybe that'll make you happy. We can have a proper honeymoon someplace nice like San Francisco. With the money these horses'll bring, I can afford that. Damn tired of living out here, to be honest. Maybe we could just sell out and move to a real town, have a big house on Nob Hill. I was there once. Loved the clothes, the fancy restaurants . . . You'd like it, too, Mae. You're too fine a woman to waste your life out here. With the sale of these horses, I can give you all that."

Mae swallowed hard, again confused. She asked, "I'd have thought the Lazy C gives you enough money to afford anything you want. If you don't like the West, why didn't you sell out and move to California as soon as your father died?"

"Gambling debts drained the farm," Comstock answered. He stared into the flames, lost in anger. "Stupid old man—couldn't seem to stop himself. Didn't matter he was frittering everything away."

"But I thought . . ." Mae caught herself and didn't finish her question. It was her own father who'd had the gambling debts, not Jared's.

He seemed to come back to the present. "Thought what, Mae?"

She tried to force a smile. "Oh, nothing. Just making conversation. Trying to get to know you, like you want."

His eyes narrowed at her lie. "Are you really? Or are you offering one of those mirages we talked about, Mae?" He reached out and caught her hand. "Mae, I could make you a good husband, if you only gave me half a chance. What with the money from these horses and your grandfather's farm, we could build an empire together."

"My granddad's farm . . . ?" She tried to pull her hand back, but he wouldn't let her. "What has that to do with—" She started to say *us*, but the word stuck on her tongue. Instead she said, "—your plans?"

He shrugged. "He's an old man. It's sad, Mae, but people die. My father did."

"And mine," she gritted out. "Murdered like a dog, or do you fail to recall?"

He took the plate from her hand and placed it atop his own. "Mae, you should forget all about the past. It just upsets you when you speak of it. I don't like to see you unhappy. If things were diff—"

She jumped to her feet, yanking her hand from his grasp. "You want me happy, and yet you keep me prisoner. You forced me to marry you with a gun to my father's head! I warned you about Morgan and you ignored me. He killed my father and you did nothing. You have a lot to learn about women, Jared Comstock. I am not some horse to be broken. Not to mention, you don't beat an animal with a blacksnake whip and expect him to *love* you." She swallowed hard, biting back further, angrier words. There was no use arguing with this man; there was something not right in his thinking. Everything that had happened since she'd come to the Lazy C was increasingly confusing.

"Aw, Mae, honey," he said, reaching for her. He had a strange look in his eyes.

She tried to back up but the tent was behind her. She started to lose her balance and fall. Jared caught her. Instead of releasing her when she was again on her feet, he pulled her against him, hard. His mouth came down on hers. She grimaced at the kiss and shoved at his chest, but that didn't move him. His unyielding hands pulled her even closer.

Panicked, Mae did the only thing she could think of: she bit down on his lip and then stomped on the inside of his foot with her boot heel. "You brute!" she shrieked.

He backhanded her, driving her to the ground. Mae stared up into his eyes, terrified. Those eyes were tinged with madness. Panic exploded within her. Jared had sent Preacher off with Chip to fill the water barrels. Trace was out in the hills and hadn't returned. There were only a few riders in camp, finishing up supper, and they believed she was married to this monster. They wouldn't lift a hand in assistance.

"You she-bitch." Jared's hand moved to the whip at his waist. "I ought to learn you how to behave—"

From behind Jared came a metallic sound. He froze, then slowly turned. Slade stood there, his gun drawn. He wasn't pointing it at Jared, was just standing there smiling and spinning the cylinder of his revolver. The sound seemed to break through Jared's peculiar mood.

"You're interrupting, Slade," he said lowly, fixing his attention on the young man.

The gunslinger gave a small jerk of his upper lip against his long white teeth, as if thinking. "Uh, yeah. Guess I am. You're making a lot of racket. Upsets my digestion, don't you know? Seeing as you ran off that old man with the Winchester, giving him work, I figured I'd better stick close to Miss Ahern. Never know when my gun might come in handy. Like, when some sidewinder come sneaking around where he ain't wanted."

"*Mrs. Comstock*," Jared corrected.

Slade pushed his black felt hat back on his head. "Funny thing about names, don't you think? Once you're used to one name, sort of hard to switch to another. Ain't that so, ma'am? Don't you still think of yourself as Mae Ahern?"

Mae's eyes shifted between the two men, feeling a meaning present far beyond the simple words. She didn't necessarily understand it. "Frankly, since you ask . . . yes, I do."

Slade flashed her a big grin. "See there? I was right about that. You might could be surprised what else I'm right about. My gran—she was from Scotland—used to tell me that back there women never took their husband's names until the English came in and forced their way of doing things down the Scots' throats. I guess that's part of why I took to carrying my guns slung so low—I never cottoned to having anyone try to ram their ideas down my throat. See what I mean?"

Mae was glad for Slade's intervention, but that didn't make her trust him a bit more than she did Comstock. Something odd was going on here. But what? All Jared had to do was order his man to leave them alone, threaten not to pay him, but he wasn't doing that. Why not? Once again, Mae was curious and alarmed by Jared's reactions to the insolence of his hired hand.

She took a step away from Jared, the bells jingling on the bizarre anklet he'd fashioned for her. Slade's eyes went immediately to her boot. Spinning the cylinder again, he asked, "Miss Ahern, you enjoy wearing that fool thing?"

She glanced up to see Jared's reaction, but Comstock was standing stone-still, his hand on his whip, clearly trying to gauge if he could use it before Slade shot him. Stupid. Still, Mae was not above playing an advantage.

"Actually, I detest it. It's humiliating," she replied.

Slade sauntered close. With a tilt of his head he said, "Why don'tcha take it off?"

"Beg pardon?" She blinked, hearing an unmistakable command in his deep voice.

"I cannot imagine any man"—he flashed Jared a look of disdain—"doing that to his woman. Sort of treating her like a dog."

Mae didn't hesitate another moment. She sat down on the wooden box she'd been using as a stool and unlaced the anklet chain.

"Mae!" Jared cautioned, clearly warning her not to take it off.

She looked up and flashed him a smile, finished removing the anklet, then stood. "Thank you, Michael Slade. Now if you gentlemen will excuse me? It's been a long day and I need my rest if I'm to join the horse roundup."

"Good night, Miss Ahern." Slade tipped his hat to her.

"Good night, Mr. Slade." She paused to study the gunslinger, not fooled by his recent actions. He was deadly if handsome, and anyone who didn't see that was a fool. Long, sooty black eyelashes or not, he could kill Comstock in his sleep, and deep down she was terrified that he could do the same to Trace.

Swallowing hard, she turned to go inside her tent. Jared reached out and caught her upper arm.

"Mae—"

The clicks from the slow rolling of the gun cylinder came again, silencing whatever else Jared was going to say. A moment later Slade said, "Miss Mae's tired and needs to rest for tomorrow. You heard her say that, right? Sounds right intelligent, don't you think?"

Jared spun on his heel and walked toward the chuck wagon. He didn't look back.

Slade slowly smiled. "Good night again, Miss Mae."

Mae hurried to her tent. Inside, she quickly closed her eyes and pretended to go to sleep, but there was no way she could find rest. Where was Trace? She wanted him here. The situation with Jared was a total riddle, with more questions appearing every time he acted or opened his mouth.

Just as she started to drift off, she felt something digging at the back of the tent. She almost cried out, thinking it was a coyote or some other creature. A voice said in a hoarse whisper, "Just me. Here." The edge of the tent

lifted, and a derringer appeared. A moment later she
heard Preacher move off.

The gun was small. A gambler's weapon, she'd heard
tell. Most had had two shots, but as she fingered the gun,
she realized it was a bit bigger than the one her grandfather owned. This one had four bullets. One shot for
Jared, one shot for Slade? Two other shots would be left.
Who were they for?

Grimacing, she tucked the derringer under the edge
of the bedroll.

Chapter Twenty

The roundup is no place for a woman," Trace argued, voicing his opinion on Comstock's plan to bring Mae along. His words fell on deaf ears. "It's dangerous for both her and for the men. If their attention's on her and not the job . . . one misstep and someone gets dead."

In the predawn darkness, the men were huddled around the campfire. They'd had their breakfast, and were trying to shake off sleep by drinking copious amounts of coffee. Soon light would streak across the rim of the canyon and the rounding up of Standing Thunder's herd would commence.

Comstock rose from his seat. "Mae's coming and that's final."

Trace sighed. The last thing he wanted was to be worried about Mae underfoot. Jared Comstock didn't seem to have a care about the risk to her, about deliberately putting her in harm's way, which was a puzzlement. But the man was one contradiction after another. He'd noticeably increased his possessiveness of Mae, while he didn't exactly seem besotted. There was calculation in his eye, as if she were important in a fashion that eluded

Trace. All he could think was that Mae was an ace up Comstock's sleeve. But . . . against what?

There wasn't time to analyze it now, and he didn't dare put up too much of a protest about Mae coming along on the drive. Trace gave Comstock a blank stare and shrugged, as if it didn't matter to him if she got hurt. "Just keep her out of the way. The last time I spotted Standing Thunder, he was holed up on the little mesa at the east end of the canyon. We've got to go in from behind and drive him down onto the canyon floor."

"Standing Thunder, Standing Thunder," Comstock snapped. "I'm sick of hearing about him. He's one horse. There's a whole herd down there!"

"Have you ever done this before, Comstock?"

"Well, no, but—"

"You get your stock in easier ways, don't you? Much easier." Trace couldn't resist the jab, though he knew he shouldn't. He didn't know how long it would be before any backup arrived.

Comstock glared at him. "What in hell's that supposed to mean?"

"Nothing. Just that, since you don't have experience with wild horses, I'd suggest you listen to someone who does. It's what you're paying me for, after all." Trace cast a sidelong glance at Mae. She looked pale and frightened, dark circles under her eyes as though she hadn't slept. But then, he hadn't had much sleep, either, not since that first night in Echo Canyon. He doubted Preacher was sleeping much, either.

He pushed on with the discussion. "Standing Thunder leads that herd. He's the key to everything. Those mares follow him. If you get the mares and don't get him, he'll call the mares to him and they'll kill themselves trying to get back to him. My plan is to get to him to lead those horses off that mesa. White Eagle's riders will fan out wide on the flatland to either side, fire their rifles, and push those horses toward that gap. You boys should ride in close from the left flank, making sure they don't turn. Once they all get moving in the right direction, it'll be a flood rolling down the canyon. When they start to close in on the corral, they're going to balk. Hang back and fire your guns in the air to keep them running. Don't fire too early, though, or they'll panic and break through the Indians' line on the other flank. We'll have to start all over again."

Trace turned. "That means you, Slade. You act stupid and I'll shoot those irons right out of your hands. You got that?"

The gunslinger made no reply, just flashed him a cold-eyed stare.

Trace turned to Comstock. "Get the mustangs into the big corral with as little damage as possible, then close the gate so they can't turn and crash back through. With a hundred or more head of stampeding horseflesh, there isn't room for error. Remember any mistake's a quick way to get dead. Any questions?"

"Yeah. Where are those Injuns?" Comstock complained. "The sun's coming up."

"They'll be here, don't worry," said Trace. "No other questions? I suggest we gather up what we need and get in the saddle." He moseyed over to the chuck wagon. "I do believe I could live on your biscuits, Preacher," he said loudly, snatching up the last one remaining and taking a bite. It was the best excuse he could think of.

Preacher was washing up the cook pans. "Seems like you already do. Biscuits and beans—what built the West, eh?" He took Trace's cup and poured him the last of the coffee. With a lowered voice, he said, "Comstock has ordered me to stay here in camp. I'm supposed to get a meal ready for after the hoedown."

Trace sighed. "I know you and your sense of adventure would like to be in the thick of things, but it's better if you stay out of the way. I've got this itch crawling up my spine like things may go bad."

"If they do, you need me and that Winchester."

Trace shook his head. "Despite his love for your cooking and the fact that you're too old to meddle with his wife, Comstock don't trust you any more than me. Your coming to the Lazy C with me probably still rankles him."

"That man's wasp-bit for sure. Acting strange enough lately. And Slade . . . ?" Preacher frowned and shook his head. "I been thinking about him more and more. Why's he here? A man like that lives by his guns, not playing cowpuncher. That's beneath him. His guns are for hire, not his wrangling abilities. But he's riding along, though he resents every step of the way. Something ain't right about the lot of them. It don't make sense, Trace. A mad dog should behave a certain way, if you take my drift."

Trace paused before taking a sip of coffee. It was more bitter than usual, but he supposed that was because it was the dregs. "Yeah, I get that same feeling. The more I see, the less any of this makes sense. Comstock's edgy. He keeps looking around like he's expecting trouble. At first I thought he was jumpy about the Indians, or suspected I contacted those other ranchers, but now I'm not so convinced. There's something else. And you're damn right about Slade. Babying cows and horses and dealing with dust from their trail? That's not for him. He's no cowpuncher. That pail don't hold water."

Preacher gave Trace a level stare before taking the coffepot and dumping it out. "One last thing. You can call me crazy, but I have the strange sensation we're being followed. It may just be a feeling, but . . ."

Trace had lived in the West since the war. He knew never to doubt the animalistic instincts men developed. Foolishly dismissing them got a body killed. "Near or far?" he asked.

Preacher shrugged. "Far, I guess. Ain't seen nothing outside of them two riders."

"What two riders?" Trace hissed.

"Yesterday, when you were out with White Eagle, I spotted two men on horseback. Too far away to see anything much. They were just sitting on the ridge, watching. At first I dismissed it—thought it was you with White Eagle, surveying the area. But then you came riding in on Diablo a short time later from the opposite direction."

"Why didn't you say something?"

Preacher gave him a look as if Trace had gone simple. "Like I had a chance to speak to you! Comstock's eyes never leave you. He watches you more than he does Mae."

Trace nodded. "Point taken."

"I've a mind to circle back after you head out, see if someone comes closer to the camp while you folks are off wrangling."

Trace handed back his tin. "It might be those ranchers. Thorne is close enough for his boys to have gotten here. I sure the hell hope so. But be careful, you hear?"

"Ord, I thought you were ready to move out," Comstock barked, riding up on his roan.

Trace gave Preacher a nod. "Just hate to see good biscuits go to waste. Going to be a long time until the next meal."

Mae was mounted on a packhorse, the animal standing quietly next to Jared's. Her eyes met his, and fear and questions were both clear in their brown depth. It hurt, but he answered with a curt nod, then walked on past.

Any hopes Mae had of speaking with Trace alone before they broke camp were dashed the minute Jared put her on the packhorse. Comstock now rode beside her, and it was clear he expected her to stay close at all times.

Frowning, she spared a glance back toward camp. It bothered her that Preacher had remained behind. She hadn't gotten a chance to talk to him lately, either, and that worried her greatly. He was her only ally, and he could get a message to Trace even if she couldn't. She'd hate to have that line of communication entirely severed.

She spotted the Indians atop the canyon rim but moving like wraiths within the pearly haze of first light. As one might expect of wraiths, they made no sound. It was odd. She'd heard so many horrific stories about this breed who'd owned these lands before the white man came, yet she found a comfort in their presence when compared to Comstock or Slade. Maybe that wasn't so odd, now that she thought of it.

Her eyes were drawn to the far end of the canyon and two figures on horseback who seemed to be watching. They were at the wrong end of the draw to be of any use to the roundup. "Jared," she asked, "who are those men, and what are they doing over there?"

Comstock's head snapped around, and he stared at the two riders. His expression went nearly as white as his shirt. "Stay here, Mae. I mean it. Don't go anywhere else; it could be very dangerous." And with no explanation, he spurred his roan and headed off. It was a reminder that Mae understood nothing about the man or what was going on here. Gooseflesh crawled over her skin.

Staring after him, she shielded her eyes, scarcely able to believe that he'd just left her unattended. The sun was beating down, but she had the sense of a coming storm. The air was stifling, almost if it wasn't air she drew into her lungs but dry heat.

Reaching up, she swiped beads of perspiration off her brow. Scanning the skies, she saw big puffy clouds in the distance, sort of like beaten egg whites—thunder pillars, her granddad called them. Of course, sometimes these clouds moved across the sky and not a drop of rain ever fell.

Damn, but she wished the drive were over. Of course, she had no idea what would happen after. Trace seemed unhurried. Had he gotten word to the ranchers who'd hired him? Maybe they were the men on the far ridge who upset Jared so much. If they were, though, what were they waiting for? Why not move in immediately?

She glanced down, searching both the canyon rim and the gap below; the horses would soon be driven down that narrow corridor of the draw, toward the open area at the end that would be used as a pen. On the far side, she spotted Trace. Almost as if he sensed her eyes on him, he turned and looked back. The distance seemed too narrow as they stared at each other. She felt the pull, the connection that said this man was different from all others.

He turned toward the pair of riders she'd just pointed out to Jared. Did he suspect they were the ranchers he'd summoned? Did they all have some sort of scheme and were simply waiting for Jared and his men to fall into the trap, much as Jared was trying to snare those wild horses? She was furious that she had been left out of the plan.

She glanced after Jared. At the same time, he glanced back toward her. His head turned and he was clearly looking off past her, and he grimaced, but he didn't slow his horse; he simply spun back around and kept riding. As Mae turned back, she caught Trace staring off to her right as well.

Slade. That was what both men had been looking at. He sat on the ridge slightly below Mae, his black hat cockily pushed to the back of his head. He flashed Trace a big grin, then lifted his gun and touched the tip of the barrel to his forehead in a salute, which, despite the hot sun, sent a chill over Mae. Cautiously she slid her hand into the pocket of her split skirt, her fingers closing around her derringer. Its presence gave her a small comfort, just as Preacher had intended.

Her horse's head bobbed, and he gave a soft nicker. In the distance rose a dust cloud: the Indians driving the wild horses toward the canyon. The waiting was over. Finally something would happen.

As the storm of dust drew closer, the riders started firing their guns. Mae felt sorry for the horses, all of them free spirits like Diablo. In an odd sense, she had been driven just like these animals. From the instant she'd stepped off the train from Kentucky, though she hadn't recognized it, men had been herding her forward. Everything had been a trap. She had to fight the urge to descend the canyon trails before the herd and fire her derringer desperately, all in hope of turning the beasts back toward freedom.

The two riders were gone when she looked back at them. Trace was gone, too, and Jared. "Horse," Mae said quietly to her mount, "I wish Slade would go away, too. Then it'd be just us."

"And me." The voice came from the rocks nearby, so softly that she wondered if she'd imagined it. "Keep on looking straight ahead, like you was."

From the corner of her eye she searched the rocks, but she couldn't see anything. Then, as if by magic, she saw the old man.

"Preacher! You frightened me!" she accused, clutching her breast as though to keep her heart from escaping. "What are you doing here?"

"Trace seemed happy that Comstock ordered me to stay behind at the camp, but I'm a-thinking something big is going to happen. Me and my Winchester will be needed."

"Preacher, something's wrong," Mae said. "I spotted a couple riders on that far rim and called Jared's attention to them. He took off like he'd seen a ghost."

"A ghost? Might be at that. I've been trying to track them, too. Saw them on the ridge t'other day, thought it was Trace and White Eagle. Then Trace came moseying in from the opposite direction. I'm a damn fine tracker, but those two riders are being especially careful. Wasn't easy, but I followed them in this direction. That's why I'm here with you. Trace would want me to protect you."

"Could they be the ranchers who hired Trace? Did he get word to them when he went to Flat Springs? Do you know?"

Preacher didn't move. With her horse blocking him from Slade's view, he was entirely hidden from the gunman, which was what he surely wanted. "He got word to them. That's why he prodded Jared into sending him. And it's been time enough for one outfit to reach here. But them two men ain't part of Thorne's bunch. They're loners. There's only the two of them, and Thorne will come barreling in here with fifty riders or more."

"So who are they?"

"No idea, missy. Don't like it, though, can tell you that. This whole business seems to get more and more twisted. Two men watching us, Comstock watching Trace, Slade, and you . . . Slade's watching right back. That's a lot of watching! I get this odd sense that Comstock is alone and feeling it, too. He can't trust anyone, not even the men he's paying. I don't pretend to know what's going on, so I'm just watching, too. . . ."

There was no sign of the ranchers or the U.S. marshal, and Trace had given up trying to make the distant ho-

rizon give birth to them. It was too late for them anyway, at least for today. Comstock's men had already
circled the mesa and the roundup had begun.

Though the rest of the outfit was made up of green-
horns and rattlers, Trace didn't give the Indians a second
thought. They had taken their places and knew what to
do. There were no finer wild horse wranglers in the Arizona Territory than the Walapai. But danger rode on the
edge of those storm clouds. He could taste brimstone,
and he wondered what difficulties the weather would
add to what they were trying to accomplish.

He hadn't exaggerated when he spoke of Standing
Thunder's cunning. He had no doubt the horse was
well aware of their presence. The animal could pick up
his scent from clear across the canyon, and there seemed
no question that he knew right where they were, what
they wanted, and wasn't going to give up easily.

For several hours they all played hide-and-seek
among the rocks and fissures that led down from the
mesa to the canyon floor. A glimpse of tail, a flash of
mane tossed on the wind—a wayward wind that didn't
seem to have a direction, kicking up dust everywhere.
There was never a sign of the herd, only the mighty
broomtail stallion, who kept teasing them like a light-
skirt stripping for her client.

Then Trace heard it: a roar so loud and constant it
couldn't be thunder rumbling through the canyon. No,
this sound was made by horses—*hundreds* of horses,
more than they'd initially thought—swarming over
the mesa in a mighty show of force. Great clouds of
rust-colored dust obscured their pounding hooves and

rippling flanks, churned up from the parched canyon floor; the air was thick with it. Standing Thunder was in the lead.

Trace covered his nose and mouth with his bandana and signaled the others to look sharp. One by one the riders fell into line; they made up two columns, one on either side of the herd.

"Steady!" Trace shouted. "Hold them in!"

Leaning over Diablo's neck, he gave the horse its rein. Diablo's great, long-legged stride carried him well ahead of the others, down over the rocky mesa and onto a path wild horse hooves had carved over time, a path Trace had scoped out earlier. It emptied onto the canyon floor below and was a different path than the rest were taking. The narrow shortcut gave him an advantage, and he came out ahead, with Standing Thunder within striking distance of Trace's lasso.

Gunshots rang out, driving the herd faster. There were more horses than he'd anticipated: five . . . no, maybe even six hundred. Trace's nose and throat were clogged with dust, the bandana being of little help. He could scarcely see the herd for the wind-and-horse-driven cloud. Out of the corner of his eye he spied Comstock wielding his blacksnake, and the man turned in a blur, driving part of the herd ahead of him, toward Trace and in the wrong direction. What was he doing?

"Son of a bitch!" Trace raged.

He lost sight of everyone else. Though it had to be at least midafternoon, the air around him was eerily yellow, though it was becoming orange with the mix of red rock dust from below. The gunshots had grown distant, muted, drowned out by the hooves of the galloping herd. The horses' screams grew louder.

A loud crack of thunder boomed overhead, and lightning streaked the sky. Trace glanced up, then back down, horrified. Part of the herd Comstock was controlling was spooked, spinning around and crashing into each other. Some went down with cries of agony. But the rest—thousands of pounds of unstoppable horseflesh—were pounding right toward him.

Chapter Twenty-one

Mae stood up in the stirrups, staring at the steady stream of horses pouring down into the gap. She had been raised on a large working horse farm in Kentucky, but she'd never seen anything like this. She doubted if her grandfather had, either.

Her gaze moved along the canyon, though she couldn't make out any of the riders clearly, except for Trace astride Diablo, and to the rear Comstock, cracking his blacksnake. His shirt was glaringly white through the odd pink haze that rose from the canyon floor. Trace landed a rope on the most magnificent creature she had ever seen: a stallion the color of wet red rock, with the most exquisite jet-black mane and a long tail that swept the ground. It was surely Standing Thunder, the horse Trace kept talking about. She could see why. He was a true rival to Diablo in both power and sheer beauty.

From her vantage, it looked as though Trace and Standing Thunder were in the middle of the stamping herd. She assumed Trace was trying to gain control of the stallion in order to turn the horses back into the box canyon. Only, Standing Thunder struck out with sharp teeth at Diablo. The black fought back.

Trace held his seat, despite the equine combat—her grandfather would love how the man sat a horse. Mae could neither watch nor look away. Her hands over her eyes, she peeked through her fingers and watched as horses flooded past Trace, and as the sorrel stallion deliberately pushed Diablo close to the steep wall. The cloud of dust was so thick that she lost sight of Comstock; there was only the two stallions locked in a duel, and Trace directly in harm's way.

Diablo went down. Mae screamed and turned away, moaning Trace's name. Her cry wouldn't reach him, not with the rumbling of thunder from the coming storm and the deafening sound of the horses' hooves on the canyon floor, but she muttered a prayer that something would protect him.

For a terrible moment there was nothing but the rumbling pandemonium of horses in motion, the cacophony of their wild shrieks, and the desperate whistles of cowboys fighting to keep from being trampled, all echoing through the canyon and carried aloft on the wind. Mae nearly fainted as she spotted Diablo again: this time he was running neck and neck with Standing Thunder—without a rider.

Without hesitation, Mae dug her heels into the sides of the packhorse and sent it rushing down the hillside to the canyon, praying to reach Trace before it was too late.

Maybe it was already too late.

* * *

The other riders, both Indian and white, scattered as the herd poured back through the narrow channel, leaping over broken corral rails, trampling the staved-in wood. Fallen from Diablo, Trace couldn't see for all the blinding dust. He did the only thing he could—flattened himself to the canyon wall, finding a crevice where water had once flooded over the top of the cliff and cut its way through the rock face.

Trapped, pinned against a rocky fissure too small to hold his whole body, he dug his fingers and heels into loose dirt and roots, whatever he could get a grip on, in a desperate attempt to keep from being sucked back into the wave of galloping horses. They were crowding seven abreast in a space not meant to accommodate half that number, and he was continuously buffeted by the wind of them racing past. He crushed himself farther against the rocks, scarcely able to breathe for the pressure and the dust and the lack of air.

At last there was some relief. The equine flood had trampled down what remained of the makeshift corral, many streaking out through the grove of saplings and over the wash beyond. Trace sank dizzily to his knees. He still couldn't see very well, but the distant rumble of the horses' heavy hoofbeats vibrated through him. His heart sank. As if they had become one body, the wild herd were stampeding back through the canyon in a billowing cloud of dirt and then disappearing into the strange yellow twilight of the coming storm. Then they were gone, almost as if they had never existed.

Trace groaned again. He was alone. He'd lost. Again. The herd, Diablo, Standing Thunder . . . Damn, if it didn't feel as if Standing Thunder was almost thumbing his nose at him, having saved his herd and even stolen Trace's horse. When he was small, his mama had told him bedtime stories about knights of old, of the magnificent chargers these men owned, how those animals fought beside their masters and never left their side in battle. If a warrior fell, his horse would stay and watch over him.

"Guess Diablo's mama didn't tell him the same stories." Trace tried to laugh but choked on dust. "I'm beginning to take it personal."

He struggled to his feet, stiff-legged and favoring his left arm. He tried to flex his shoulder and winced. There were no broken bones. It wasn't dislocated, but the pain was excruciating. He wiggled his shoulder again, then wound his arm in cautious circles. There was a throbbing ache in the joint. He'd feel it tomorrow for sure, maybe a week or two to come, but the stabbing pain was already fading. Fortunately, it wasn't his right shoulder, the one he'd need for his gun hand; he hadn't forgotten the danger he was in.

He glanced down and noticed his pistol was missing from its holster. "Double damn." He turned in a circle, trying to find the gun, kicking at the dust, but nothing. No telling when he'd lost it.

A prickly warning crawled over his skin, the survival sense that had saved him from death more than once. It warned him everything was out of control, that the trouble with the horses was merely a start. He turned just in time to see a whip unfurling toward him. His left arm burned as that lash coiled around it, and with a jerk, he was twisted around and nearly off his feet.

Despite the pain searing through his brain, Trace's right hand reached out and caught hold of the braided leather and didn't let go. Comstock gave a grunt of surprise. At the same moment, Trace gave a hard tug that was strong enough to drag Jared off his roan. But instead of falling to the ground, Comstock launched himself forward. Both men landed hard in the powdery dust, rolling around in the midst of the straggling horses still trying to escape the corral.

Trace planted a punch in Comstock's belly, and air left the man's lungs in a grunt. Good! He owed the bastard for beating Diablo. The second blow Trace struck was to that pretty face. It was for Mae. But another spate of horses came galloping through, rushing to catch up to the rest of the herd, and that ended his assault. Trace and Comstock were forced to roll apart to escape their deadly hooves, one of which barely missed coming down on Trace's head.

Comstock took the moment to right himself, and he was on his feet a shade faster than Trace. In a blink, he'd drawn his gun, but Trace kicked it out of his hand. Jared's hand went to his thigh, coming up with his bowie knife. Trace froze, considered his options. His gun was lost. His knife was strapped to his saddle, long gone with Diablo. The only weapons he had were his guile and wits.

A smile spread over Jared Comstock's face. "Not such a big mouth on you now, eh, Ord?" He kept the knife held out before him while he moved to pick up his gun.

There came the sound of pounding hooves, this time coming from outside the canyon. Trace's heart fell as he saw Mae rushing toward him. Brave, foolish Mae. He loved her, but he wished her a thousand miles away.

She reined up when she saw the gun trained on Trace. She raised a derringer and pointed it at Jared's chest. "You know, I've always hated your white shirts—you're a pretty boy who never lifts a finger to work, just lets everyone else get dirty for you. My granddaddy always said never to trust a man who thinks he's too good to get dirty. It'd be a real shame to stain it red, wouldn't it, Jared?"

The muscles in Jared's jaw twitched, and his eyes shifted to Trace. "If you so much as twitch, I'll shoot you where you stand."

"You're not going to shoot Trace," Mae insisted, "because I will kill you if you do, Jared. And you don't want to die. Plain and simple."

Comstock spared her a brief glance. "I never trusted your story that he was coming back with you. I've seen you watching him when you didn't know I was looking. I know your feelings . . . But it makes no never mind. I'm your *husband*. You won't shoot me. You won't shoot your husband."

Mae's eyes flashed with fury. "Calling my bluff, are you? You were never my husband. Don't think I'm so stupid. I found out about your little deception."

Astonishment lit his face. "How? When . . . ?"

"That's moot now, though I'd love to know what you were thinking. Put down the gun." When he refused to obey, she snapped. "Drop it!"

He shook his head. "I think I will shoot Trace, let you watch him d—"

In a quick movement she fired one shot. The bullet

struck the rock beside Jared's head. "I warned you," she said. "The next one goes right into that black heart. I swear it, Jared."

Comstock's expression changed. His facial muscles seemed to sag, and his eyes showed true defeat. "So be it, Mae. You win." Jared's hand started to lower the gun.

It was then Mae made her mistake. In that heartbeat, everything moved too slow and everything moved too fast. She risked a look to see if Trace was unhurt. Another horse clattered down the rocky canyon and came around the bend. Mae's packhorse shied and began to dance sideways, even gave a small buck. She had to fight to stay in the saddle. Which was time for Jared to lift his Colt.

Trace felt the breath of death blow across him. He looked down that blue steel barrel, saw Jared's finger squeeze the trigger. He flung himself to the side. Two shots rang out.

He landed on his shoulder. His teeth ground together as blinding pain transfixed him, and for an instant he thought Jared's bullet had struck home. Then realization sank in that he'd landed on his injured left arm; Jared's shot had gone wild. Trace blinked away the stars before opening his eyes. Comstock stood frozen, a red stain spreading across his shirt, just as Mae had warned. The man's surprise was clear, and he stared mutely down at the vivid scarlet spreading across the white cotton. Then his knees buckled and he went down.

Trace glanced around. It wasn't smoke from Mae's derringer he saw; it was from Slade's gun. Slade had shot Jared!

Not hesitating, the gunslinger rode over and knocked Mae's gun from her hand, then wrapped an arm about her waist. He dragged her off the packhorse and across his lap. When she struggled, looking as though she was ready to scratch his eyes out, he growled, "Don't. I'll kill Trace."

His warning stopped her cold. Mae's head snapped around and she stared at Trace, reassuring herself that he hadn't already been killed.

Trace tried to keep calm. This whole damn day had seemed to go from bad to worse. "You won't be collecting your pay, Slade. Shooting the boss closes up the bank." It was an inane thing to say, but he was fighting pain that was making him dizzy and struggling just to stay on his feet. Where was White Eagle? He wished now that he'd told Preacher to tag along. The old man had warned him that he'd need that Winchester at his back someday.

"Never figured on a payday from Comstock." The gunslinger shrugged and turned his gun so that the barrel was under Mae's jaw. "It's your left that's injured?" he asked Trace.

It took every ounce of willpower to remain composed. Trace gave a slow nod.

"So your gun hand is fine?" Slade grinned.

Trace coldly returned the expression. "Hand me a gun and I'll be happy to show you."

Slade laughed. "I think I'll leave you to find your own gun. It's still too busy down here in the canyon. I prefer a place where the dust don't choke you or sting your eyes." Lightning arced overhead, streaked along the canyon rim, and caused Slade's horse to dance on its hooves. "Catch me when you can. I won't harm her. Might upset some people if I do. But if you want her back, you'll have to earn her freedom. Don't take too long or you'll never see her again."

With that, the gunslinger dug the spurs into his horse and galloped away.

Chapter Twenty-two

Trace leaned over and scooped up Mae's derringer before walking to the rancher lying prostrate on the canyon floor. Comstock was still alive, but he wouldn't last much longer. A mix of emotions milled inside Trace. He knew he should hate Jared, had wished more than once that he could kill him. He had wanted to take his whip to the man for what he'd done to Diablo, to do worse for what Jared had put Mae through. Yet his anger diminished as he watched the dying man's labored breathing. His rage drained away like Comstock's blood from his body.

Upon reflection, Jared could have been a lot rougher in his handling of Mae. He had, for whatever reason, failed to rape her. The man had permitted her to keep him at arm's length. Trace wondered if that was a spark of good in him, or if there was more to the story. Maybe a bit of both? Jared Comstock had done a lot of wrong in his life—killed at least one man Trace knew about, maybe others—yet there was no longer any need to balance the books. The man was going to die.

Still, it ticked Trace when, using his remaining

strength, Jared lifted his arm to point his revolver at him. The hand holding it shook.

Trace reached over and jerked the gun out of the man's fingers. There was hardly any resistance. He had the derringer, but that was only good for a short distance. He needed a Colt to go after Slade.

"Mae . . ." The name came out with a gurgle of Jared's blood.

Trace nodded. "I'm going after her. I'll get her back."

"Protect . . . her." Jared's eyes were starting to get a glassy look, and he fought to get the words out. "I know what . . . you think . . . of . . . me, Ord. But I . . . never . . . hurt her."

"You have my word on it, I will protect her. I'll see her back to that farm in Kentucky where she belongs." Trace swallowed back the urge to tell the dying man he'd be taking Mae to wife. The taunt tasted bitter in his mouth. A bizarre sensation, something along the lines of what a priest must feel when he promises forgiveness during last rites, was washing over him.

"Save . . . her from . . . him." Comstock's hand dropped to the dusty ground.

How odd. He was swearing to Jared to protect Mae after all that the man had done himself to her. "I'll kill Slade," he vowed. "Don't you worry about her."

Instead of the words giving Comstock comfort, the rancher suddenly struggled upright, fighting to grab Trace's pant leg to raise himself up. "No! Not *Slade*. . . ." The hand fisted in a spasm on the material, then slowly released, and with a raspy sigh Jared Comstock fell back and gave his last breath.

Trace grimaced. There wasn't much he could do for

the dead man. He obviously couldn't take the time to bury him, but, looking around, he grabbed the man's arm and dragged him a few steps into a crevice. Rolling the body inside, he pulled up some shrubs and collected others dislodged by the passing horses, and he covered Jared the best he could. Perhaps he'd run into some of the Lazy C drovers and send them back to bury their boss.

Opening the cylinder of Jared's Colt, he checked to see how many bullets were chambered. Two were missing. He replaced those, then spun the cylinder and tested the gun's weight and balance. Shoving the revolver into his holster, he drew it and then repeated the processes several times to get used to the feel of the gun. Facing Slade would call for every advantage. Using an unfamiliar weapon would be no help whatsoever.

Looking around, he muttered, "Now I walk." Maybe his luck would turn and he'd find a mount.

It didn't. On foot, the long coulee seemed three times the original distance, especially while lightning kept flashing overhead. He'd seen storms like this one, thunder and lightning, people holding their breath and praying for rain yet nary a drop would fall. Other times the skies opened and it poured like there was no tomorrow—you'd almost expect Jonah and the whale to come floating by! These flash floods could catch a man in the wrong spot, drown him in a river where none had existed moments before: The earth was hard-baked by the blistering sun, and the rain didn't soak it; the water just ran off like it was spilling across stone. Eyeing the high, sheer walls, noting especially the gouges cut through the stone from just such runoffs, Trace hoped this storm was the former. He didn't need to deal with a torrential downpour either killing him or washing away Slade's tracks.

Hearing the sound of hooves echoing against the canyon walls, Trace pulled the Colt and stepped into one of the rain-formed hollows. He held his breath until the horse came round the bend, but then Trace's mouth spread into a grin. Maybe his chain of bad luck was finally broken.

He stepped into plain sight and let out a shrill whistle. Diablo's head jerked up, ears pricking as he saw Trace. The silly horse nickered lowly and then pranced forward, going straight to Trace. Reaching out, he snagged the reins as he spoke to the animal, running his hand over him. "I guess you might have the blood of one of those ancient warhorses after all. I figured you'd stolen a gaggle of Standing Thunder's mares and were halfway to California by now."

Trace took a moment to check the stallion over, to assure himself the horse's legs were fine. There were couple of bite marks in his neck that would require care, but otherwise the animal's run-in with the sorrel reflected no permanent damage. Trace adjusted the cinch on the saddle and then swung himself up on the horse's back.

"Come, boy," he said. "We've got to get my wife back."

As Trace crested the ridge, a smile crossed his lips. His luck had truly turned. In front of him were Preacher and his Winchester. "Yeah, sometimes it's good to have someone watching your back, Diablo," he said, patting the horse's withers.

Keeping out of sight, his friend was pressed up against an odd stand of red rock that the Indians called Old Man Watching, which struck Trace as humorously apt. Dismounting, he led Diablo far to the right flank, using the high rock as a shield so no one could see him approach. Preacher clearly was hiding from someone.

The old man gave him a grin as he tied Diablo to a shrub. "Well, if that don't beat all," Preacher said. "Saw him runnin' riderless. . . . Figured that black would be long gone, that you'd never see him again. Where'd you find him?"

"I didn't. He found me. Came prancing down the canyon just as fancy as a show horse. Don't tell him, but I was damn glad to see him." He inched past, to the edge of the rock around which Preacher had been peering. "Since you're hiding here, I assume Slade's up there?"

"Sure as hell is—with your gal, too. She looked like she would spit in his eye. That woman's got spunk." He gave a chuckle. "Of course, takes a special breed of filly to fall for a man who shoots her, eh?"

Trace studied the land, seeking out any advantages. "Where did you come from? I thought you were staying behind in camp."

Preacher reached up and rubbed the back of his neck. "Comstock and you thought that. I had different ideas. You weren't gone long before I got to thinking what I told you earlier: it never hurts to have a gun at your back. One *covering* it, not pointed at it, mind. I sneaked up here, Injun-style, keeping to the rocks.

Stayed close to your Mae. Figured you'd appreciate me keeping an eye on her. Of course, then she run off—"

"Slade see you?" Trace interrupted.

The old-timer shook his head. "Nope, just Mae. Comstock left her up here when he went down to handle the horses. Slade didn't go, even after he was ordered. He sat on his sorrel over there by the bluff, where he could keep one eye on the drive and t'other on Mae. I don't get it. Mighty contrary, if'n you ask me. Gunslingers are an arrogant lot, but they usually listen to the folks who pay them."

"There's a lot I don't get about this crew," Trace agreed.

"Where's Comstock?"

Trace's answer was short. "Dead."

"You kill him? You said you would," Preacher admitted.

Trace shook his head, still troubled by what had happened. "Slade took the honor. Jared would have killed me, but Slade shot him first. He saved my life. Then, with his dying breath, Jared was asking me to save Mae. From Slade." But that wasn't quite right. Not Slade . . .

Preacher squinted, his forehead wrinkling. "Wonder why he did a fool thing like that. Mae saw you go down in the stampede and lit out like the devil gave her spurs. Slade was a bit more careful going down that rocky path. Damn puzzler if'n you ask me. He killed Comstock but left you alive. Why?"

"Professional courtesy, maybe."

The old man's head pulled back slightly. "He wants a showdown, to see which one of you is the fastest? So what do you want me to do?"

Trace didn't like how little influence he had in these events, but it seemed ever since he'd shot Mae while she was stealing Diablo, his whole life had spun out of control. With a sinking heart he tried to think of some way to take charge and dictate events to Slade, not the other way around, but as long as the gunslinger held Mae, Trace could only follow his lead.

"Do you know where White Eagle or his men are?"

"Last I saw, they were hot on the trail of Standing Thunder."

Trace frowned. There'd be no help from his friends. "Slade expects me to head straight for him," he said to Preacher.

"He's got Mae stuffed under that small ledge," the old man replied. "It's not quite a cave, as you will see."

"I'm going out, and will demand we meet on that level spit of land. You flank around to the right and see if you can get to Mae when he agrees."

Preacher shook his head. "You're taking a big risk there, partner. You look worse for the wear after dancing the two-step with them mustangs."

Trace dusted red powder off himself. "I am that, but I want Mae safe. Something just ain't right about all of this. When Comstock was dying, he was begging me to save Mae . . . but not from Slade."

Preacher scratched the side of his face. "Huh? Just who are you supposed to be saving her from? Maybe Comstock wasn't quite right in his right head. He was shot and all."

Trace doubted it. "No, he knew what he was saying. Just didn't live long enough to say what he needed."

"Trace, I seen them two riders again, hanging off in

the distance. They don't come any closer, but they sure are sticking with us."

Turning, Trace scanned the far horizon, searching for anything that moved. Lightning flashed overhead. "This situation is mighty peculiar," he said one last time. "Has been from the start. I don't have time to unravel the whys, but I have a feeling the answers will come calling shortly."

A bolt of lightning struck close by, sparking off the rocks higher up. Trace determined to get Mae away from Slade before the storm broke. He didn't want to risk the skies breaking open and Slade stealing away in the deluge.

"You circle around to the right. I'll give you time to get up there, and then I'll draw Slade out, demand we face each other on that flat spit. I'll get him turned around; you see if you can slip Mae away."

"And then what?" Preacher asked.

"Get her out of here. Put her on Diablo and you take Slade's horse. Ride. Don't look back. Don't stop until she's on a train to Kentucky." Trace gave him a nod. "If I'm lucky, I'll catch up."

Preacher laughed. "That sounds high and noble, you sacrificing yourself to save the woman you love, but you ain't taking that little gal into account. She ain't going to hop on any horse and ride off and leave you—I'd bet my back teeth on that."

Knowing the old man was right, Trace laughed. "Okay, how about this? You keep Mae out of the way so I don't worry about her becoming a tool for Slade to use against me. If he kills me, you kill him. Don't be honorable. Back-shoot him if you have to."

"Now, that might work—except the part where you get yourself killed. I don't cotton to that. Doubt Mae will, neither. I'd prefer to see you again."

Trace paused, wanting to tell Preacher how much he appreciated everything the old-timer had done to help him since their paths crossed. He'd been helping all the way and never once asked anything for himself.

Preacher seemed to sense his gratitude. "No need for words, Trace. Let's go fetch that woman of yours."

Lightning splintered into bony fingers crawling across the rim of the canyon. Trace knew they couldn't wait any longer, as the dark clouds were already making the afternoon into twilight, but he forced himself to give Preacher time to reach the upper edge. Once he saw the old man in place, he leaned low and used a dip in the land to race to the other side of the small plateau. He held still there, hiding against a small outcrop while he got his wind back. Finally he straightened and stalked toward up toward Slade.

Seeing a large boulder, he made a dash for it, knowing he was in the gunslinger's view the whole way. "Let her go, Slade!" he called once he reached cover. "You're not one to hide behind a woman's skirts."

"You're right, I'm not," the gunman called back. "But I wasn't going to let Comstock make off with her. I was here to prevent him from doing just that. I knew he'd make a run at her if the need arose—she was his ace in the whole. I just bided my time until he made his move."

Trace stilled. He still didn't understand what was going on here. "Let her go. Then we can get down to what you want."

Mae stepped tentatively out from the deep impression in the rocky cliff, her eyes wide with worry and fear. Slade, his left hand on her throat, was right behind. Since the gunman was only of medium height, there wasn't much left unshielded—precisely what Slade was counting on.

"Let her go. Then we can talk," Trace repeated. He knew it was useless, but like the damn roundup he was locked into going through the motions.

"Talk? There's nothing to talk about. There's only one thing I want from you."

Trace laughed. "Somehow I figured out that much. The woman's in the way. Let her go, and we can finally answer your question of who's the faster gun."

"So, how do you want to accomplish it? I send her away and you shoot me. My mama didn't raise me to be no stupid cowpuncher." Slade laughed.

His words made sense. Slade wasn't going to shoot him while hiding behind Mae; he could have killed him unarmed while they were still in the canyon. The gunslinger wanted one thing, and one thing only: to face Trace and settle the question burning through his brain.

"What do you suggest?" Trace called.

"How about I send her away and keep my gun trained on her?" Slade replied. "You come out and face me. I'll have my gun on her the whole time. If you shoot me, I *will* still shoot her, so you better not take the coward's way out. Face me. You have to be as curious as I am who's the quicker hand. Besides, you owe me. I could have let Comstock kill you, but then we'd never have known the truth."

Lightning tore across the sky, struck the ground a short ways off in the distance. Out in the open like this, they were targets of its wrath.

Trace raised two fingers in salute. "Send the woman away and let's get this done. That storm's almost upon us. How about we start walking and meet on that flat spot in the rock?"

"Deal!" Slade gave Mae a push, yet kept his pistol trained on her just as he'd warned.

Matching the gunman's stride, Trace headed out to the point halfway between them. As they reached the flat outcropping, they stopped and appraised each other. Trace shifted to Slade's left, so the gunman would have a harder time keeping his eye on Mae.

"So how do we do this?" he called, stalling, watching Mae edge backward. Lightning crackled once again, followed by an earthshaking boom. An idea occurred: "How about we let the lightning make the call? The next strike and we draw."

The corner of Slade's mouth quirked upward. "Agreed."

A gust of wind swept up the hillside, the smell of rain pushed before it. Trace wanted to look at Mae, didn't want to die without seeing her beautiful face again. Yet he dared not take his eyes off his opponent. Slade was too damn fast.

Old-timers said life passed by your eyes at times like this. Not so for Trace. He saw Mae's beautiful face, almost saw her horse farm in Kentucky and the life they would have together if he just survived this next moment.

Slade was all focus. His eyes burned holes in Trace. His fingers at his side wiggled faintly, keeping them lose and ready to draw. By his expression, he could already taste victory. Then, in that heartbeat, a jagged streak of lightning rose from the ground, traveling skyward, so close that Trace felt the hairs rise on the back of his neck.

Trace's gun left its holster in a fluid motion, fired without thought but instinct. And a prayer. Slade himself moved so fast that Trace barely saw the gun clearing leather. For a long moment they stood frozen in this strange shard of time, not breathing, neither moving; then Michael Slade looked down at the front of his shirt. He brushed the fingers of his left hand across the black fabric and then pulled them back, stared at the red staining his hand. Blood. His expression seemed puzzled. Then his legs folded up.

Trace moved cautiously toward the kneeling man. He was smart enough to know a wounded animal was dangerous, and the gun was still clutched in Slade's right hand. But then, without letting go, the gunman tilted sideways and fell to the ground.

He heard Mae cry out but he didn't trust Slade. Cocking the hammer of his Colt, Trace moved to the fallen gunman's side. Unlike Comstock, Slade didn't raise his pistol. Trace's aim had been true. Up close, he could see a small hole that was dead center in the man's chest. Slade wouldn't last but a few more heartbeats.

"I was . . . fast," he said, with an odd expression.

Trace nodded. "Yes," was all he could think to say.

"Trace Ord . . ." Slade closed his eyes.

"I'm here."

"Protect . . . her . . ." Whatever else Slade intended to say, it died on his lips.

Trace looked up to see Mae running toward him, Preacher on her heels. She practically jumped into his arms, knocking him backward. He was forced to retreat a step to keep from going down with her. He spoke her name in a hoarse whisper, his hand reaching to comb through her hair, and he kissed away the tears streaking down her cheeks.

She pulled free, her fingers flitting over the contours of his face as if she scarcely believed he was alive. She had to be sure.

"I . . . I saw you go down," she murmured. "The horses . . . I saw them trample you. Then Jared was going to kill you. Now this 'I'm the fastest gun around these parts' nonsense. Trace Ord, if you ever—!"

"Hush, Mae." He laughed. "This is one hell of a way to conduct a courtship. I shoot you and then end up nearly getting killed by one bastard after another, each with the dying request that I protect you. I think *I'm* the one who needs protecting."

"Hush? Don't you dare tell me to—"

"Just hush so I can say what I need to. Marry me, Mae." Maybe it wasn't the proposal women dreamed of, but she didn't seem to object. Mae Ahern gasped, and her reply seemed lodged in her throat. She did manage to nod.

Preacher just laughed.

Chapter Twenty-three

Mae wiggled her toes in the water, giddy with excitement. Married. She had stood next to Trace and said the words, "I do," all in front of a preacher. A *real* preacher. The preacher of Timber Junction, the biggest town in the area. She had thought it would never happen, what with the events of the last few days. They'd met up with the U.S. marshal and the northern ranchers who'd hired Trace, and they'd straightened out the entire situation with the rustling. They'd taken Comstock's men in for questioning—those they could find. Of course, justice had been served earlier. Jared and Michael Slade, the leaders of the group, were already dead.

Trace had spoken to White Eagle, too. The Walapai had managed to round up a number of horses despite the storm, although Standing Thunder of course eluded them. Trace, Preacher, and the Indian leader had all spoken at great length about the stallion, and Mae realized how they all coveted the beast. She'd had a moment of terror that they would go out after the horse once more. But then they'd spoken about something else—a woman. White Eagle's daughter? Preacher had said the girl just needed a firm hand, and Trace had nodded. White Eagle had looked sad. That had been the end of it.

A firm hand. That's what Trace had provided for Mae. He'd brought her right back here to be wed, dispelling all her fears about him putting the horses first. He'd seemed to have only one thing on his mind: making her an honest woman. Her heart fluttered at the memory, and her body tingled. Afterward, he'd ordered a bath for her and gone off to check on the horses and make sure all was in readiness for transport of Diablo and Duchess and themselves on the train back East. They were going home to Grandfather, he'd said. He wouldn't have her endangered one more moment in the West.

It wasn't a full bathtub but a half bath, hardly more than an elongated washtub. Still, she was delighted with such luxury after being on the trail. And Trace was right: it did ease the pain of having had him in her body.

She knew she should blush at that image, but she didn't. She couldn't. Such thoughts only provoked a deep warmth inside her, a need to take him into her again and again. As a young girl she'd seen stallions mounting mares, a cumbersome process that always seemed over before it started. Thus, she wasn't totally unaware of what would happen. She felt sorry for those poor mares now, for the act between humans in love was nothing like the mating of animals. Oh, there were animalistic impulses—she blushed and wondered if the sounds she'd made had carried through the hotel walls.

And he'd been so worried about hurting her, but the pain had been exquisitely brief. Then she was part of him. The love had woven around them and made it more. So much more.

The water was still warm, the fluffy lather gliding over her wet skin. The sponge fell from her hand and drifted to the side of the tub. Totally relaxed for the first time since she left Kentucky, her arms floating at her sides, she let the warmth lull her to sleep in a gently lapping womb of lavender and rosewater.

Vaguely she grew aware of the pins being pulled from her hair. As the third was tugged free and her long tresses fell loose, she seized the sides of the tub and attempted to sit upright. Water sloshed onto the floor. Strong hands held her back.

A familiar voice softly crooned, "Shhhhh. From the first moment I clapped eyes upon you, I knew it would come to this."

She laughed. Trace was on his knees at the side of the tub. "Silly man," she said. "The first moment you saw me, you thought I was a man—a horse thief—and you shot me."

"True. So, maybe the second?" he teased, unbuttoning his shirt and rolling his sleeves above his elbows. When she didn't comment, he added, "Surely the third."

Her brows lifted in challenge, as she drank in this handsome man who was now her husband. He was clean shaven and dressed in black breeches and a white shirt. No longer a renegade rider, he might be a captain of a pirate ship—no, a privateer, for her husband would always be on the right side of the law. While his hair was still long, he'd had several inches trimmed away.

The rest was now pushed back, dark waves curling about his earlobes and two locks falling rakishly over his forehead.

Sunlight streaming through the thin lacy curtains defined the angles and planes of his bronzed face, played wickedly about the sensual shape of his lips and deepened the shadowy hint of a cleft in his strong chin. No doubt about it, she'd cut out the prize stallion from the herd in claiming Trace Ord as her mate. No, that wasn't right—Trevor Guilliard. Still, he would always be Trace to her. But she was Mrs. Trevor Guilliard. That would take some getting used to, just as it would take a little getting used to, being a wife.

That thought brought another smile to her lips. She had a lifetime to get used to it.

Trace took up the sponge and soaped it, moving it up her arm and onto her shoulder in slow circles. It seemed wicked, that she should allow a man to do these things to her. That would take getting used to as well.

His sleeves were rolled back to the biceps, exposing the hard rippling muscles that clenched as he continued to soap her. The shirt gaped open in front, giving her a glimpse of the hair pointing arrow-straight downward to disappear into the waistband of his breeches, and Mae swallowed, hunger constricting her throat. Last night when they had made love—their wedding night—it had been in the shadows and silver moonbeams filtering into their room. This was in the brilliant light of morning.

She gasped as the sponge reached her breasts, and then she writhed as he allowed the suds to trickle over nipples. The scented water was silken, his touch as light as air. Though his fingers trembled as they grazed those hard, tawny buds, he played them as a skilled musician plays his instrument, with reverence and adoration.

It was bewitching and frightening all at once to stare into his eyes, to see the passion rise in them. That expression took her breath away. Set her heart to pounding. Oh, how handsome he was! Yes, his was a handsome face, but ruggedly handsome, all angles and planes—the kind of face an artist would love to paint, she admitted to herself. She'd ask Trace to sit for a painting for her birthday present next spring. So easily she imagined that portrait hanging on a wall at Foxtail Hall.

When his hand slipped beneath the water and settled upon the V between her thighs, Mae's breath caught in her throat. Slowly at first, with the lightest touch, he began to stroke her there, probing beneath the curls to the sensitive flesh beneath. She leaned into those fingers that spread shock waves of drenching fire through her loins, and the delicious sensation radiated outward over her belly and thighs, like ripples in a quiet pond when a skimmed stone breaks the surface of still water.

Trace took her lips in a smoldering kiss, all while his fingers deftly stroked her sex—faster, deeper—causing sensations to rush at her very core until she arched her spine into the friction causing the ecstasy and groaned as release washed over her like waves of liquid fire. It was then, while she was in the throes of deep contractions, that his fingers first slipped inside her, first one and then another, gliding on the silk of her inner wetness.

She wanted to tell him how much she loved him, yet she couldn't bring herself to speak the words, not when his hands were roaming her body, not while his lips were tugging at her nipples. Dizzy, she clung to him as he lifted her out of the water and scooped her up in his arms to carry her to the bed. The feather mattress and counterpane were cool against her damp skin as he laid her down. Not used to a man looking at her nude, she started to reach for the blanket.

Trace caught her wrist. "No, don't," he said, yanking off his boots. "I want to see you bathed in sunlight. I want to make love to you and see those beautiful brown eyes as I am inside you."

Mae lay still, watching while he stripped off his wet shirt and breeches. He was aroused, and the sight of him took her breath away. He was perfectly formed and strongly made, from his broad shoulders to his well-turned, corded thighs. Her wild stallion. Mae's fingers itched to touch him. It was scandalous to feel this way; it had to be. But the minute he climbed in beside her, she reached to stroke his strong back, followed the curve of his spine to that narrow waist and firm buttocks.

His hands roaming her body brought her to the brink of ecstasy again. His fiery kiss, blazing a searing trail from the base of her throat to the hardened buds of her nipples, seemed to set her very soul ablaze. She was malleable in his hands, and everywhere he touched, every line and curve of her body throbbed with an inner fire. Her very bones were melting.

Trace crushed her close, his strong arms molding their bodies together. Easing himself between her legs, he guided them around his waist, lifting the rounds of her buttocks as he penetrated her in one, long perfect thrust like a sword into its scabbard. Mae moved to his rhythm, taking him deeper as he plunged and swayed and undulated atop her. All the while, his hooded gaze was riveted to her face, his dark eyes catching glints from the sun's rays. Mae couldn't keep her hands from riding up and down his spine, from greedily gripping his buttocks as he filled her.

All at once he rolled over, taking her with him. He was on his back now; she straddled him, her long hair teasing his thighs as she matched his pistoning thrusts.

"Ride me," he whispered harshly. "My renegade rider."

His eyes still devoured her. She met his gaze as he cupped her breasts, crushing her tender, hardened nipples against the thick, rough cushion of his palms until she feared she would faint for the firestorm of sensation.

Trace pulled her forward until his lips closed around one turgid bud, laving it with his tongue. The tug resonated to her very core, triggering a release that all but drained her sense, and he gripped her waist and took her deeper still, riding her wetness, raising her up and down, his rapid thrusts hammering into her until he groaned and held her down upon his hard shaft as his climax pumped him dry. Mae felt the pulse of him, the very beat of his life force inside her as his seed spilled forth. Her hands splayed out over his taut, heaving chest, felt the pounding of his heart, which shuddered against her soft skin so violently she feared it would burst from his chest. His breath short, he rolled her onto her side and gathered her to him.

Nothing mattered but those arms, those searching lips, the anxious pressure of his manhood within her. He didn't speak except to say her name, again and again, against her lips, against her hair, against her breast. The murmur spoken so reverently, like a prayer—a litany of his love—thrilled her to the core.

Vertigo starred her vision. He was hard again, already? They had not separated. Her breath caught. Her heart, hammering against his heaving chest, seemed about to explode as he began to thrust inside her again, his groan resonating through her body. How he filled her. How perfectly they fit together. How easily she moved to the rhythm of his love.

Shifting until he was over her, he raised her hips with his massive hands and she wrapped her legs around his waist, taking him deeper still, undulating in a way that made him cry out in pleasure. Moments later he shuddered to a second pulsating climax inside her. The sound ran her through like a javelin, and waves of icy fire coursed through her loins, her belly, and her thighs, and she followed him into ecstasy.

Again and again he took her, each coupling a nourishment of their passion. It was like mating with a lightning bolt that struck again and again, never needing to recharge. Time didn't exist—nothing did but the rapture of his embrace.

Mae's body still throbbed to his pulse long after they lay sated in each other's arms. Her head rested on Trace's chest. The heart beneath her ear had slowed to a steady thudding rhythm; his breathing was deep and contented. He imparted gentle caresses, sliding his hand along her arm.

She wanted him. She had always wanted him. Would never stop wanting him.

* * *

Trace shifted up in bed, pulling the covers around his hips, not sure Mae was yet fully used to seeing him in the altogether. One day she would be, but he would allow her to reach that point on her own. Theirs had hardly been a romance of courtship, hearts, and flowers. There would be plenty of days for her to lose her shyness. And lose it she would. Mae had grit. She had battled lying men seeking to use her and kept her head.

But she'd lost her heart. He smiled at that thought. Mae. His woman. His wife.

He leaned over and placed a kiss on her bare shoulder, which was still healing—he'd been as careful as he could while they made love. His body clenched in desire, but also in pain at the thought of having shot her. Her body would forevermore bear the scar of their first meeting.

She'd seen the look of pain in his eyes as he'd bathed her, and joked about what grand tales they'd have to tell their children and grandchildren about how they'd met. True to her dauntless spirit, Mae had laughed it off. For him, it wasn't so easy. He loved her. God, how he loved her. He wanted to cherish and protect her like one of those knights of old his mother had told him about; she was his lady and he would die to defend her.

With Comstock and Slade dead, he should feel some measure of peace. But he was too much a renegade rider, ever mindful of danger lurking around the next bend, behind the far boulder; he simply couldn't shake the feeling this nightmare wasn't behind them quite yet. Silly. There was no one left to pose a threat to their happiness. Even so, he chafed that they had to wait for the train traveling east. Perhaps it was how close he had come to dying and losing her, but he wouldn't draw a full, peaceful breath until their horses were loaded and they were miles down the track, heading back East. Hell, he wouldn't let down his guard until they crossed the wide Mississippi and spotted the bluegrass of Kentucky.

No matter how he told himself that this episode of their life was done, something didn't fit, and no matter how he tried to explain it away, the dying words of those two men haunted and mocked him. Oh, he might assume they regretted their deeds and simply wanted to know the object of their lust and perhaps twisted affection was safe, and in some ways he could accept that. Only, Jared hadn't been warning him against Slade. So, who? And Slade saying something similar . . . Oh, he would like to dismiss them both, but he had a deep sense he would regret it if he did. Business unfinished loomed dark on the horizon, but damned if he knew what it was.

Mae was sleeping deeply, half on her stomach, her face buried against her pillow. He kissed her again, but lightly, not wanting to awaken her. His darling wife was exhausted from their lovemaking. His blood surged hot, possessive, but there was too much to do before they got on the train and left all of this behind.

Reaching for his pants, he slid quietly out of bed. He wanted to go check on the horses and Preacher, make sure they would be ready to board the train the instant they could. It would seem odd to leave the West after being out here for so many years, and in going back he would have to face the ghost of young Trevor Guilliard, the man who grew too old before his time. And yet he couldn't wait to get packed up and gone. He would have the long ride back to Kentucky to come to grips with everything he'd fled after the war. Right now, he simply wanted Mae safely away from here.

The desk clerk was already on duty as Trace came downstairs. The balding man gave a smile and said, "Good morning, Mr. Ord. I trust you and the missus rested well? Anything you'll be needing before breakfast?"

"Thank you, we did rest well." It was a white lie, and Trace felt a blush tinge his cheeks. "I'm heading over to check on the livestock. My black hasn't been housed in a stable before. Not sure how he'll take to the confines of a boxcar."

The clerk just nodded and smiled.

Trace strode outside and across the dusty street, his eyes moving restlessly. The morning was clear, the harsh western sun already bright. His destination the livery, he might appear a man on a casual stroll, but he couldn't rid himself of the feeling that eyes watched his every move. Trouble seemed to lurk around the very next corner.

"I'll be damn glad when we're out of here," he said under his breath, trying to calm his jangling nerves.

Everything about the changes in his life still felt odd, almost unreal. He'd never expected to marry, never considered he could fall in love. So much of his young soul had died in the war and the horrible aftermath, that part of a man who wanted a wife, a home, children. Long ago he had given up his dreams. But Mae had given them back to him. He was married and going back to a real life.

Preacher was already awake, rubbing down Diablo

with straw. He glanced up and said, "This black of yours is antsy, like the devil knows you plan to shove his hiney in a boxcar for a *loooong* ride."

Trace gave the old-timer an easy smile. "Now, don't you go putting grumpy ideas in his head. I'm taking him back to a life of luxury. He'll get to sleep in a barn that's better than any house you or I have lived in for more years than I care to count, will have a green pasture to eat his fill of grass the likes of which he's never seen, and a whole bevy of Kentucky belles just waiting to make his close acquaintance." He reached out and ran his hand down the stallion's neck. "Yes, you spawn of Satan, you're going to think I took you to heaven."

Preacher's hand dropped from his currying. "Trace?" Unease was written clear on his face.

"What is it, old-timer?" Trace reached into his shirt pocket for the sugar cubes he'd taken from the hotel dining room. He put two on his palm, which he held out flat, and let the stallion's velvety muzzle find them.

With a sigh, Preacher rubbed the back of his neck. "I know Slade is dead. Saw it with my own eyes. And you said Jared is dead, that you got one of his hands to go back and bury him. But something you said to Mae got me thinking, and I'd just as soon get shed of it. It was about those two men asking for protection for Mae. I might see Jared saying protect her from Slade. The part I don't get is, who was Slade warning you about? He said—"

"I know what he said. I was there," Trace snapped. He wasn't upset at Preacher, but the sourdough's misgivings echoed his own—which magnified his recent discomfort.

The old-timer made a sour face. "Sorry, don't mean to gnaw on your nerves, but . . . who, Trace? Who did Slade mean? He told you to *protect* her, not to take care of her. He was warning you against someone. Only, everyone who's a threat to her is dead. Right? It don't make no sense to me. I thought about keeping my trap shut, but I've got me one of those queer itches on my scalp like a red man is thinking it'd look mighty fine hanging in his lodge. We don't ignore those feelings, Trace. No matter how much we'd like to. That's why you and I are still alive."

"I'm not ignoring them," Trace growled. "I just don't have any answers for you." He put his hands on his hips and threw his head back, staring up at the barn's loft. "I go in circles until I get plum loco."

A train whistle blew, alerting the whole town that a locomotive was arriving in Timber Junction. Both Preacher and Trace walked out and saw the black monster slowing rolling past toward the town's high water tower. Trace wasn't sure he'd ever seen a more welcome sight.

"Let's get on the train, and then the words of those two dying men won't matter much. They don't matter much anyway. I *will* protect Mae. She's my wife. I'll get Mae up and ready, and then I'll come back to help you with Diablo. I have a feeling he's going to be a pain in the backside to get on board. They have a two-hour stop for the passengers getting off, and to allow the driver and engineer to get some grub in their bellies, to get the mail loaded and take on wood and water. I'll go get Mae dressed and fed and then meet you back here in a little over an hour. If you have anything you need to do, get it done."

Trace strode from cool shade near the stable into the harsh rays of the morning sun, the day already promising to be a hot one. A small bead of sweat trickled down his spine, but when he shivered, it wasn't from an itch the drop of moisture provoked. Nope, it was the damn recurrent feeling that eyes still watched him, were following his every move.

Chapter Twenty-four

Time to board, miss," the conductor called to Mae. She shot Trace a worried look, and he couldn't help admiring the sweetness of her face as she gnawed on the corner of her lip.

He was walking Diablo in circles. When a horse proved too stubborn to go where you wanted, you turned him around and around until the fool animal forgot where he was headed. Only, the black wasn't falling for the trick. This was the third time he'd led the animal in a loop, and the stallion was no closer to allowing Trace to get him into the boxcar.

"Damn fool critter! I'm the one who's getting dizzy. Would serve you right if I left you behind, sold you to some farmer for a plow horse."

The horse's eyes seemed to go wide and flash Trace a shocked expression, and he actually shook his head. When Trace glared, Diablo shoved out his nose and gave Trace's chest a gentle push. Just then, Duchess nickered from the boxcar, calling out to the stallion.

"Yeah, your lady love is summoning you. Why don't you do us all a favor and listen to her? Or I might have to ride you all the way back to Kentucky," Trace threatened.

"Hey, you two. We're set to roll. You coming or not?" the conductor called from the platform steps of the train.

"Trace!" Preacher yelled from inside the boxcar where he was settling the mare. "Maybe if I get behind him, you lead and I push, we can get the blasted varmint to load hisself."

"He'll kick you like a mule that's been bee-stung," Trace predicted, laughing, then once again turned the stud in a tight circle.

Preacher appeared. He took off his hat, wiped the sweat from his brow, and then gave Trace a big grin. "Then I'll lead him and you can push."

"Folks, we're already ten minutes late," the conductor announced, pocketing his watch. "You all better hurry up. When the engineer gives me the signal—which will be any minute now—that'll be all she wrote; this iron horse moves out."

Mae glared at him. "Mr. Conductor, you'll be waiting for my husband to load his stallion. As long as it takes. We're the only ones boarding the train here, and from the looks of that passenger car we're your only passengers anyway, so no one is waiting on us. These delays sometimes happen. There's no point in being a horse's behind. Am I clear?"

The man's Adam's apple bobbed and he nodded, cowed. "Yes, ma'am. Anything you say, ma'am. I'll just tell the engineer to wait, that there's a small delay."

Trace chuckled to himself, shaking his head as the conductor hurried off. Yes, he and Mae certainly would have stories to tell their children and grandchildren. He'd never wanted anything as much as to hold their first baby in his arms, to watch Mae's expression as she cradled their son or daughter to her breast. Like any man he hungered for a son, but a precious little girl who was a small copy of Mae would be worth all the gold in the world.

Diablo suddenly jerked hard against the lead shank, his nostrils flaring, his eyes wild. Trace struggled to keep the horse from pulling the leather strap out of his hands. "Easy . . . easy," he said. "Something sure has you spooked, boy."

The world suddenly moved in slow motion. Trace half turned his head, hearing the cock of a gun hammer behind him. Mae called out a warning—or tried; her words never had the chance to leave her lips. From the corner of his eye Trace saw a man step out from between two railcars. He ducked behind Mae and put a gun to her temple, clamping his left hand over her mouth.

Trace released his hold on Diablo's shank, so his hands were free. The horse snorted, stomped, and then trotted away. Trace didn't spare the stallion a second glance. He flexed the fingers of his right hand, planning to spin around and shoot his wife's assailant on the count of three.

"No, you don't. I ain't stupid," another stranger said, a white-haired man stepping into the open. "I heard you killed Slade, so I ain't takin' any chances. You turn around real slowlike."

There was something familiar about that voice; Trace had heard it before. Biding his time, he did as he was told, racking his memory for when he'd heard that gravelly bark. Even when he looked the man in the face, he still couldn't place him.

Finally truth hit him. His forehead creasing in confusion, Trace guessed, "Morgan?" The man had aged quite a bit, still looked a tad unsteady on his feet, which Trace attributed to the grievous injuries Comstock had inflicted on him.

"Yeah. Morgan. Bet you thought you'd never see the likes of me again, eh?"

"I wonder if that's what Lazarus said to Jesus," Trace said, a bit inanely. He was stalling, giving himself time to assess the situation. What did these two want?

Morgan gave a laugh. "You can ask old Jesus when you see him. Of course, that's assuming you make it past the Pearly Gates."

"How did you achieve this miraculous rise from the dead?" Trace asked.

"I wasn't really dead when Wally dragged me out to bury me. I paid him to get me away from the Lazy C."

"What do you want?" Trace demanded. "It's not to avenge Jared. We both know he wasn't your boss, and he tried to kill you. There was no love lost between you and Slade, either, so I don't imagine that's the reason you're here . . ."

"Slade," Morgan muttered. "Anyone stupid enough to go up against him should have the survival instinct to back-shoot him. You don't give someone like Slade the chance to clear leather! Only, you're the Whisperer—that's what them Injuns call you. You're that renegade rider. Worse than Texas Rangers, they are . . . You're likely jug-headed and principled enough to face Slade man-to-man."

Morgan grinned and continued. "Slade once told me never to trust speed alone, that you should always look for the advantage. Well, we have the advantage—we have your woman. I figure that'll rattle you a bit."

"She's not my woman—she's my wife," Trace corrected.

"Wife?" Morgan glanced at her and leered. "Is she really your wife, or did you marry her like Jared married her?" He glanced with amusement toward the man holding Mae.

"She's my wife. And I'm going to kill any man who tries to hurt her," Trace promised. His voice held a softness that belied the cold fury rolling through him.

"All aboard!" the conductor shouted from inside the train, clearly not wanting to come out and risk another confrontation with Mae.

Morgan called over his shoulder to his partner, "You go ahead. Get her on board. I'll deal with Ord and catch up at the next station."

"Yeah, you do that," his accomplice replied.

Suddenly Mae stomped on the inside of her captor's foot and shoved away from him. Spinning, she confronted the man . . . and a mixture of shock, horror, and revulsion crossed her beautiful face. "You? My God. I thought you were dead. Murdered. They told me you were dead!" Tears filled her eyes and choked her voice. "Father. Why?"

Trace was taken aback. It was peculiar enough to face one man returned from the dead, but two? "Your father? Seems Lazarus here wasn't alone. Is there some resurrectionist around here selling potions?"

Now that more pieces were falling into place, things

were beginning to make a little bit of sense. Morgan had never worked for Jared. He'd been working for Mae's father all along.

"Michael Slade," Trace told the older man. "He was your man, too. None of these people ever worked for Jared."

"How could they work for Jared when he didn't own the Lazy C? Jared worked for *me*. A pretty boy with smooth ways—if he couldn't sweet-talk you, he'd scare you half to death with that blacksnake." Jack Ahern laughed.

"But none too bright, eh?" Trace shook his head. "He didn't realize you were using him. If those ranchers came looking for all those horses, the first person they'd go after would be Jared Comstock. Your hands were kept clean."

"As much as you'd like to drag this out, I can't stand here all day. Come, Mae. We're getting on the train." Jack Ahern reached out and grabbed her upper arm.

She tried to jerk away. "Like hell we are."

"You're my daughter. You will do as I say," he barked.

Mae shook her head. "You're not my father. I'm the daughter of no man who allows me to be terrorized and nearly raped by your hired hand over there." She pointed to Morgan.

The white-haired man's eyes narrowed and he turned to stare at Morgan. "Is this true? I told you and Slade to protect her from Jared."

"Jared?" Mae's laugh was harsh. "Jared Comstock was a gentleman compared to Morgan. Your hired vermin was always putting his hands on my body, grabbing and squeezing. . . . Why do you think Jared took a whip to him? He found out how Morgan was treating me. He was the reason I ran the first time. I see by the expression on your face your lackey didn't explain everything."

Her father looked furious, but he mastered himself. "I tried to protect you by—I'll deal with this later, Mae. Get on the train. Now."

Mae dug the heels of her boots into the dry soil, resisting. "I'm not going anywhere with you."

"You'll do as I say, this instant, or I'll shoot Ord down like a dog, right before your eyes. We're getting on this train. Now."

"Hold it right there! Don't either of you polecats move!" Preacher called from the darkness of the boxcar. "A Winchester is pointed at what's left of your back, Will Morgan. One move and I'll shoot you like the yellow-bellied varmint you are."

Instead of holding still as Preacher ordered, Morgan drew. Trace was faster; his gun was in his hand and fired by the time Morgan's finger found the trigger. The train gave a loud lurch and began to move. The herky-jerky motion sent Preacher falling backward, spread-eagle and trying to balance on one leg. His Winchester barked. The bullet splintered wood as it went through the slatted side of the boxcar.

Morgan stood, stunned, his gun trained on Trace. Unfired. He reached up to his chest with his left hand and touched the stain spreading across his green shirt. Then, in one breath, all strength seemed to drain from him. He dropped to his knees, his gun falling into the dirt. "I'll . . . be damned."

"You got that." Trace stalked forward and kicked the

man's gun away, not trusting Morgan not to back-shoot him.

Jack Ahern swung Mae around hard, tossing her to her hands and knees on the metal stairs of the coach car. Grabbing the metal railing, he jumped onto the bottom step. The train started to roll in earnest. The wheels were spinning, the locomotive fast gaining speed, and the engineer blew the ear-piercing whistle to alert everyone to clear the tracks. Trace dashed after it.

Wooden crates that had been off-loaded sat at the end of the station's platform and he was forced to vault over them, which cost him precious time. Ahern was pressing Mae up the steps toward the door of the coach. Her father looked back, staring straight at him. Then, giving a half smile of victory, he slowly raised his pistol and took aim.

Mae grabbed her father's gun arm, causing the shot to go wild. Even so, the bullet went buzzing by so close that Trace could hear the whir. It hit a strut of the water tower and ricocheted off in another direction. A moment later, Jack shoved Mae through the door and into the railcar.

Trace was actually gaining ground and catching up with the train, though it was still increasing speed. The train's bell clanged a warning for some kids playing along the tracks. The kids scattered right into Trace's path. He was forced to pull up or they all would've col-lided.

Cursing, Trace sensed the train reach full speed. He was losing more and more ground, the distance in-creasing between him and Mae. His eyes searched fran-tically for an option. He could see her standing in the middle of the train car, the white of her dress brilliant in the shadowed interior, her beautiful face growing farther and farther away. He made one last push, running with all his energy.

The iron bar railing was there, almost in grasp . . . His fingertips brushed it as he stretched to grab hold, but then the toe of his boot caught on a dead honeysuckle root and sent him sprawling to the ground. He slammed into the red dust, so stunned that he had to shake his head before he even attempted to sit up. Anguish gripped his soul as he observed the train growing smaller and smaller on the horizon.

Rage boiled up inside him, and he lifted his head to the sky and bellowed. Satan seemed to be breathing down his neck today. Now what? Was he to sprout wings?

A nicker came from off in the distance, and suddenly things weren't looking so bad. He saw Diablo cantering his way, and he let out a shrill whistle. The animal walked up to Trace. Giving him a nudge with his nose, the horse rumbled a deep-throated murmur.

"For once you do what you're supposed to. I could kiss you." Trace almost laughed. Picking up his Colt from the dirt, he holstered it. He then snatched the dangling lead shank and vaulted up on the horse's bare back. "Sorry about your spine, but this is likely going to hurt me more than you. Ride like the wind, you devil's child. That piece of filth—hmmm, my father-in-law—has our Mae."

He leaned forward, giving the horse his head, and they raced to catch up to the rolling train. Trace wasn't sure how far it was to the next station, but he wasn't about to hope he caught up by then. He needed to move faster. Mae was his. He didn't care what it took to see her safe, even if he had to kill the low-life skunk who happened to be her father.

Diablo flat-out galloped, running with his whole heart as though he knew Mae's safety depended upon them catching up. They were making up the distance, despite the engine's huffing and puffing and its plume of black smoke. Cinders hit Trace's face, stinging his skin, but he paid them little mind. His sole focus was on catching up.

Yard by yard, he did just that. He moved past the caboose, then the baggage car. There was no sign of Preacher anywhere. That bothered Trace. That nosy old man would be trying to do something if he was able. Since Trace couldn't spot him, he feared something had happened. He couldn't take time to find his friend now, however; he was almost even with the boxcar. Only a few feet more.

Diablo stretched out his neck, finding a second wind to sprint alongside the train car. "That's it, fella!" Trace said. "Come on, come on!"

At last, he pulled close enough. Trace grabbed the vertical railing of the platform. His fist closed around the wrought-iron bar and held tight, and he inclined forward and allowed the onward motion of the train to haul him from Diablo's back. He grabbed for the short railing with his right hand and missed. For a moment he seemed to dangle in midair, and then he dropped hard, his thighs slamming against the edge of the metal steps. The toes of his boots dragged in the dust and rocks.

Gritting his teeth, Trace held on, for to let go would be to lose all. His arm felt as if it was being yanked from the socket, yet still he struggled not to lose his grip. Only by sheer will did he reach up and hook the small railing. Once that hold was established with his right hand, he was able to haul the rest of his body onto the steps.

For a long moment, he sucked in the cinder-filled air, trying to summon enough strength to finish what he must do. Taking his Colt from its holster, he removed the spent shell and replaced the bullet fired into Morgan. He definitely wanted all six shots for this encounter.

Looking up, he felt a weak smile spreading across his mouth. "Damn fool horse," he muttered. Though Diablo had slowed his pace and dropped back, he was trailing after the train. "He likely doesn't give a tinker's damn about me, though. He wants Mae back. Well, so do I. So do I," he laughed.

As he mounted the final two steps, he could see movement inside the coach. Jack Ahern had his beautiful daughter, his left arm crooked around her throat and the nose of his revolver pointed to her temple. As Mae had pointed out earlier, it didn't seem there was anyone else inside.

His wife's eyes were frightened, reminding Trace of the long-ago night he'd shot her. Her pretty white dress was speckled by the flecks of soot floating back through the open windows. How could any man use his daughter in this fashion? But then, Trace supposed the man had used Mae in worse ways.

"Keep back! Keep back, I say!" Ahern commanded

as Trace opened the door and entered, though he kept himself behind cover. That cocksure smile was gone, replaced with nervous anger.

Trace smiled in challenge. "Or you will what? Shoot Mae down in cold blood? You may be the sorriest excuse for a father I've ever laid eyes on, but I don't for one minute believe you'll shoot your daughter when she's helpless. Besides, you know the moment you shoot her, your shield is gone and I'll empty my Peacemaker into you."

"I'm warning you, Ord." Jack's gaze darted around, looking for an avenue of escape.

"Yep, you are. And I'm calling your bluff, Ahern. You won't kill Mae. Because I will make you *pay* if you harm so much as a hair on her head. And I'm a much harder man than you, gramps."

While he didn't believe Jack Ahern would shoot his daughter in cold blood, the cornered man could get her killed in all this foolishness. Mae's eyes watched Trace, surely trying to judge what he was planning, to glean some clue as to what he wanted her to do. He wished he could assure her that everything would be all right or give her some brilliant directive, but he'd have to trust she would act with common sense and on the spur of a moment when an opening presented itself.

He stepped out into the open to press his claim. "You should have cut your losses, Jack. You could be halfway to California or Oregon now. No one knows you're alive. All the blame has come down on Jared's shoulders—as you intended all along. He was your dupe. You had him pretend to marry your daughter to protect her, though that didn't work quite how you expected. And you were going to use him to sell all those rustled horses. Perhaps he was the worse gambler of the two of you. I reckon he was. Did he get into debt and owe you his soul? I suppose it doesn't matter. He's dead and gone. Now maybe you should turn yourself in and we can end this all nice and easy. Isn't it time?"

Jack Ahern scowled. "The trouble with a lone wolf—and that is what you are, Trace Ord—is that it hangs back and watches instead of having proper fear. It just keeps watching and guessing how its prey will jump. Well, you judge correctly how I'll jump. You're right. I won't kill Mae, because even as low down a varmint as you think I am, I'm still her pa. But those family ties don't extend to you, even if you're my son by marriage. I won't kill Mae, but I damn sure can put a hole in you." He raised his gun hand.

Mae acted. She struck backward with the heel of her dainty boot, catching her father in the shinbone of his right leg. At the same instant, she sank her teeth into the hand under her chin and struck out at her father's arm. The action changed the path of his shot. Instead of hitting Trace in the chest, his bullet struck Trace's gun. The impact sent the Colt flying out of his hand and spinning away into the shadows.

There was no time to worry about where it went. Trace leapt forward, catching hold of Ahern's arm and jerking the man's gun barrel away from Mae. But Jack Ahern was a tough man, despite the thick thatch of snowy white hair, hardened by the years of living in the West. With his fingers locked on the stock of the Peacemaker, Jack Ahern was determined not to let go, and while Trace had the advantage of youth, his arms had been nearly ripped from their sockets after he'd jumped from the back of Diablo. That fatigue was an edge for Ahern. Compounding that, Trace's right hand was numb from the gun being shot from his grip.

Trace jerked forward and then pushed against Jack's hold, but only succeeded in lifting the gun barrel. The Colt barked, putting a bullet through the ceiling of the railcar. He and Ahern spun around and around in some bizarre dance, each resolute to be the victor.

Mae lunged for the emergency cord and pulled it. As the massive engine fought to come to a stop, the whole train gave a lurch, wheels locking up and screaming as the long cars jump-bucked against their couplings. That herky-jerky bouncing tossed Trace and Jack sideways, each still struggling for control of the revolver. They slammed against the seats on the left side. With Trace bearing the brunt of the fall, a sharp wooden edge bore into his hip. He grimaced in pain but kept struggling.

"Don't move." Mae stepped forward, dropping her reticule, and in her hand was the derringer. Without hesitation she pointed the small gun at her father's head, much as he had done to her just moments before.

Glancing over his shoulder, Jack Ahern rose slowly and gave his daughter a smile. "Now, Mae, honey, you should know that pistol is practically a toy."

Mae frowned. "This is a Sharps .32-caliber derringer. A little old, possibly older than I am, but it'll still do its job. John Wilkes Booth assassinated President Lincoln with a derringer, so I would hardly dismiss it as a mere toy, Father. Especially at this range."

"Now, Mae . . . you wouldn't shoot your old papa,"

Ahern said. "Not when you know I wouldn't harm a hair on that pretty head of yours."

"No, you might not. But you apparently would drag me halfway across the country and away from the only home I've known, away from the safety and protection of Grandfather. You saw me 'married' to a coward—a bully with a blacksnake whip instead of a spine. You put my life at risk for some scheme for you to get rich—or should I say richer, since I'm assuming the Lazy C belongs to you? You used me, lied to me. You allowed me to think you were murdered, all just to swindle Foxtail Farms from its rightful owner and steal my inheritance. Worse, you put my husband's life in peril." Mae was furious, her face pale with two high spots of color on her cheeks.

The door to the front of the car jerked opened and the conductor appeared. "What in the heck is the problem, folks? The engineer is—" He pulled up short when he noticed Trace and Jack still fighting over the Colt, neither willing to let go and give the other the advantage, and Mae with her gun pointed to her father's head. "Oh!"

Trace spoke up. "How far to the next town? Someplace that has a lawman?"

"Comanche Wells . . . uh . . . that's the next place we stop to take on wood. They have a sheriff there." The conductor gulped.

Ahern's jaw muscles flexed. "You ain't turning me over to no lawman. They'll hang me." The old man moved fast. He released the Colt so quickly that Trace was suddenly falling backward, his arm slamming into a seat, which sent the revolver flying in the air. It landed on the floor several feet away and spun out of sight.

Ahern latched on to his daughter's wrist, trying to take the derringer. She fought. The derringer discharged once, sending the conductor scurrying behind one of the seats, and then a second bullet whizzed across the carriage, hit the metal framework, and ricocheted. White-hot pain slammed into Trace's shoulder.

Trace almost laughed, as his luck couldn't get much worse. But he couldn't care about the agonizing throb of his bruised hip or his numb hand or the wound in his shoulder. Fighting light-headedness, he struggled to his feet and toward Mae. There were two shots left in her pistol.

Ahern shoved his daughter, knocking her back, then whipped around to point the short barrel at Trace as Trace fought to rise. "This ends here and now, Ord."

"Don't. I wouldn't squeeze that trigger unless you want your daughter to see the mess a Winchester makes of a man's chest." Preacher stood in the doorway. "Drop it, or by God I'll drop you."

For a moment, the thought surely crossed Ahern's mind to go out in a blaze of glory; it was clear in his angry blue eyes. But finally he gave a nod and dropped the derringer. He seemed to age right before their eyes.

"Here." Preacher tossed a length of rope to Trace. "Figured you might need this."

"You always seem to be right there when I need you," Trace said, awed.

The old-timer shook his head. "Not this time. I was a bit late. Sorry. Bashed myself on the bean. Wasn't knocked out, exactly, just stunned, but I sure couldn't move. Plumb fool horse—Duchess kept licking my cheek trying to get me up. Horse breath sure ain't sweet."

Trace tied Ahern's wrists, then ankles. Mae's father didn't resist, nor did he utter a word. Trace reached out and patted his thigh. "Now, don't you go anywhere, hear?"

"Oh, Trace! You're bleeding." Mae rushed to him, pushing on his good shoulder until he sat down on the opposite site of the car. It didn't take much effort, as loss of blood was quickly getting to him. She immediately reached down and started ripping up her petticoat to form a bandage. "Hold still, so I can press on this to stop the bleeding. What happened? I thought his bullet hit your gun."

Preacher was laughing. "Well, if'n this ain't a fine howdy-do! You shot Trace!"

Her spine straightened and she paled. "I did not!" Then, as her mind went through the sequence of events, she asked, "Did I?"

Trace gave her an easy smile but grimaced as she applied pressure to the wound. "Yes, my love, you shot me. The ricochet from the derringer—which goes to prove that gun isn't a toy. I'm living testament. Damn, but that hurts."

"Oh, Trace." Mae looked horrified, then sad. "I think I'm going to faint."

"No, don't. You faint, I'll bleed to death," Trace teased.

"What should I do? As I recall, you dug the bullet out and then cauterized the wound." She gulped. "Trace, I don't think I can do that."

"No need." The conductor finally came out from his

hiding place. "We'll get the engine going again. They have a doc in the town up ahead. Just keep doing what you are. Your man will be fine until then, miss." Taking out his watch, he shook his head. "Well, we sure are going to be late today."

"Oh, Trace," she whispered.

He reached out with his right hand and brushed her cheek. "Hush, everything will be fine. Just think of the stories for our children: 'Your father shot your mother because she was stealing his horse—yes, that's how we met! Then, on the day after our wedding, your mama shot me in return.'" He couldn't help it; he laughed, then groaned because the vibration hurt his shoulder.

Preacher joined the chuckling. "Danged if'n you two won't have matching shoulder scars. What're the odds on that?"

Trace leaned his head back, closing his eyes and fighting the pain. "Whatever the odds, I'll take them. Our love is a sure bet." Suddenly, however, he remembered his horse. "Diablo—"

"Not to worry. He caught up. I put down a ramp on my way up here. Blasted horse walked right up it without the first word of encouragement. I think he just wanted to see Duchess."

Trace shook his head, and he couldn't help but smile. "There's an important lesson there: never try to keep a man from his woman."

Epilogue

Trace leaned with his arm on the top rail of the white-washed fence, studying the rolling hills of the Kentucky landscape. Diablo was alone in one small pasture, prancing around with his tail high, for in the far pasture were the mares. They were showing off for him, as well. Some would trot toward the fence, whinnying, but then Duchess would charge forward and run them back.

"Looks as though Diablo belongs to her," Preacher commented as he walked up.

Trace watched with a wistful smile. "It does seem that way. We may have to take Duchess out for a long ride while we slip Diablo into the breeding paddock. Mae's grandfather truly thinks he has the blood to breed a winner in this new race they're having, the Kentucky Derby. He thinks it would up the price of the stock if we could win, and the way Diablo runs . . ."

"I think the old man has the right of it. No one is faster than that horse except maybe Standing Thunder."

Preacher was worrying the lobe of his ear. Trace had noticed the gesture before, and his friend did it when he had something on his mind that he didn't know how to approach. But Preacher didn't have to; Trace already knew what burr was under the man's saddle. His friend was restless. While he'd enjoyed his stay in Kentucky, the place wasn't for him.

"You finish your game of chess with Sean?" he asked, stalling.

"That I did," Preacher replied. "It's been a long time since I played chess. Damn near forgot how. He finally took pity on me and we switched to checkers, but the sly old dog is too good. At least with chess I could sometimes outfox him and get a draw. I suppose if we keep it up all summer long I would get to where I could beat him sometimes, but . . ." His words trailed off, and with a frown he looked into the sunset. West.

"But what?" Trace finally asked. "I never knew you to keep your mouth shut when you have something riding your mind."

Preacher exhaled in frustration. "I am damn happy for you, Trace. You know that. You've found yourself again through Mae. You belong here. After all you told me . . . well, it's easy to see Trevor Guilliard has finally shaken off the horrors of that stupid war—as much as anyone of us ever will. You didn't belong out West any more than that beautiful gal. The planter's son is at home here. This is your element. You're returning to life, to a life where you belong. And you know what? I think you're going to breed that black son of Satan to a good mare and win that derby for that old man. It's a good life you've found. Be damn happy the good Lord saw fit to give it to you."

"Now I remember why I called you Preacher," Trace

joked. "But there's a place for you here, too." He spoke the words hoping he could convince his friend, but knew it wouldn't be enough; the old-timer had wander-lust in his eyes.

Preacher smiled, though the expression was a bit sad. "I thank you and Mae, kindly, but if I spend the rest of my days on that porch playing cards and chess with her grandpappy, you might as well take that shovel propped next to the barn over there and bury me out in the pasture. Trace Ord was running from the war and how it destroyed everything you loved. Mae is the salve for that wound in your heart. She'll watch your back now, though she'll use a derringer instead of your Winchester." He winked and held out his hand. "I never told you my real name in all our travels, though I implied I had a past. Shake hands with John Mercer. I think it's time."

Curious, Trace reached out. The two men shook.

"I buried a lot of me back there in the Shenandoah," Preacher continued. "My oldest boy was killed in the Wilderness. That was damn hard to take. Such an ugly campaign. Then Yanks came through one night. They burned my house and crops, drove off the livestock, and robbed me of everything. I worked my whole life to make that farm something to be proud of, something to leave my sons, and they took it all away.

"My youngest wasn't even fourteen. . . ." The old man swallowed, his eyes glassy. "He took his brother's death hard, so to watch them Union soldiers ruin our home was more than he could stand. Tad was the apple of his mother's eye, so when one of the soldiers snatched the cameo off my wife's neck, he grabbed an old musket off the wall . . . Damn thing was left over from the War of Independence—my pappy fought with Lighthorse Harry Lee, Robert E. Lee's sire. Tad rushed forward to defend his mama, and that bluecoat captain shot him down like a dog.

"I went crazy, killed two soldiers. That captain drew his long Colt and pulled the hammer back. My wife jumped in front of me, took the bullet. I can still hear him laughing as he rode off, leaving me holding Carrie in my arms. Said I could live the rest of my life knowing what I'd done. John Mercer died that night. I buried him with my family in the light of my burning house. Then I walked away."

The old man sighed and looked down at the ground before fixing his gaze once more upon Trace. "I don't really recall much, wandering across the countryside afterward. I guess I went plumb crazy for a time. Years later I came across that captain up near the panhandle. I could see it in his eyes that he didn't recall my face. Even when I prodded him, he just laughed and said it was war. He wasn't laughing when I killed him. . . ."

Trace shook his head. "I am sorry for your losses, John Mercer." There was nothing else he could say.

"I thank you kindly, Trevor Guilliard." The old-timer gave his hand a squeeze and then released it. "I am fine now. Helping you and Mae get back here sort of put paid to a lot of my sorrows. Only, I cannot live here. Reminds me too much of things that hurt to remember. Out in the territory I found peace. I'm not sure what I want to do now, maybe find a spread like the Lazy C—a good one that might need an old sourdough. . . ."

"I understand." Trace reached into his back pocket,

pulled out a letter, and unfolded it. "I was kind of thinking along the same lines, and maybe this will be the answer. The Lazy C is now Mae's. She got this letter from her father. I guess prison is making him sorry for a lot of things he did. He tells her how he's found religion, though I figure that's just another lie. I reckon Mae thinks so, too, since she gave me the letter and asked me to deal with it. She doesn't want to face anything to do with that ranch right now—maybe never. Too many bad memories. Still, I hate to let it go. It's a fine spread. It would need someone with an even temper and a strong determination to turn it back around. But it could be done."

"There's no stock, no hands. Jared's men will have done claimed all the horses that weren't returned to the ranchers they was rustled from," Preacher pointed out.

"Yeah, but I was thinking that maybe White Eagle might like to move his tribe onto the range. There's plenty of room. It'd be a good home for them. They would be safe and able to stop moving around. You'd get no better horse wranglers—"

"Me?" the old man asked.

Trace nodded. "I figured you were getting a restless urge in your blood. Only, I don't care much to turn you loose to wander. You might take a fool notion in your noggin to go out to Death Valley. Rounding up those mustangs that got away and breaking them should give you all the adventure you need—wouldn't you think? I was considering making you a half partner in the Lazy C. You and the Indians can catch Standing Thunder and gather up his herd. You'd have a great start to stock that could equal anything back here in the East. You like the notion? Maybe if they keep holding this derby going every year, you could bring one of your colts back and race against Mae's father, maybe even beat the pants off him. That'd sure make up for losing at checkers."

Preacher paused for a moment, thinking.

Trace jumped to add one more thing: "Perhaps you could even turn your hand to gentling a certain Indian woman. Provided she'll have you, maybe you can show Breath Feather just what it's like to be well treated. Her anger might take a wander if someone were to just show her a bit of kindness, and we know she has a fondness for the ways of the whites. There's no white man I know who has a kinder heart than you. White Eagle will see that. And if Breath Feather doesn't want you . . . well, there's plenty to be done just running the ranch."

Preacher nodded, a smile crawling across his face. "I like that, Trace. I like it mighty fine. Maybe it will heal my wounds as well. Maybe there's time yet for this ol' sourdough to start again. Maybe the two of us can find the happiness you and Mae have. I wouldn't mind seeing what she thinks of the idea."

Trace held out his hand to shake again. "We have a deal?"

The old-timer's leathery hand took his. "Deal."

A short time later Trace was sitting on the top rail next to the gate, watching Duchess and Diablo rubbing noses. He supposed that was a horse's equivalent to kissing. For a mare, she was a match for the black stallion. So intent was he on watching the courting couple, he failed to notice the lasso until it descended around his arms and then snugged down. He turned to find Mae reeling in the slack.

"Good grief, she's gone cowgirl!" he teased as she walked toward him.

Her eyes were flashing as she gave a strong tug on the rope, not enough to pull him off his perch but enough to let him know he was caught. "You're lucky I was practicing my roping and not my shooting. You have a faraway look in your eye, Trevor Guilliard." She usually called him Trace, so her use of his real name was pointed. "Ever since I told you we own the Lazy C, I can see the hunger in your eyes. You're thinking of going back and rounding up those mustangs."

Trace sighed. "I am. That herd was twice the size I thought it would be. Do you know how much money that would bring us—not to mention the thrill of capturing Standing Thunder?"

Hurt flickered in Mae's eyes, along with a touch of fear. Her hand whipped out, and in her fingers was the derringer that Preacher had given her. She pointed it out into the distance. "Maybe I'll need to work on my shooting after all."

Trace leaned down and brushed his lips against hers, and his fingers closed around her gun hand. "I think you need to give me that. You might accidentally shoot me. Again."

"Accidentally? No, it would be quite deliberate. It would take you months to heal before you go west again. Maybe by that time you won't want to go. Let Standing Thunder live free, Trace."

"I can't do that," Trace said. "If we don't get him, some other wrangler will—someone maybe like Comstock. I won't see that king of the canyons condemned to such a fate."

Mae's lower lip trembled. "Trace, I don't want to go back. Maybe someday years from now, but . . . And don't you dare tell me I can stay here while you go. You're my husband. If you go, I'll go."

"Hush, my little renegade rider. Our trail ends here. As you say, we might want to go back . . . someday, not now."

"But I don't understand."

"Preacher's not happy here. I offered him half of the Lazy C to run it. He can go back, get White Eagle and the Indians to round up the wild horses, restock the Lazy C, and Standing Thunder can live free there. He can spend his days keeping his mares happy."

"Oh, Trace!" She threw her arms around his neck and hugged him, almost pulling him off the fence.

Regaining his balance he climbed down. Putting one arm around his happy wife, he reached out with his free hand and slid the lock on the gate back, then swung it wide, allowing Diablo into the pasture with Duchess. The stallion and the mare did a victory lap around the field.

"Renegade hearts, all of us." Trace was thinking about himself and Mae, about Preacher and Breath Feather, about Diablo and Duchess. He wondered who was Standing Thunder's mate, and if the stallion had discovered her yet. Maybe that would come in time. Shrugging, he smiled and kissed Mae. "Every renegade needs someone to love. I'm so glad I found you."

INTERACT WITH DORCHESTER ONLINE!

Want to learn more about your favorite books and authors?
Want to talk with other readers that like to read the same books as you?
Want to see up-to-the-minute Dorchester news?

VISIT DORCHESTER AT:

DorchesterPub.com
Twitter.com/DorchesterPub
Facebook.com (Search Pages)

DISCUSS DORCHESTER'S NOVELS AT:

Dorchester Forums at DorchesterPub.com
GoodReads.com
LibraryThing.com
Myspace.com/books
Shelfari.com
WeRead.com

☐ YES!

Sign me up for the Historical Romance Book Club and send my FREE BOOKS! If I choose to stay in the club, I will pay only $8.50* each month, a savings of $6.48!

NAME: _____

ADDRESS: _____

TELEPHONE: _____

EMAIL: _____

☐ I want to pay by credit card.

☐ **VISA**   ☐ **MasterCard**   ☐ **DISCOVER**

ACCOUNT #: _____

EXPIRATION DATE: _____

SIGNATURE: _____

Mail this page along with $2.00 shipping and handling to:
Historical Romance Book Club
PO Box 6640
Wayne, PA 19087
Or fax (must include credit card information) to:
610-995-9274

You can also sign up online at **www.dorchesterpub.com**.
*Plus $2.00 for shipping. Offer open to residents of the U.S. and Canada only.
Canadian residents please call 1-800-481-9191 for pricing information.
If under 18, a parent or guardian must sign. Terms, prices and conditions subject to change. Subscription subject to acceptance. Dorchester Publishing reserves the right to reject any order or cancel any subscription.